Troy

Troy

Richard Matturro

Walker and Company
New York

First published in the United States of America in 1989 by Walker Publishing Company, Inc.

Published simultaneously in Canada by Thomas Allen & Son Canada, Limited, Markham, Ontario.

Library of Congress Cataloging-in-Publication Data

Matturro, Richard.
  Troy.

  1. Troy (Ancient city)—Fiction. 2. Trojan War—Fiction. I. Title.
PS3563.A8664T76 1989   813'.54   88-27991
ISBN 0-8027-1079-4

Printed in the United States of America

10 9 8 7 6 5 4 3 2 1

For Barbara

οὔ τοι ἀπόβλητ᾽ ἐστὶ θεῶν ἐρικυδέα δῶρα.

Iliad III.65

Contents

I

The Chief

A HORSE WHINNIED. The young man turned his head and peered in the direction of the sound, but could see nothing along the still, dark coastline. No sailor by trade, he had tied the halter knot poorly the evening before, and one beast had managed to loosen it and steal away. Realizing what had happened, he slipped out of camp early and walked up the beach to try to find the mount before one of the officers discovered it missing.

He stopped next to the black hull of a ship, a stationary ship, pulled completely up on shore and tipped slightly to one side, supported by poles. It was an ancient ship, surprising in its smallness. The sun, rising now over the lower shoulder of Mt. Ida far in the east, glinted off a piece of bronze hung by a leather strap on the yardarm. The bronze was a greave, a piece of leg armor. When new, it could be used as a medium of exchange like gold, but now its brightness was worn off by use, and it was stained black from blood dried in the sea breezes overnight.

Thinking that he might have inadvertently passed the horse in the dark, the young man looked back in the direction from which he had come. He could see a whole line of vessels, all pulled up on shore and propped up on poles. There were not a thousand ships, as the poets have said, nor even half that many, but the armada lying at rest here represented the largest assemblage of seagoing vessels since shipbuilding had been practiced. They had come to this Asian shore from every state in Greece for the only pursuit that ever joins together men of differing nations—war.

Seeing nothing from where he stood, the young man clambered up to the deck of the ship to get a better vantage. From here he could look over the barricade toward the plain and the Trojan camp. If the horse had wandered into the enemy lines, there would be no getting him back. He scanned the field between himself and the row of campfires, and then beyond the campfires toward the walled city.

A star-shaped fortress of rock and timber, Troy was situated on a small rise halfway between the sea and the hills in the distance, which, at this hour, appeared merely as a black outline against the sky. During the day it was possible to view from here the red tile roofs of some of the more prominent buildings, and, because of a natural incline within the city, almost the whole of the great Temple to Athena. But in the gray light of dawn, all the young man could see was the dark silhouette of the wall.

He shivered in the cold breeze blowing down from the straits, and wrapped his cloak more tightly about him. Troy stood at the windy northwestern tip of Asia Minor, just below the narrow sea boundary between Europe and Asia, the Dardanelles, or the Hellespont, as it was called in 1184 B.C. Troy's fortuitous location had made it a mercantile center where ships stopped on their voyages from the Mediterranean to the Black Sea and back again. Merchandise had made it a rich city, and wealth had brought it fame. Troy also stood at another boundary, that between history and prehistory.

The young man heard a snort close by. He leapt to the ground and saw the horse behind the ship, scraping with its hoof a small, weedy patch of grass that had managed to attain a foothold in the sand. It pulled the grass up with its teeth and chewed tranquilly.

"You could've gotten me in a lot of trouble," the young man whispered as he patted the horse and took hold of the rope dragging at its feet. He was just about to lead the mount back to the camp when he heard another sound, unusual at this hour, footfalls from far up the beach. He squinted to make out the figure in the early morning twilight. When he recognized the face, however, he lowered his eyes and offered no greeting, but quietly went about his business. It would not have been proper to address his superior before being addressed himself. But he did wonder why the chief was walking alone so early.

Agamemnon was a powerfully-built man, older than most of the other warriors, approaching fifty, in fact, but living in a time when middle age did not exempt a man from hand-to-hand combat. He was a king, like most of the leaders camped on this shore, and his kingdom was Mycenae, the most prominent of all the independent states that divided up the Greek peninsula. Here, however, by common consent of his fellow kings, he was commander-in-chief of all the allied Greek forces. He accepted his role, but learned, like many after him, that the requirements of leadership are more complex than those of fighting alone. He had at best only a tenuous hold over the royal warrior captains under him, who fought for their own glory and for booty more than they did for him or for their united cause. What respect he did get from the others had more to do with the size of his army, which was far and away the largest.

He passed the hull of the ship without speaking to the puzzled young man. Down the beach there was activity in the camp now, shadows moving about in their early morning rituals. As Agamemnon reentered its confines, however, he seemed oblivious to his surroundings, the cooking fires, the heaps of weapons and armor, the paddocks, the cattle, and the piles of debris that an armed force produces in such abundance. Nor did he acknowledge the people whom he passed, soldiers waking on the ground, women and other camp followers up and working, officers standing in the entrances of their tents, but they all noticed him. Though they did not stare, they whispered among themselves once he was past, speculating about his thoughts during so solitary a walk. The kings, and this king of kings, were no strangers to the lower-born. They had all lived together for nine long years on this littered beach.

When Agamemnon reached his own tent, his brother Menelaus was waiting for him.

"Looking over the defenses?" Menelaus asked.

Agamemnon glanced at him, his reverie not quite broken. "Yes."

Menelaus was only a few years younger than his brother. If there was a family resemblance between the two men, it was most noticeable in the mouth, for both had very full lips, visible even though they wore beards, as did nearly all men of that time and place. But the most impressive thing about Menelaus was his shocking red hair, which he wore long. Were he a less able warrior, the unusual color might have been a source of humor among his fellow captains. Menelaus was king of Sparta, an allied province that could safely be ruled by a younger brother of meaner stature.

If there were any envy in Menelaus for his elder's better fortune, it was never expressed. Menelaus was not ambitious for another man's state; he wanted only what was his own. If he sometimes seemed less sure of himself than his brother, it was because the thought seldom strayed too far from his mind that the whole bloody business they were engaged in, whose outcome after a nine-year siege was still in doubt, was precipitated by his inability to keep what was his own—Helen, his wife.

"The wall we built will keep them out," Menelaus said confidently.

"If it keeps them out as well as theirs has kept us out, we could stay here another nine years," Agamemnon said dryly.

Menelaus was about to smile, but stifled it. The mere presence of their ramshackle barricade, a hastily thrown-up affair of scrap wood, metal, and stone set behind a trench, was a testament to the Greeks' failure. After all, the Greeks were the besieging army, who should have had freedom of movement while they penned the Trojan warriors in their city; instead, the Trojans had beaten them further and further down the field until the only territory the Greeks now held was the thin margin of beach around their camp. It was a humiliation, and one not lost on the various captains, who increasingly began to think of their farms back home.

Ten days earlier, the Greeks had the run of the plain, as they had during most of the war, but then Agamemnon had a falling-out with his best captain, Achilles. Consequently, Achilles withdrew himself and his whole contingent from the fighting. The blow to morale in the Greek army was as great as the diminishment of their numbers, and the Trojans quickly capitalized on the situation. Now the soldiers were grumbling, and the captains, whether they sided with Agamemnon in the dispute or not, resented putting themselves in danger while Achilles sat safely in his tent.

Agamemnon gazed up the field. The Trojan army, camped no more than a hundred yards from his own, was awakening and preparing for the day's fighting. He squinted at the morning sun. It was rising earlier now each day. Soon it would be the spring equinox. Back home it would be planting time, but here it was merely the beginning of another fighting season, the tenth his army had endured. The winter had been severe. The incessant winds blowing down from the straits had made Troy a bitter place for besiegers and besieged alike.

Agamemnon looked beyond the Trojan camp. In the distance the city loomed behind its wall. It was an ancient wall, far older than the collective memory of the people who lived within its circuit. The Trojans said it had been constructed by Poseidon himself, the god of the sea, when he and Apollo were condemned to hard labor for having offended Zeus, the king of the gods. The Trojans told this story about the wall because they could not otherwise account for its presence.

However the wall came into being, it stood as a barrier to Agamemnon's immortal aspirations. If he could succeed in conquering Troy, his name and his triumph would live forever. This story would become the archetype for all stories, this war the archetype for all wars. His name would ring down through the centuries—his name, in every land, in every language, for as long as human beings walked upon the earth. All that stood between him and his glorious fate was a wall.

But a wall in those days, when men fought with spears, swords, bows and arrows, was enough. At the beginning of the war, the Greeks had cheered the first time they drove the Trojans back up the field to seek refuge inside their city. Arriving at midsummer, the Greeks thought this would be but a brief contest and they would be home by harvesttime. No one could dispute that they had the larger and stronger army. Indeed, few Trojans outside the royal family had any military training at all. Even their best fighter, Hector, was more at home on his farm than he was on the battlefield. So the second time the Trojans were driven behind their wall, the Greeks cheered again, but as this pattern repeated itself over and over, the Greeks realized that the wall might forever frustrate their attempt to take the city. To make matters worse, when Troy's allies saw that the Trojans were successfully weathering the siege, they began to arrive in great numbers from the landward direction to fight against the Greeks. So the fighting wore on, and now after nine years it was the attacking army that faced extinction.

Agamemnon lowered his eyes from the citadel to his own flimsy barricade. His face hardened. "Maybe it *is* time we went home," he said, as much to himself as to his brother.

Menelaus betrayed no emotion, but he felt a constricting pain in his stomach. Agamemnon had been his staunchest ally, his only ally at times. If his brother now decided to abandon the siege, all hope was lost. Menelaus thought of Helen. He tried to imagine a future in which he would never see her again. He even tried to convince himself that it might be better not to get her back. She could hardly be the same Helen he had married many years ago. Even he knew that. She was older now, to be sure. And what else? Wiser? More worldly? How could it not be so if she lived for a decade among the Trojans? The Trojans were a clever people, a sophisticated people. Everyone said so. They were known throughout the Aegean for the beautiful buildings they constructed, the lovely painted statues and vases they created, the songs they sang. He had feared from the very beginning that if she returned to him, she would find his country ways rude and uncouth by comparison. Yet the thought of never seeing her again was intolerable. His mind raced for something to say to his brother that would change his mind.

From down the beach, a burly figure was making his way toward Agamemnon's tent. There was no doubt that this balding, vigorous man was a sailor, for his short legs and rolling gait seemed more accustomed to the sea than dry land. His calves and thighs were thick with muscles formed by the thousand motions and counter-motions necessary to keep steady on a pitching ship. Even on solid earth they seemed to swing and pivot as if ready at any moment for the ground to move under them.

"Odysseus," the chief called out to him.

He came to a stop and nodded a greeting to Agamemnon, then to Menelaus.

The chief looked in the direction from which Odysseus had come. "What are the others saying?"

The newcomer lowered his eyes and smiled shyly. It was a habitual mannerism with him, and belied the facility he had with words. "There's a lot of talk about furrows."

"Furrows?"

"Yes," he laughed, "furrows. About how crooked they are when they're left to servants, and how ill the crops grow when the furrows are crooked. Something about the blessed Demeter not liking crooked rows, and cursing the ground. The goddess wants the rows to be neat and straight, or she considers it an insult and doesn't provide grain. Oh, yes," he said, "I hear an awful lot about furrows, and how poorly they're plowed when the master's away."

Agamemnon's face darkened again. Automatically his gaze turned toward the plain and fell on the distant wall. Maybe even Odysseus thought it was time to leave. Odysseus ruled over Ithaca, a small, rocky island off the western shores of the Greek mainland. He brought with him to Troy only a small contingent of soldiers, but Agamemnon valued him for the quality of his mind, a quality that had made him famous throughout Greece. He had a wealth of knowledge, and a wily intelligence that was without rival. Few enterprises were embarked upon without his counsel. If he now considered victory impossible, continuing the war might be futile.

8

Menelaus, as if conscious of his brother's thoughts, now said abruptly, "Let me offer them a challenge."

Agamemnon looked at him.

"Me against Paris, for Helen. If I win, they give her up and we go home. If he wins, we go home without her."

"And in either case we go home without taking the city," said Agamemnon flatly.

"We only came here for Helen," Menelaus reminded him. "If we leave with her, there's no shame in that."

"He'll never accept," the chief said, turning away.

"Then he'll look like a coward in front of his own people."

Agamemnon suspected that the Trojans already considered the young prince a coward, but that did not really concern him, nor did he seriously care about getting Helen back. What concerned him was the possibility that such a negotiated settlement would end the war without his having obtained the ultimate prize he sought.

"What would you do if Hector accepted in his place?" the chief asked, frowning at his brother.

Menelaus hesitated for a moment, then said with less conviction, "I'd fight Hector."

The chief wanted to forbid it, and was about to, but he was interrupted by the Ithacan, who had been eyeing this exchange with keen interest.

"It's a private quarrel; Hector's got no place in it. Besides," he added, "we stand to benefit no matter what happens. If Paris accepts, he'll lose. He's not half the fighter Lord Menelaus is. And if Paris refuses, at least the Trojans will suspend the battle while they consider the proposal. If we fight again today, I'm afraid we'll make our beds in seawater tonight."

The chief scowled. He still didn't like the idea.

Odysseus smiled and said in lowered tones, "Don't

worry, my lord. Should the duel take place, what we do afterward is still up to us.''

Agamemnon glanced once more at the field, where the Trojan campfires, so ominously close to his own, were now fading from view in the growing light of day.

''All right,'' he said with a sigh, ''I'll send the challenge. We'll see what they say.'' With that, he turned and disappeared into his tent.

Aulis. It was Aulis that kept coming back to him this morning, like a dream he couldn't quite forget. Agamemnon didn't know why. He thought he'd put that to rest years ago, but this morning during his solitary walk, and now lying in his tent, he kept thinking about it—Aulis.

There was nothing special about the town, really. It was just a small port on the east coast of Greece. Situated on the narrow channel separating the Greek mainland from the island of Euboea, it provided a good sheltered harbor. It was chosen as a point of departure for the fleet because it stood at a more or less central location for the armies from all the far-off states. The little town, for its part, had never seen so many ships at one time in its harbor, and every day more and more arrived. Ships from nearby Athens and Thebes, ships from Mycenae, ships from Sparta, ships from Ithaca, ships even from the mystical isle of Crete, the seat of the old empire. Hundreds of ships.

And heroes, men whose names were well known throughout Greece, but who no one at Aulis had ever hoped to see in real life. There was the great Ajax from Salamis. There was the fierce Diomedes from the citadel of Tiryns. There was the famous navigator Nauplius, who had piloted Jason's ship in quest of the Golden Fleece. There was wily Odysseus. There was old Nestor, king of Pylos, the oldest man to join the expedition. His fighting days over, he brought his wise counsel and his two sons who would fight in his place. There was the archer Philoctetes, leader of the Thessalians, who carried the bow of Hercules. And most notable of all, there was Achilles, said to be the greatest warrior on earth.

All these heroes converged on Aulis, and a holiday atmosphere prevailed. Though the Greek states were used to scrapping among themselves, there was nothing like a common enemy to unite them. Besides, their destination was the richest city in the world, known everywhere for its wealth, beauty, and splendor. Few had ever actually seen it, of course, in those times of little travel, but all had heard of it—Troy, the great walled town. It conjured up visions of gold, shining bronze, colorful statues, intricate stone carving, and magnificent horses. Bards who sang of the city praised Troy as another Olympus, a home that would be suitable for the gods if the gods chose to live on earth. This fabled city with all its wealth was their destination. There was reason to celebrate.

Agamemnon was the natural choice to be leader of the expedition since he was both ruler of the most powerful Greek state, and also the elder brother of the offended party. At that time, nearly a decade ago, he was delighted with the office, as who would not be? He was supreme head of the greatest fighting force ever assembled. Seeing fresh armies arrive each day and pay homage to him, he began to have dreams which surpassed even the conquest of Troy. He imagined himself conquering the whole of Asia, then uniting all the ragtag Greek states into one great empire. He would be a good ruler of that empire, too, firm but kind, as he had been with his own children. He would establish a monarchy to perpetuate the empire after his death, and he would train his son to be a worthy inheritor of that monarchy. And when he finally died, he would become the subject of song and story in ages to come.

Thus ran his vision, and when the last of the armies arrived at Aulis, and the ships were loaded with provisions, and all was secured and made ready for the passage to Troy, imagine his dismay when a violent wind suddenly blew up from the east, binding his great army to the shore. Contrary winds happen, of course, to all sailors, and they must simply be waited out. But this wind continued for days, and then the days lengthened into weeks. The restless armies, not prepared for the rigors of peace, began to fight among themselves. Brawls had to be stopped every night as soldiers from rival contingents debated the respective merits of their homelands. The captains, too, became restless, and some began to say that the gods were against them and didn't want them to set out for Troy. It was to stem talk like this that Agamemnon called upon Calchas to find out why the winds blew against them.

Calchas was a prophet, a man who was believed to have insight into the will of the gods. The Greeks had invited him to join the expedition because they would no more attempt to navigate the shoals of the world without a prophet than they would to guide a ship through the Hellespont without a pilot.

Doubtless there have been some atheists in every age, but the Greeks by and large (and the Trojans too, for that matter) accepted the existence of the gods. They believed in a host of divine and semidivine entities all around them who interfered regularly in earthly matters. In those days gods did not remain aloof and removed from human affairs as gods of a later time. Gods had favorites and they took sides in human conflict. They protected those they liked and inflicted harm on those they didn't. A concept of justice that allowed gods to be uncommitted, to show equanimity to all sides, would have seemed like no justice at all.

Thus, when a man threw a spear farther than seemed

humanly possible to throw, his fellows believed that a god loved him and endowed him with his superior ability. When one driver's chariot wheel broke in the midst of a race, the spectators could be fairly confident that a watching deity wanted a different driver to win. When a warrior stumbled in battle and thereby was killed, his companions assumed that a god had seen fit to trip him and so end his life. This system of belief was less a religion than it was an explanation for the otherwise random and inexplicable turns in human life.

The prophet, for his part, provided the only view, however dark or distorted, into the mind of the gods. He attempted to decipher their will and to predict the future by examining a variety of natural phenomena. He would look at a flight of birds, for instance, and predict by the chance pattern they made in the sky whether an earthly endeavor would succeed or fail. He would examine the entrails of a sacrificed animal, and read in the color and condition of the viscera whether the gods smiled on a particular human exploit. By such means, Calchas had originally predicted that Agamemnon would lead the great enterprise, and that Troy would eventually fall to him. Now Agamemnon called upon Calchas's powers again.

Calchas performed a sacrifice and divination in the sight of all the assembled captains. When he was done, he announced to the chief that it was the goddess Artemis who was responsible for the adverse winds. Artemis was the virgin goddess of the moon, who was thought to haunt isolated glens and lonely wooded hills. Though sometimes called "the Huntress," she was considered also to be a protector of animals, and the beast most sacred to her was the stag. Agamemnon had killed such a beast on a hunt shortly after he arrived at Aulis. Calchas told him that the goddess was angry and would on no account allow favorable winds unless Agamemnon paid her in full for what he had taken from her.

"What does the goddess want?" the chief had asked.

"In exchange for one most dear to her, she demands the death of the one most dear to you, your daughter Iphigenia."

Iphigenia, his firstborn, a gentle, soft-spoken, lovely girl, just then reaching marriageable age. Kill her? The idea was unthinkable. He could never do it. He said so. He said so loudly, and the other captains agreed. They too were fathers, most of them, and they were appalled at the cruelty the goddess demanded. They understood what a child means to a man.

There were many things Greeks of the twelfth century B.C. did not know. They didn't know the shape of the earth; they didn't know the cause of disease; they didn't know that if you cut down a forest and plant no more trees, you denude your land for a hundred generations. But one thing they did know was that the killing of your own offspring was unparalleled evil. No captain would blame Agamemnon for refusing the goddess's demands, even if it meant that he would have to give over the expedition.

But he did not give over the expedition. After his refusals, Agamemnon retired to a place by himself to think. He thought for days, and spoke to no one. The other captains, now more restless than before, could not see the reason for staying at Aulis any longer. If the goddess's demand was not to be fulfilled, why didn't Agamemnon release them so they could go home? But the chief remained by himself and thought.

He recalled Clytemnestra as the young wife she had been before the birth of their first child, and how happy they had been when the pregnancy was first realized. He thought of how he had marveled at the increasing swell of her belly as the baby grew. He thought of his momentary disappointment when the child was born and turned out to be a girl instead of a boy, but then he thought of the joy the child quickly became when her personality began to emerge. He thought of the girl's first steps, and then, what seemed to follow soon after, her first words, which she almost immediately put into the form of a song.

Iphigenia loved to sing. As a little girl, when she was gone from the palace, her father could usually find her merely by listening for her voice. She would invariably be singing at the top of her lungs on the forest paths around Mycenae. So natural did she seem there that Agamemnon called her a wood nymph, like one of the immortals. As she grew older, he would ask her to sing for visiting chieftains as they sat around his table.

He loved the girl, and even after a son was born to him, and another daughter, Iphigenia remained his favorite. She was the least like him of the three, to be sure, for she was exceedingly gentle, even to the animals, and loved the outdoors more than the palace. There was something in her that her father recognized as true beauty and goodness, a quality not present in himself, his wife, nor his other children.

Indeed, it amazed him that he could even produce such a child, when he considered the sordid history of his family. Every generation had seen one atrocious crime or other. His father, Atreus, and his uncle Thyestes had killed a bastard brother at the instigation of their mother, and when the deed came to light their mother killed herself. Later, Thyestes cuckolded Atreus and tried to steal his kingdom. In revenge, Atreus killed Thyestes' sons and displayed their hacked bodies to him.

Agamemnon's grandfather, Pelops, was indebted to a charioteer who, through a clever ruse, helped Pelops obtain the wife he wanted. To make sure no one ever learned of the stratagem, he drowned the charioteer.

Pelops's sister, Niobe, blessed with a large and handsome family, disparaged one of the gods, and saw all fourteen of her children carried off by disease. It was even said of Tantalus, Agamemnon's great-grandfather and founder of the house, that he had gone mad and baked his child in a pie, then invited the gods to partake of it.

Yet, from this cursed garden, one pure, innocent flower had grown. Kill her? It was unimaginable. She owed nothing to him; he owed everything to her. Never could he harm her.

But if this were true, why did Agamemnon hesitate to disband the army and go home? He had no obligation to Menelaus that this divine demand did not cancel. Besides, his brother was free to lead the expedition himself if he wished. Agamemnon had no obligation to anyone. He was free to pack up his army and head back to Mycenae. Yet he did not go.

Perhaps it was because he knew all along that he would fulfill the goddess's demand. Perhaps he knew in his heart that he would kill his daughter, even while proclaiming to the captains that he would not. Perhaps he knew it the moment Calchas pronounced the goddess's will. A man, after all, may have many children, but destiny rarely gives him the opportunity for immortality. Undying fame was being offered to Agamemnon, and he could not refuse. Killing his daughter would be the most sinful act he had ever committed, more sinful even than the gruesome dish mad Tantalus had prepared for the gods, because Agamemnon was not mad. But by committing this sin, would he not ultimately achieve a greater good? The union of the Greek people, the conquest of an empire. The gods had promised him victory; this was but their price.

Agamemnon stayed by himself seven days, and when he once again joined his captains, he told them that he had decided to accede to the goddess's demand. He said he feared eternal retribution from the goddess on the rest of his family if he did not make the sacrifice. He cited the many examples of the gods' anger at his family in the past, and he said he did not dare to anger them again. He said all this sadly, and some of the captains believed him. No one, at any rate, voiced an objection.

Iphigenia was brought to Aulis by means of a lie. Agamemnon sent a message to his wife that there was to be a marriage between their daughter and Achilles before the fleet set sail. Clytemnestra, delighted with the match, accordingly sent Iphigenia overland, with a large retinue of servants. Agamemnon met the procession himself and welcomed his daughter to Aulis.

The very next morning, a fine, summer day in which the wind, as always, blew incessantly from the east, Iphigenia, decked in her wedding gown and the jewelry her mother had selected, was accompanied by her family servants to the altar on a rock promontory standing between the forest and the sea. Agamemnon had kept his plan a secret, shared only with his most trusted captains. They were all present that morning. Achilles was there, and Odysseus, and Ajax, and Diomedes, and Nestor, and Menelaus. They all looked grave, but Iphigenia was radiant with happiness. She followed her father's instructions and stood close to the altar, facing out to sea. The wind blew back her hair, which touched Agamemnon's chest as he stepped up behind her.

For decorum's sake, Iphigenia for once repressed the urge to sing, but in her joy she couldn't help humming snatches of her favorite songs. In the midst of one of these, she felt her father reach around with his left hand and gently lift her chin. It might have been a caress, or the prelude to some last-minute fatherly advice about the married state. It might have been merely a way of drawing her close to him for a kiss, a blessing for her wedding, a wish for children. It might have been any of these things, but it was not. For even as he lifted the delicate chin, and felt the smooth skin in his left hand, his right hand, grasping a knife, drew the blade across his daughter's throat. She made not a sound, but her body jerked hideously in his arms as blood spurted onto her bridal gown. Agamemnon dropped the knife to the ground, partly so he could support her convulsing body and partly to resist the temptation to plunge the same knife into his own neck. Behind him, the family servants shrieked in horror.

When the girl stopped twitching, Agamemnon laid her on the altar, and even as he did so, the wind shifted. A great, billowing wind rose from out of the west to blow the fleet to its destination. The captains looked at each other wild-eyed. Menelaus hastened them down the hill to make ready their ships, but he himself went to his brother. He stood by him awhile looking down at his niece, then gave instructions to the astonished servants to dig her a grave.

Neither of the brothers stayed to watch the interment. They joined their now-jubilant men and left what had become for them a hated place. It was the last Greek soil they trod for nine years. For many, it was the last Greek soil they would ever tread.

A mild sea breeze rattled the flap of Agamemnon's tent. He wondered what Iphigenia would be like, if she had lived. Surely, she would be married to a young prince now, maybe Achilles indeed. Probably she would be a mother, singing lullabies to Agamemnon's first grandchild. What a feast he would have held for that birth! All his fellow kings would be invited. And he would bestow presents on the child, gold cups, painted vases, and if a boy, bronze armor. The child would want for nothing.

18

But of course there was no child, and there would be no lullabies. There was just this grizzled, lonely old soldier lying where he had lain for nine long years—in an armed camp outside the walls of Troy.

II

The City

TALTHYBIUS SLOWED HIS horse to an easy walk as he picked his way across the field. He didn't want there to be any question about his purposes. When he reached the foremost lines of the Trojans, he nodded to individuals as he passed, for he'd met some of them before on other visits to the city. For many of them, he was the only Greek they'd ever spoken to, and none had ever encountered him in battle.

He enjoyed his occasional missions to Troy, and sometimes found it amusing that he could do what the whole Greek army could not—enter the gates of the city. But that was the privilege of a herald. He had been a young servant in Agamemnon's palace in Mycenae, and had once astonished his master with his precise memory of the contents of the larder. After that, the king began employing him as a messenger, and his life became easier. Now in his thirtieth year he carried the herald's staff of office.

In an age before writing, the ability to memorize things exactly was highly valued, and Talthybius had developed his skill to a fine art. Sometimes he associated certain words with others that sounded like them, and thereby remembered them. Sometimes he reorganized a list of items into a rhythmic verse, and remembered it that way. And sometimes, when he felt least creative, he merely repeated the material over and over in his mind until it was burned in his memory like a brand on leather. The process had gotten easier over the years, and it was now nearly automatic. The particular message he carried today was quite brief; he had memorized it entirely while making ready his horse.

The only thing that puzzled him was the correct protocol for getting into the city now that the Trojan army was camped outside. Whenever he had gone to Troy before, he had approached the gates directly, confident that he would be espied from the walls long before he got there, and the gates would be opened for him. Today, however, the army blocked his way, and he didn't think it right that he should pass through their lines without at least telling someone in charge what his business was. He stopped his horse and looked around to see if any of the princes were making their way toward him.

On the whole, Talthybius liked the Trojans. They had always treated him courteously. There were some, of course, for whom he didn't care, Prince Paris, for one, and Queen Hecuba for another. He prided himself on being the only one in the Greek army who knew the names of all the Trojan princes. The Greeks, dismayed by the number of Priam's offspring, claimed the king had fifty sons, but Talthybius knew better. No woman could have borne fifty sons. But Queen Hecuba had borne Priam many sons, the last, Polites, only thirteen years ago, when everyone thought she had reached the end of her childbearing years.

On his left, Talthybius saw a small party of Trojans approaching him, so he dismounted. He thought he recognized their leader, Hector, the king's eldest son and head of Priam's armies. As the group got closer, however, the herald realized it was not Hector, but his cousin, Aeneas. Talthybius knew there was some long-standing feud between the two branches of the royal family that kept the two cousins at arm's length. Aeneas's branch didn't even live in the palace. They made their home instead in the easternmost suburbs of the city, and though Aeneas was at least on speaking terms with Priam and his sons, his father, Anchises, never set foot in the palace.

"Talthybius," called Aeneas, "have you come to surrender?"

It was said as a joke, but the herald maintained a serious expression. "Not yet, Lord Aeneas. I have a message from Agamemnon for Priam."

"I like your new wall," said Aeneas. "We were just trying to guess which of the gods helped you to build it."

"It was Silenus," said Talthybius dryly. The Trojans burst into laughter, for Silenus was a minor deity known only for his rotundity, drunkenness, and sloth.

Aeneas clapped Talthybius on the shoulder. "I'll take you to the palace." He directed one of his companions to fetch his own horse. Then he walked Talthybius aside. "I hear that Achilles is sick."

The herald nodded. "Yes, Achilles is ill."

"And his whole army too."

"Yes, they're all ill."

"Not a plague, I hope."

"No."

Aeneas smiled. "Talthybius, what will you do if we breach your wall?"

The herald shrugged his shoulders. "Me? Run, I suppose, with everyone else."

"Where do you stay during the fighting? In the camp?"

"Sometimes. Other times I walk up the beach."

"You don't watch the battle?"

"No. I used to, but I don't anymore."

"What's there to see up the beach?"

The herald glanced away momentarily. "Actually, there's a grave I visit."

"Whose?"

"Protesilaus's. There's no reason you'd know him."

"Who was he?"

"He was from Phylace. Don't ask me where Phylace is. He told me once, but it was after quite a bit of wine, and I can't remember anymore. I met him at Aulis. He looked me up because he wanted a poem for his wife. He'd just gotten married before he left home, and when he returned, he wanted to be able to recite a poem to her."

"Did you compose one for him?"

Talthybius snorted. "No, no. I'm no poet. But he knew I'd memorized a few poems. All he wanted me to do was insert her name in one I already knew. Her name was Laodamia. So I recited some for him, and he chose one. It was an awful thing, one of those dreadful verses comparing a woman's qualities to an assortment of vegetables. Cheeks like apples, lips like radishes, that sort of thing."

Aeneas laughed.

"Yes, that's what I thought too," said Talthybius, "but Protesilaus seemed tickled with it and repeated it over and over again until he memorized it. We became friends after that."

"He died in battle?" asked Aeneas.

"If you can call it that. Actually, he was never in a battle. We'd heard a prophesy that the first Greek to land here would die. Most of us thought it was a rumor started by one of your people."

"It probably was."

"Still, no one wanted to test it, so Agamemnon offered a prize to the first ashore. Protesilaus wasn't particularly superstitious, and decided it was an easy way to win a souvenir to take home to Laodamia. On the day we arrived, he made sure his ship was in front of all the rest, and when it was within range he leapt off and bade everyone else follow. The beach looked deserted, but there was a small party of Trojans hiding among the rocks. They didn't stay to fight really, just threw a few spears and left. But one of the spears hit Protesilaus.'' The herald paused. ''We buried him near the spot where he fell.''

Aeneas was silent for a moment, then asked, ''What was the prize?''

''A shield. A nice one with the likeness of Aphrodite on it. The goddess of love: he would have liked that. The chief had it sent to Laodamia.''

Aeneas looked over his shoulder and saw his man returning with a handsome chestnut mare. He turned back to the Greek. ''If we get through your wall, I'll keep an eye out for you. I'll save you if I can.''

Talthybius smiled at the Trojan, but did not reply. He had seen enough of warfare to know that death, in all its painful forms, was much more common than escape in a melee. That he had never lifted a sword against the Trojans would not save him if there were a general slaughter.

The two men mounted their horses and made their way along the path that led to the city. At one time, this path had meandered through farms and meadows, trees and cottages, but now it led merely through devastation. Nine years of conflict had seen all the human habitations burned, the crops trampled, the trees chopped down for firewood, and even the low stone fences that divided one farm from another thrown over and left in disarray.

As the two men climbed the small rise to the plateau on which the city was built, the great wall loomed larger. Talthybius marveled at it, and almost believed the story that Poseidon had built it. It was a full thirty feet tall, and angled in slightly from bottom to top. It was constructed of large limestone blocks, squared off and smoothed on the outside to prevent an enemy from getting a foothold. The wall followed the outline of an irregular star, with points projecting out on either side of its several gates. These projections allowed Trojan warriors on the ramparts to catch enemies approaching a gate in a cross fire. There were four portals in all: the Thymbraean Gates, which faced north to the Hellespont; the Dardanian Gates far on the other side of town, which faced inland toward Mt. Ida in the east; the Ilian Gates, which looked south toward the River Scamander; and finally, between the two most formidable of the projecting points on the western side of the city, the Scaean Gates, the main entrance into Troy. These were the gates the two men now approached. Talthybius could make out figures moving around on the battlements and on the two great towers that flanked the gates. He saw the massive wooden doors begin to open. They dismounted, and Aeneas allowed the herald to precede him over the threshold while he paused momentarily to speak to the guards and to entrust the horses to their care.

The Scaean Gates opened onto a large, open marketplace, the terminus of several broad streets. In later times, such a plaza might have had as its focus an elaborately carved fountain, with stone dolphins, birds, and mythological figures cavorting amidst jets of water. But the Trojans contented themselves with an ancient oak tree, beneath which wooden benches had provided shady comfort once for merchants from all over the Mediterranean.

Talthybius tried to imagine what the marketplace must have looked like before his countrymen arrived: the streets thronged with people; noise, shouting, laughter. Wagons coming from the harbor laden with jars as tall as a man, filled with oil, grain, and wine. Buyers from lands beyond the Black Sea came here to purchase the famous

Trojan blue cloth and of course Trojan horses. It was universally acknowledged that Troy bred the very finest horses.

But with the coming of the Greeks, all commerce stopped. The Scaean Gates were closed, and the population, both city-dwellers and those who made their homes outside the walls, were confined within the citadel. Troy was not a large city by modern standards. The wall was little more than a mile and a quarter in circumference, and it enclosed only a few thousand souls in an area of barely a hundred acres. Yet, the city had been designed to weather a siege. It had numerous wells for water, herds of livestock, and vast storehouses of food. Furthermore, Troy was never altogether cut off from the outside. The Greeks could completely surround the city only at the risk of spreading their forces dangerously thin. Rather than do this, they camped their main force on the shore west of the city and manned only token outposts at other locations around the perimeter. Consequently, armed bands of Trojans were able to supplement their city's supplies by occasional forays outside the wall. Nevertheless, the siege had taken its toll. The Trojans were a people used to freedom of movement, used to a lively commerce with foreign travelers; now they had to accept a kind of imprisonment within their own city limits. Like birds caged too late in life, many gave way to despondency in the long years of the war.

There was little movement in the marketplace this morning. A woman with a jar balanced on one shoulder and a child tagging after was making her way to the well. A boy led a solitary cow into a side street. An old couple sat in silence on the benches beneath the great oak.

"Talthybius!"

The herald turned his head, and saw Aeneas beckoning him to follow toward the palace. He took one more glance at the plaza, and then followed his Trojan guide up the broad avenue that led to the central part of the city.

Like most ancient towns, Troy followed no regular pattern. It had grown in a haphazard fashion, each new generation building on the last as its fancy or needs dictated. Most of the city was still a maze of narrow streets, dusty in summer, frozen in winter, or muddy, as they were now in early spring. Its crowded buildings were made of wood, with mortarless stone walls for foundations. But this present race of Trojans, either through the wealth they had acquired, or through knowledge they gathered from commerce, or perhaps just from an extraordinary love of beauty, had begun to transform their city. They had thoroughly rebuilt large sections of town, and had torn down those buildings falling into disrepair. They had constructed fine and graceful public buildings and lovely private residences. They had planted trees and small parks throughout the city. They had paved their principal streets with stone, and widened them so they would be filled with sunlight, and they dotted their houses with windows to let the sun indoors.

The particular thoroughfare Talthybius and his companion were traveling was lined on both sides by a series of stone pedestals which supported beautiful painted figures of the Trojan gods. The herald marveled each time he visited the city, and he understood why travelers from the farthest reaches of the Mediterranean used to come here, and why they would bring home tales of Troy's splendor. Troy may have begun as merely a walled town, convenient for trade and secure from invasion, but its citizens had turned it into a city men and women were proud to live in.

Before he had seen Troy, Talthybius considered Mycenae, where he came from, as the standard for all human art and architecture. The grim lions carved over the entrance to Agamemnon's palace, the cone-shaped tombs of the bygone kings filled him with a terrible awe. But after he saw Troy, Mycenae seemed primitive and crude by comparison. Here in Troy art inspired gaiety instead of fear; architecture served the living, not the dead. As he looked around, the herald wondered which he dreaded more: losing his own life if the Trojans prevailed, or watching this glorious city be destroyed should the Greeks conquer. He sent a silent prayer up to Zeus that the diplomatic mission he was engaged in might prevent either event.

The palace of Priam, which was at the terminus of the street they had taken, was not the most prominent building in Troy. That distinction went to the temple to the goddess Athena which stood close by, on the highest promontory in the city. But the royal palace was a lofty enough structure, and easily the largest building for human inhabitants. Its size was somewhat justified by Priam's large family, most of whom lived under his roof. At the main entrance to the palace, Aeneas again spoke to the guards to explain the presence of a Greek. One of the guards was dispatched to alert Priam of the herald's presence, and Aeneas accompanied Talthybius inside. The palace, too, had gone through different periods of construction, and therefore followed no uniform pattern. Its various wings and apartments, however, were arranged around a large, central courtyard, and it was through this that Aeneas led the herald.

Trojans had a great love for gardens. Every private home that had room contained either a courtyard like this one, or some small, green area behind or beside the residence. Trojans lavished great care on these, planting ornamental bushes and shrubs, laying gracefully curved paths, and erecting small, painted statues of the gods to preside there. This particular garden had in one corner a laurel tree and an altar to Zeus, the king of the gods. It was considered a sacred precinct, and residents of the palace would repair to it when they sought guidance or comfort. No one was in the courtyard today, however, as the two men passed through it on one of the winding paths.

Aeneas led the herald back inside, and then through an anteroom into the main audience chamber. This room was the most ornate in the palace. In a later age, doubtless, such a hall might seem low and ill-lit, and the throne itself a modest, if not downright uncomfortable chair, but in Talthybius the chamber inspired awe. The floor was polished stone, carefully fitted together by an artisan who had no knowledge of mortar. On the walls, illuminated by torches and by their own bright colors, was painted a series of scenes depicting Troy's history. As the two waited for the king's appearance, Talthybius studied these. He was a keen student of the iconography of the time, and he found an intense pleasure in deciphering such pictures.

On one panel was the god Poseidon, easily recognizable by the trident he carried in one hand; in the other he held a great square stone as he was shown building the walls of Troy. On an adjoining panel the god Apollo characteristically strummed his lyre at the foot of the new structure, thereby casting a charm on the wall so that it would protect the city as long as it stood unbroken. In another panel, the goddess Athena wearing full armor carried a statue of herself as a gift to the city. It was called the Palladium.

Then began a series of five panels devoted to the line of Trojan kings. The first was Dardanus, the progenitor of the royal family and the first to settle here. He had escaped the great flood by floating on an inflated skin, and he was pictured arriving on the deserted Asian shore still clinging to it. The next painting was of his son, the wealthy Erichthonius, surrounded by horses. These represented some of the three thousand he bred on the broad plains beneath Mt. Ida. They were said to be the offspring of Boreas, the North Wind, who fathered the swift breed that Troy became famous for. Then came the great King Tros, who built the city which now bore his name. He was pictured holding a team of regal, snowy white horses while Zeus, enthroned in glory, sat amidst the clouds overhead. Next came Tros's son Ilus, who was shown, sword in hand, subduing the surrounding province, which came to be known as Ilion after him. And finally, in the last panel was Laomedon, the father of the present king of Troy. He was shown standing upon the walls as the demigod Hercules rescued his daughter from the sea monster. There was no mistaking Hercules, who was clad in a lion skin and wielding a club.

Talthybius was pleased with himself. There was probably no one else outside of Troy who could read this pictorial history so clearly. Something nagged at him, though. He knitted his brows and scanned the panels again, stopping at the painting of King Tros. There was something he didn't understand in this one. Between Tros on the ground and Zeus in the clouds, there was a beautiful young boy who seemed to be suspended in midair. At first Talthybius thought it might be Eros, the mischievous love god, but Eros was almost always pictured with a bow and arrow. Furthermore, the herald knew of no story connecting Tros and Eros.

He didn't like to admit ignorance about such things, but curiosity finally got the better of him. Talthybius turned to his companion. "Who is the boy?" he asked, gesturing with his staff of office toward the painting. "Is it Eros?"

"No," said Aeneas, smiling. "That's Ganymede, King Tros's younger son. Zeus took him up to Olympus, the story goes. They say he was too beautiful to live on the earth, so Zeus took him away."

Talthybius had not heard this story before, and he

30

committed it to memory, as was his wont, while he stared at the picture. Yet he knew something was still unexplained, because ancient painters did not put details in unless they meant something. "What do the horses have to do with it?" he asked.

"Zeus gave them to Tros in exchange."

At that moment, King Tros's great-grandson entered the audience chamber through a small door to the left of the throne. Along with him came a hastily assembled group of his sons and counsellors.

Priam looked old, older than his seventy-odd years. The cares of a nine-year siege had thinned both his white hair and his body. His face was haggard and drawn. Yet he was tall, and still carried himself with the authority and dignity he had inherited from a long line of kings.

Talthybius quickly scanned the group that had accompanied the king. He recognized Priam's old counsellor, Antenor, and several of Priam's sons, including his youngest, Polites. Once again he did not see Hector. Nor did he see Paris. But of necessity he cut short his inventory to bow his head as Priam mounted the small platform that supported the throne.

When the king was seated, without preliminaries he said to the Greek, "You have something for me from Agamemnon?"

Talthybius, his moment now arrived, began to spin out the string of words he had memorized earlier that morning: "King Priam, Lord Agamemnon salutes you, and sends to you this message: The Lord Menelaus challenges Prince Paris to single combat in sight of both our armies for the possession of Helen. At the successful completion of the combat, when one man has either surrendered or given up the ghost, and Helen has been entrusted to the care of the other, the Greek forces will depart for home and consider the war over. If you agree to these terms, you may appoint the day of combat yourself, and we will make the appropriate sacrifices and take oaths with you to seal our pact before the most high Zeus."

There was a stir among Priam's companions, but the king himself showed no emotion. He looked at the herald in silence for several moments, and then, without shifting his gaze, put his hand on the arm of Polites, who stood next to him. This was the only indication Talthybius had that the next words Priam spoke were directed to the boy and not to him.

"Go to Hector," the king said. "He's on the right flank of the battle line. Tell him there is to be no fighting today, and that he must come to the palace." The words were said calmly, with no sense of urgency, but his son rushed out the door, and only after his hurried footfalls were no longer heard in the hall did Priam once more address the herald. "My council and I will consider Agamemnon's proposal, and I will have an answer for him shortly." The king then turned to his kinsman, who was still by the herald's side. "Aeneas, see to the Greek's comfort while he remains in Troy." With that, he rose and was out of the chamber almost before Talthybius could bow his head a second time.

Priam looked around at the score or more of sons, counsellors, and allied leaders assembled in front of him, who were at this very moment debating the offer that had come from the Greeks. He wondered what his father, Laomedon, would have thought. The old king would not have approved of this. The king who had bargained with Hercules to rescue his daughter and then withheld the reward, the king who had alienated even the gods with his cruelty and miserliness, that king would never have allowed his sons, let alone the city elders, to make a decision for him.

But the habits of peace are hard to break. Priam had formed this council shortly after he had become king, when the foremost questions to be decided were how to deal with the increased mercantile traffic through the city, how to accommodate so many visitors, and how to improve the harborage. He knew little about these things, and so he called in those citizens who did know to advise him. The council had worked well, too. Once the citizens so honored saw that the king really did want their opinions, they offered them freely, and then defended them just as freely when other citizens expressed contrary views. Priam did not like the arguments that erupted in front of him, but he learned to suffer them, because the right course of action would often emerge thereby. He required his sons to attend the council sessions too, even when they were quite young, as Polites was now, but he forbade them to speak until they attained adulthood.

Then the Greeks came, and this odd assortment of landowners and merchants, most of whom had never held a sword in anger in their lives, suddenly became a war council. Men who had advised the king about well-digging and road-building began debating the strategies of man-slaying. Priam shook his head slightly in amazement. No, Laomedon would not have approved. He would have considered it weakness in a king, and who's to say that he would be wrong? But Priam had come to depend on them now. He had grown old with some of these men, and he was grateful that the fate of the city did not rest on his shoulders alone.

After the war began, Priam had of necessity increased the size of the council by inviting the allied leaders to join. It was one of these who now had the floor, Sarpedon, the leader of the Lycians. Sarpedon was a fierce fighter, and he was dead set against accepting the Greek offer. Priam watched him speak, and tried to determine if his opinion was motivated by interest in saving the city, or by the lure of booty so temptingly close now in the Greek camp. The king wished Hector would arrive, but when the door opened in the midst of Sarpedon's speech, it was his son Paris who entered instead.

The Lycian leader paused, and Priam said, "Sit down, Paris. We have received a challenge from Agamemnon that concerns you."

"I've heard it," his son said, placing himself in one of the preferred seats near the king, "and I accept."

"That's not for you to decide," said Priam.

Paris scowled, but even that unflattering demeanor could not diminish the prince's good looks. He had a boyish face still, though now already in his thirties, and he had a vigorous and graceful body. Since his weapon was the bow, he did not have to fight in the front lines, and therefore his smooth skin was still unbroken by the scars that laced the bodies of so many of his contemporaries. His good looks, however, were no source of joy to Priam. The king could not forget that his son was responsible for bringing his city to the brink of oblivion. He resumed his attention to the Lycian leader.

"My lord, as I was saying, there is no denying Prince Paris's skill with a bow, but in hand-to-hand combat Menelaus is much the stronger man, if only because of his size and experience. I've fought—"

"Don't worry about me, Sarpedon," interrupted Paris. "I can take care of myself."

Sarpedon leveled his gaze at the prince and continued more slowly. "I've fought the man. He is strong and skillful. Don't underestimate him."

"Menelaus is old and slow," countered Paris. "If he was too much for a Lycian, what's that to me?"

Sarpedon fumed. "If my men weren't within spitting distance of the Greek ships, I'd be happy to clear out right now and let that 'old and slow' Spartan rip your ass off!"

Paris, enraged, leapt to his feet.

"Sit down!" said Priam.

34

The prince hesitated a moment, glaring at Sarpedon, then slumped in his chair again. Priam looked once more to the Lycian leader, but Sarpedon, disgusted now, said no more.

Priam understood how Sarpedon felt. The Lycians had come to Troy on their own. Their particular reasons for coming had something to do with allied loyalty, but they also had an interest in keeping the Greeks from building an empire in Asia. They were not mercenaries, had received no pay from Priam. The Trojans merely provided their food, and there was an implicit agreement that if the Trojans prevailed, the Greek spoils would be shared equally among the allies. Now that they were closer to those spoils than they had ever been before, Sarpedon was loath to relinquish them in a negotiated settlement.

The next to speak was a corpulent, balding man standing near the Lycian. "I agree with my countryman, Lord Sarpedon. We've nearly driven the Greeks into the sea. They only proposed this duel to keep us from finishing the job." He spoke in a slightly wheezing voice, which made it sound like he was out of breath.

"Are you so certain of victory, Lord Pandarus, that you'd turn down the first opportunity we've had in nine years to end this war?" The speaker was Antenor, a man nearly as old as Priam. He was the brother of Priam's wife, Hecuba, but his friendship with Priam predated the king's marriage, for they had been companions even in their youth. He had now been Priam's counsellor for close to half a century. In peace, the two had watched their numerous sons grow to manhood, and in war they had watched them die. Priam had seen a change take place in his old friend during the course of the war. At the beginning Antenor, like many an old man who could no longer wield a sword, was eager to battle the Greeks and show them once and for all that Trojans were superior. But now Priam's most faithful counsellor counseled peace.

"Are you so trusting, Lord Antenor," said Pandarus, "that you believe the Greeks will leave whether or not they win the duel? If they kill Prince Paris and are rewarded with Helen, do you expect them, in the flush of victory, to depart as if they'd lost the war? Or if Prince Paris gets off a lucky blow and kills Menelaus, do you think Agamemnon won't want to revenge his brother's death?"

"Then we'll be no worse off than we are right now," countered Antenor.

"I disagree," said Pandarus, shaking his head, but bearing a mirthless smile on his face. "Right now the Greeks are scared. They're scared they can't win without Achilles, and they don't have the motive of revenge, or the motivation of victory to spur them on to try. Why else would they offer a duel? Would a winning army stake everything on a single combat? I say we should waste no more time discussing it, because time is what they're after. I say we should attack now, and with the help of the gods, by nighttime we'll see the glow of their ships burning on the shore."

There was a murmur of agreement around the room, but then a familiar voice was heard coming from the doorway. "And will Achilles sit by and watch as you burn his ships?" All eyes turned to the new speaker, a black-haired man in battle gear, his helmet dangling from one hand.

"Oh, my lord Hector, I didn't see you come in," wheezed Pandarus, still smiling.

Priam watched his eldest son as he strode into the room and took the place reserved for him by the king's side. He was a man past forty, and his much-scarred body and muscular arms and legs testified to nearly a decade of constant warfare. Yet as Priam looked at him, he remembered a different Hector in the time before the Greeks came. When the king allowed himself to think back on those days, he was shocked by the transformation that had taken place in his son.

Before the war, Hector seemed to have only two interests outside of his family. One was his farm. He had purchased fields in the broad plain before Troy and supervised their cultivation himself, often working side by side with his servants. He enjoyed experimenting with crops to see what would grow and what would not at that windy crossroads of the world. He learned storage techniques, what conditions were necessary to keep produce uncorrupted. He had even established city granaries as a precaution against lean times, little knowing that they would eventually be used to weather a siege.

His other interest was horses. In a nation of horse breeders and horse tamers, he became the best of both. He had a natural affinity for horses, and could ride almost before he could walk. He delighted in taking a spirited animal and teaching it to be a good riding horse or a good chariot horse without breaking the beast's spirit. He became so expert at it that Trojans used to call him "the horse tamer."

But now as Priam looked at his son, he saw a stranger. That earlier Hector, quick to smile, quick to laugh, would have liked nothing better than to inherit his father's crown in the course of time, reign over a peaceful city, and at the end of his own life to pass that same crown peacefully on to his son. But that Hector was gone. The man Priam saw now was not a farmer, not a horse tamer, maybe not even a son anymore. He was a warrior, and in his eyes was the hollow, dead look of all warriors in every age, the look of men who have seen what men should not see, done what men should not do. Priam regretted the war with every part of his being, but no regret tore at his soul more than that his son had been sacrificed to it.

When Hector was seated, Priam said, "You've heard the Greeks' proposal?"

"Yes," Hector nodded.

"I'm going to accept," said Paris to his brother.

"That's not for you to decide," said Hector, without looking at him.

"Do you think we can trust the Greeks to keep their oath and leave after the duel?" asked his father.

Hector sighed and then was silent for a moment. "No," he said finally.

"There you are, then," said Pandarus. "Even the Lord Hector agrees with me. The Greeks don't care about Helen. They never did. She's just an excuse. They came here out of greed, and they won't leave until they've sacked this city and taken all the gold they can carry back to their wretched homes in Greece. Or until we drive them away."

"I don't suppose there's any greed on your part," said Paris, "nothing in the Greek camp you've got your eye on?"

"And why not?" asked Pandarus, still smiling. "We've all certainly earned it."

"But what about Achilles?" asked Deiphobus, Priam's second eldest son, who had not yet spoken. "Hector's right. Achilles won't sit by and let us burn his ships."

"If Achilles isn't fighting us," responded Pandarus, "then there's no reason for us to burn his ships. Our quarrel isn't with him. His camp is at the very end of the beach, and there's no reason why we can't keep a safe distance from him."

"What do you think, Hector?" asked Sarpedon, entering the discussion again. "Can we trust Achilles to stay out?"

Hector shook his head. "I don't know. We don't know

why he retired in the first place. There's no telling what might bring him back."

"But you think we should reject the offer anyway," said Antenor.

"I didn't say that."

"I thought you said we couldn't trust the Greeks to keep their oath," said Deiphobus.

"Yes. Their oath won't bind them if they see a chance of winning again."

"Then there's no reason to accept the offer," said Pandarus with finality.

The council members looked to Hector for his reply, but he leveled his gaze at his brother Paris. "There is a reason," he said.

Paris, feeling uncomfortable suddenly, avoided Hector's eyes.

"I don't know if the Greeks will leave after the duel," said Hector. "They might. They may have only proposed the duel to give them an excuse to leave without looking defeated. Or they might just be stalling for time. I don't know. But I think we should accept anyway."

"Why, in God's name?" asked Pandarus.

Never taking his eyes from the younger man seated across the table from him, Hector said, "Because Menelaus and my brother here ought to have a chance, at least once, to face each other."

There was silence around the room. Paris looked up again at the cold stare trained upon him, and Priam detected fear in his younger son's eyes for the first time.

"But if they don't keep their oath—" said Deiphobus softly after a moment.

Hector finally shifted his gaze and looked around the room. The next words he spoke were in the clarion voice all of them had heard on the field. "If they don't keep their oath, then we'll drive them to the beach again. We'll drive them into the sea, drive them to hell, Achilles and all!''

There were cheers from several quarters, but the other allied leaders waited for Sarpedon, whose expression had not changed. He stared at Hector for a long moment, then smiled and nodded his head slowly. ''All right. I'll agree to that,'' he said. ''Let's accept the offer.''

With that, the other allies spoke their assent too, and when the noise died down, all looked to the king. Priam regarded his two sons, looking from one to the other, a duel of his own going on within him. Then he drew himself up and once more looked around the room expectantly to show he was still willing to hear. When no one else spoke, he said merely, ''Then it is settled.''

While the others shuffled out of the room, Priam sat for a while. He had just let his council decide not only the fate of his city, but the fate of his son as well. The image of his stern predecessor rose in his mind again. With a mixture of guilt and resignation he thought, Yes, Laomedon, that's the way we make decisions now in Troy.

III

Helen

AS THE HERALD was led across the courtyard to begin
his journey back to the Greek camp, he was watched by
a woman from one of the palace windows. She did not
know his mission, but she knew that in one way or
another it concerned her. Everything concerned her.
Yet, despite what the poets said, she had not been born
for this. Her name need not have been bound up forever
in the crazy human confusion of love and war. Her name
need not even have been coupled with Troy. She was just
a girl from Sparta.

In the last nine years, hardly a day had gone by when
Helen hadn't asked herself how all this had happened,
why so many men, men she didn't even know and who
didn't know her, were fighting over her. She had never
wanted this, never planned on it. When she traced back
through her life to discover the chain of events which
brought her to this walled town, she could find nothing
in her actions that made it inevitable. She had been
married, she had borne a child, in a moment of passion
she had been unfaithful, and in a moment of folly she
had run away with her lover. She was not proud of her
actions, but they were far from unique. Women of every
era could tell a similar tale, and she knew it. Why should
her story lead to this conclusion when a thousand thousand others did not? She searched for the answer, and
the only answer she ever found was a word: "beautiful."

For a long time while growing up she thought the word
"beautiful" applied only to swans. Her mother loved

41

swans, and had dozens of them around the palace grounds. The little girl would watch their stately progress on the river Eurotas believing that Zeus himself had created swans so that human beings could know what true beauty was. If she ever considered her own looks, it was merely to note that she wasn't half as handsome as her sister, Clytemnestra, and even if she were, she was still far inferior to her elder brothers, the twins Castor and Pollux.

When she saw them bathing in the river or exercising together, she would admire their lean, smooth bodies, their muscles, the way they could run and leap and throw a javelin while in midair. She saw the way their bodies tapered from broad shoulders down to narrow hips, and she dreaded the day when her own body would assume a contrary form. Once when she was very young she asked her father, Tyndareus, why she couldn't grow up to be a man like her brothers, but he just laughed and told her it was the will of the gods.

Nevertheless, she imitated her brothers, learned to ride horses as they had, learned how to pace herself while running so that she didn't use up all her wind at once. She would follow them when they climbed the rocky hills around Sparta, or went hunting in the forest. They made fun of her at first, and told her she should stay home with her sister, but when she showed them that she could keep up with them they eventually accepted her as a comrade. The three of them would hunt rabbits when they were young, and deer when they got older. She didn't enjoy the killing of animals, but she loved the thrill of stalking, of walking quietly in the woods like an animal herself, and then the lively banter as the three headed home with their kill. The world seemed like a golden place to her at those times, and she hoped such a life would never end.

In her early adolescence, however, she began to hear

the word "beautiful" applied to herself. It was then that things started to change. She would often catch her parents talking about her when she entered a room, though they would stop when they noticed her. Her mother began to take more interest in the condition of Helen's hair and clothing, and her father began to limit whom she could see and where she could go unaccompanied. These actions annoyed her, because she had never seen her parents treat her brothers, or even her sister, in quite this way. Clytemnestra, in fact, began to act coldly toward her, and Castor and Pollux seemed to be more and more uncomfortable when she was around. All of these things she eventually associated with the word "beautiful," and she began to hate it.

She once looked at her reflection in her father's great polished shield and tried to see what the others saw, but she saw only a skinny, gangly girl, much less shapely and womanly than her sister. She saw a child, in fact, fresh from the errors and indignities that are the history of all children. Had they suddenly forgotten the time she was running after her brothers and had slipped and fallen in the cow dung? Or the time the old King Atreus of Mycenae was visiting and she suddenly felt sick and threw up her dinner in front of everyone? Who, she asked, knowing these things, could call her beautiful?

Yet everyone did. Visitors whom she'd never seen before, relatives who visited once a year, even house servants who saw her every day. And the more she was told she was beautiful, the more her freedom was restricted. Finally she asked her mother what was happening, and Leda told her that her father was making plans for her marriage.

Marriage! She had not thought of it before. Of course she knew that she would need to marry. Everyone married. And in a vague way she knew that she would bear children, for that was the lot of women. But she had expected it to come much later, at a time when she was ready for it. All things before had come in their season. She had not been allowed to bathe in the river alone until her parents were sure she could swim. She had not been permitted to ride a horse before her legs came halfway down Nutty's flank. Was she now to marry before— before what? What was supposed to happen? Or had it already happened without her knowing it?

She asked her mother, and Leda began talking inexplicably about blood and the moon and the great goddess Artemis. The girl didn't understand, and she pressed her mother, but Leda would say no more. Then one day the blood came, and the girl was horrified. Shortly after the blood, came the suitors.

Full-grown men from all over Greece traveled to Sparta to see her. Some were covered with scars, some ugly, some old and bald. But her father honored them all, for each was a king just as her father was, and each offered an alliance which she would seal in blood. To each one she was presented in all her finery, and asked to speak. Some laughed, some looked somber, some seemed to look deep into her eyes, and others avoided her eyes altogether.

There were so many who had requested to see her that these audiences went on for months. Her father, however, who at first was flattered by the attention paid his daughter, seemed to grow more and more anxious as time passed and the number of suitors grew. Again the girl began to hear her parents talking about her in muffled tones, and she wondered what she was doing wrong. One day in a fit of anger Tyndareus said, "To have a beautiful daughter is one thing, but why did the gods have to curse me with a daughter so beautiful that I'll risk a war if I choose one suitor over another?" It was that word "beautiful" again. She went to her room and cried.

Then, abruptly, the suitors stopped coming, and talk

of marriage ceased almost as suddenly as it had begun. Helen was puzzled, but did not question her parents. In large measure her freedom was returned to her, and she was overjoyed. Castor and Pollux would no longer let her accompany them when they went hunting, but at least the girl was free to roam on her own again, which she did every chance she got. She would often ride her horse far from the palace, taking a small bag of cheese and bread so that she would not have to return before dark.

On these solitary rides she sometimes thought about marriage, and wondered if perhaps she would never have to marry now. The idea pleased her, and she imagined herself free to live like her brothers. She prayed to the great goddess Artemis to make it come to pass, and promised eternal fealty in exchange. Her parents continued to say nothing, and as months lengthened into years, the possibility that the goddess had heard her prayer seemed more and more certain. But the word "beautiful" would not die.

Although the visits of the suitors had stopped, commerce with travelers and merchants continued, and these people kept alive the fame of her beauty. As she got older, the beautiful girl became a young woman so beautiful no one had seen her like before. Yet she did not conform to the beauty standards of her day. She never achieved full, womanly breasts like her sister, nor did her hips become very rounded. Through her constant exercise, she had remained boyish in her frame. It was only in the luxuriance of her hair and the exquisite fineness of her features that her sex was revealed.

Her father grew troubled again. The suitors, whom he hoped in time would forget his daughter and marry elsewhere, now with each report carried to them, pressed Tyndareus anew to make his choice. At length, he restricted her freedom again, keeping her within the palace boundaries so that people would not see her, but the solicitations did not stop, and they began to take on a threatening tone. Something had to be done.

Tyndareus sequestered himself for three days. When he emerged, it was with the idea of a pact. Before he chose a son-in-law, all the suitors had to agree first that they would honor the choice, and then that they would defend the marriage against any who would attempt to break it. Messengers were enlisted and dispatched to every corner of Greece. Weeks passed and the messengers returned; the suitors agreed to the pact, one and all.

But the young woman who was the subject of this agreement was not told about it until much later. She only knew that her father had ordered her not to leave the palace grounds. She asked her mother what was happening, and Leda told her that once more the king was arranging for her marriage. The news shocked her, more than it had years before. Now she had gotten used to the idea of not marrying. She went to her father and told him she had made a vow to the goddess Artemis that she would not marry, but he said she had no business making such a vow. He said she was too beautiful not to marry, and if he didn't give her in marriage to someone, his very kingdom would be in jeopardy. She went to the sacred grove behind the palace and prayed to the goddess and asked why Artemis had abandoned her, but the goddess said nothing.

Tyndareus, meanwhile, satisfied that he could make his choice without danger, chose for his daughter the red-haired, second son of King Atreus. The marriage would make a double bond between Sparta and neighboring Mycenae, for the Spartan king had already given his other daughter, Clytemnestra, to Atreus's elder son, Agamemnon. The two marriages would make their kingdoms the strongest alliance in Greece. Further, Tyndareus had determined to retire from the cares of state. Since his own sons, Castor and Pollux, had no interest in government and had left Sparta to seek their fortunes elsewhere, the king decided to resign his crown to his new son-in-law, Menelaus, at the solemnizing of the marriage.

The wedding plans, the weeks of frenzied activity, the arrival of relatives, friends, guests from all over, the marriage celebration itself were all a blur in Helen's memory. All that stood out clearly was the wedding night. Her mother had taken great care to prepare her for it. Leda warned her that it would be frightening, but told her not to act afraid. She warned Helen of the pain and the blood, and told her that it was all right to cry out from the pain, but only once. The young woman asked her about the man she was to marry, for she had met him only briefly, and that was years before. But Leda, who knew him no better, merely told her that it was sufficient he was a king's son and would be a king himself on his wedding day. She knew no fault in him, and told her daughter to be yielding to him that night in all that was seemly, but that she should not consent to do what only the animals and the courtesans do. Her husband would then respect her, and she would have a peaceful marriage.

So the ceremony was performed, and in the evening the young woman found herself in a chamber alone with the man. Menelaus was only ten years her senior, but he was already an experienced warrior, having fought in his father's war to regain the throne from his uncle Thyestes. Menelaus was also no stranger to women. As a warrior, he had enjoyed the singular prerogative of all warriors, the pleasures of captive women. But this woman was to be his wife, and from her would issue his lawful sons. This marriage would make him a king like his brother Agamemnon, an ambition he had not entertained as a young man.

He stepped up to her and put his hands on her shoulders and kissed her on the mouth. He wore a beard, and the hairs pricked her cheek and her chin. As he began to remove her wedding garments, she remembered her mother's advice to pray to the goddess Hera for strength and guidance. Hera was the wife of Zeus and patroness of marriage, but the young woman found herself silently praying to Artemis instead, the great virgin goddess of the moon, and apologizing for her broken vow.

The lovemaking itself was curious to her. The pain her mother warned her about was not severe, and she didn't cry out at all. But what surprised her most was that she could think of other things while it was going on. She had expected something as important as this to drive all other thoughts from her mind, but in the midst of it, while she felt the weight of the strange red-haired man on top of her, she was thinking about a particular hill some distance from the palace. It was her favorite destination when she went out riding with her horse. There was an outcropping there where she loved to sit and watch the hawks circle over the heated valleys below. The ease with which they soared fascinated her, for they hardly seemed to move a feather, yet they could stay aloft for hours. She used to try to get her horse to watch them too, and would lift his head up to aim it in their general direction, but once released he would just shake his mane and return to nibbling the grass at her feet. She used to wonder what kind of a world he saw through those odd rectangular slits in his eyes.

Then she became conscious of the red-haired man again, and she left her favorite spot. He groaned as if in pain, and then stopped moving and became much heavier upon her. She waited a few seconds and was about to ask him if he was all right, but then he rolled to his side without speaking to her, and shortly fell asleep. Her mother had warned her of this too, and she had advised

Helen to lie still and try to sleep also, even though sleep might be difficult.

But the young woman was wide awake. She had gone through the rite that made her a wife, and now she was trying to discover what it meant, how she was changed. She didn't feel any different. She ran her hands over her body as the man had done and tried to feel what he felt, but she couldn't. She wanted to ask him, but her mother had told her to let him sleep.

She wondered what her sister's wedding night had been like with Agamemnon. She had met Agamemnon, and he seemed much more austere than his younger brother. She was a little afraid of him, in fact. He had a fire in his eyes that Menelaus lacked. She was glad her father had chosen the red-haired man for her. Clytemnestra now lived in the great palace at Mycenae, which people said was the finest in all Greece. She had never seen it, and she wondered if her husband would ever take her there to visit.

Her husband! The word shocked her a little. Did he feel the same way about the word "wife," she wondered. She wanted to ask him. She reached her hand over to wake him, but then remembered her mother's advice and pulled it back. The words "husband" and "wife" must be two different things, though, she thought, or else they would be the same word. She had feared the word "wife." It seemed a forbidding word, and it reminded her of being confined to the palace grounds. But that had been because of another word, "beautiful." Had she now just exchanged one confining word for another? The word "beautiful" had forced her to marry, and now the word "wife" forced her to lie still so her husband could sleep.

She sat up and looked at the figure lying peacefully by her side. For a moment she hated him; she hated her father for forcing her to marry him, and her mother for telling her to be yielding. But even as she seethed in that hatred, the thought came to her. If the word "beautiful" had limited her freedom and brought her inevitably to marriage, why might not the word "wife" reclaim some of that freedom? There is a kind of rough justice in all the world. Though she had married this man unwillingly, she did make him a king by doing so, and herself a queen. And must a queen tremble in fear at the thought of waking her own husband?

She gave her mother only one more passing thought, and then said, in a voice that even surprised herself, "My lord Menelaus!"

He started, as only a soldier does when suddenly awakened. He reached instinctively for his sword, but when he remembered where he was and saw that all was still about him, he looked at her. "What's the matter?" he asked.

"What is Mycenae like?"

"What?"

"What is Mycenae like, where you come from?"

He sat up beside her and stared at her, wondering if Tyndareus's daughter might be a half-wit for all her beauty.

"Why are you asking me this?"

"People say Mycenae is the most magnificent city in all Greece. You come from there, my lord. Is it really true?"

He continued to stare at her. He had not heard her speak more than ten words before this, but now he found that he liked the sound of her voice, despite the unusualness of her questions. He smiled. "Yes, it's true," he said.

"Are you very sleepy?"

"No, not very."

"Would you like some wine? The servants left us some."

"All right."

She leapt out of bed, and Menelaus watched her as she filled two large cups at a table across the room. In the moonlight, her lithe naked body might have been that of a graceful boy, so tall and smooth and perfect. Whether she was a half-wit or not, Menelaus thought, there was something divine, godlike about her. He watched her return and accepted the offered cup from her hand.

"What is it like?" she asked him again. "I've never been away from Sparta."

He smiled again, and began to tell her about Mycenae. He told her about the famous lion gate and the great conic tombs and the treasure house. Then she asked him about his family, and he recounted their history, which went all the way back to the gods. She asked him about the war with Thyestes, and he showed her the scars he'd gotten in it. She plied him with questions, and as he drank the sweet wine and warmed to her company, he asked her questions too. He asked her about Sparta and the Spartan people he would be ruling. He asked her about her father, about the palace, and the servants who lived in it with them. He laughed at her story of the swan that once mounted her mother when she bent over to pick a flower. They talked, and they drank, and the hours passed.

It was near dawn before they resigned themselves to sleep, and past noon before they finally emerged from the chamber, but when they did, Helen did not think about Artemis anymore. Instead, she thanked Hera for sending her this good, red-haired man.

The days and months that followed were peaceful ones. Menelaus busied himself with his newfound affairs of state, and Helen, free once more to roam as she pleased, enjoyed a tranquility she had not known since childhood. Leda and Tyndareus moved to a small estate they owned on the periphery of the kingdom. That left her mistress of the palace, and she enjoyed ordering it in her own way. Best of all, she began to feel quite friendly toward the man who shared her bed. If he remained taciturn and somewhat formal in his lovemaking, he was at least a good listener and easy to make laugh. Helen did love the sound of his laughter. If things had remained like that, life would not have been so bad. But life was ultimately the problem, a new life, sown in her.

Helen had not thought much about bearing children, and was surprised when the local midwife told her she was already two months gone. Menelaus was delighted and prayed to Zeus that it would be a son, but Helen was confused. Amid the general gaiety she felt she should be happy too, but she wasn't. She was alarmed and frightened, more frightened than she'd ever been by marriage. She felt something growing inside her, taking her over, and the idea horrified her. She resented the daily sickness once it began, and when her belly started to swell hideously, she was thankful that her lean brothers were no longer there to see her.

She began to hate her body as a thing no longer her own. She could not ride, could hardly even walk sometimes, and in this grotesque condition she had to suffer the smiling gazes and good wishes of all who saw her. Worst were the attentions of other mothers, who now numbered her in their ranks, and gladly initiated her into their mysteries with stories of their own pregnancies. She didn't want to be classed with them. She wanted to flee to the hills and be alone with her horse once more, or to flee even further back to the outings with her brothers, before she was beautiful, before she was a woman, when she could pretend she was a boy, too. But she could not flee what was happening to her.

Then came the labor.

Her mother had warned her about the pain of her

wedding night, but no one could have prepared her for the pain of childbirth. The white, searing pain, exquisite in its purity, made her wish only for death. She prayed for death, prayed from her soul that the huge thing ripping her apart would just kill her and send her shade to hell. When the gods did not hear her prayer, she cursed them. She cursed them for making her a woman, for making her subject to this. She cursed Hera and Artemis both, for betraying her. She cursed all the gods she could name in her frenzy, and the midwife only stopped her mouth when she began to curse Zeus for founding the house of Atreus from which her husband had come. Then some merciful god, in one final blinding flash of pain, struck her unconscious.

When she awoke, Leda was there. She had come to visit her daughter during her confinement. She told Helen that she had given birth to a girl. Helen did not react, but seemed to look through her mother and focus on some distant object no one else could see. Her mother tried to press the infant upon her, but when Helen saw it she got such a wild look in her eyes that Leda feared for the child's safety, and gave it to a servant to take from the room. Leda tried to comfort her daughter by telling her she would in time forget the pain and take joy in what she had produced, but Helen said nothing.

It was several days before Helen would consent to hold the baby, and she would under no circumstances suckle it, so that duty continued to be performed by a wet nurse. It pleased Leda to watch her daughter hold the child, but she learned not to express any delight, or Helen would immediately give it up again.

Helen herself took no nourishment during this time. The thought of food nauseated her, and the servants stopped offering it to her for fear of her wrath. She spent most of her time alone, even after she began to get out of bed. She continued to feel the dull throb, still echoing her intense pain, and this kept alive her anger and her hatred. If she consented occasionally to hold the child, it was to see if her feelings had changed, but they had not. The child was a helpless creature, surely innocent of its own birth, and everyone said she should love it, would love it, had to love it as her own. But Helen felt nothing, and so along with the anger and resentment she felt fear, fear because she was different. She began to hate even her absent brothers, who would never have to feel what she was feeling now.

Leda began to be concerned for her daughter's life as she continued to watch her despondency. The lack of food was not only contracting her belly to its original size, but also robbing her of all vitality. Her cheeks sank and her eyes looked out of dark cavities. Menelaus had been forbidden from Helen's apartment, but now Leda consented to let him visit in hopes that he could rouse her. The sight of him threw Helen into a frenzy, however, and Leda would have led him away again, but Menelaus ushered the older woman out the door and latched it. He then produced a loaf of bread and some wine he had carried along. He set them on a table, sat down near them and watched Helen in silence.

The look on her face shocked him, for he had seen such a look only on the battlefield. Her head tilted down, she peered at him with grim eyes from beneath her brow. It was a mixture of fear and hatred, a readiness to duck if need be, flee if possible, fight if compelled to. He had seen such a look on an enemy's face, but never on a woman's.

"Helen, you must eat something," he said firmly.

She didn't answer.

More softly he said, "Helen, what's the matter?"

"I don't want to live."

"Why, in God's name?"

"I don't want to have any more children."

"That's for the gods to decide."

"No," she shouted. "That's for *me* to decide!"

He was quiet for a moment. Then, softly again, he said, "You have produced a fine daughter. We've named her Hermione. But you and I must now have a son."

"NO!" She screamed the word at him, and so pitiful and terrifying was the sound that Menelaus was abashed by the chill he felt in his own spine.

When the echo of her cry died away, he said gently, "Have some wine with me. Eat some of this bread."

She looked at him. He had a kindly expression on his face, and she found herself feeling sorry for him. Her face softened. "Menelaus, if I have another child, I'll die!"

"That's in the hands of the gods, too," he said, "but you won't die. Come and sit with me."

But she would die, she thought, whether the gods wanted her to or not. At that moment she made a vow, one which her father could not rescind. If she became pregnant again, she would take her own life. Menelaus was a good man, and she would let him lie with her again, but she would bear no more of his children. The freedom to die was the one freedom still left her.

Once committed to that, Helen felt a strange relief, a burden lifted, as when she rode away from the palace and passed over the crest of the first hill that blocked her from view. Wordlessly, she went to the table and sat beside him and took the offered wine and bread.

Menelaus felt an uncommon tenderness for her at that moment. He said, "The gods make the second one easier than the first," and Helen nodded.

But the gods had heard her prayer this time, and they sent Helen no more children.

Hermione was everything her father wanted in a girl, and he pampered her as only a father can his first daughter. If he regretted anything at all, it was that his wife took so little joy in her. He tried at first to interest her in the child, and Helen would be agreeable, but he could tell her heart wasn't in it. She continued to allow him into her bed anytime he wanted, but her heart was not in that either, if it ever had been. These things troubled him. If he were a different sort of man, a man like his elder brother, Agamemnon, for instance, he might have insisted that she behave differently, but instead he let her alone, and she spent more and more of her time by herself.

Helen, for her part, tried to find something she liked in the child, especially when Menelaus wasn't around. As the girl grew older, Helen tried to interest her in horses and had visions of their riding together someday. She wanted to share with the child the joys she had found in the hills and shady forests, but Hermione was scared of the horses and would cry when her mother tried to make her approach them. So Helen would give her back to the servants, whom the child felt much more comfortable with than she did with her mother.

Leda had told Helen not to worry if she didn't feel motherly feelings for the child right away. She said they would come. But when the child entered its fifth year, they still had not come. What came was Paris.

Helen had never met anyone from Troy, though she had of course heard of it. Everyone had. It was the almost mythical walled town across the sea. So she was excited when her husband told her that they were going to receive a visitor from there. He said one of King Priam's sons was coming to talk about trade between Troy and Sparta, and he would be staying at the palace. Helen hoped he would be a good storyteller, because she wanted to ask him many questions about his city. But the man who came was a disappointment.

He was a young man, for one thing, about her own age, and filled with the cockiness handsome young men have in such abundance. Also, his speech was annoying. He spoke Greek with a curious kind of lilting accent, and used words she was unfamiliar with, or antique words she'd only heard the bards use in poetry. She found out later that these were merely the peculiar characteristics of Trojan speech, but in Paris they seemed an affectation, and she disliked him for it. What repelled her most of all about the young prince, however, were the looks she caught him giving her when others were not watching. She avoided him, and tried never to be alone with him.

To her dismay, however, Menelaus announced after a few days that he had to leave for Crete. His maternal grandfather, Catreus, had died, and Agamemnon asked him to go there to settle the estate. Helen asked her husband if she could accompany him, but he laughed and said it would be impolite for them both to leave while they had a royal visitor. So she stayed, and she concealed as best she could the dislike she felt for the young man. She made sure to keep the servants around whenever she was with him.

What she missed most of all while Menelaus was away, though, were her daily rides on her horse. She had stopped taking them so that she could manage the entertainment of the Trojan prince and his retinue. But early one morning, determining that she could safely slip away for a few hours and leave them in the hands of her servants, she rode away from the palace. She went to her favorite hill and sat with her back to a tree to watch the hawks. For a while she thought about the annoying prince, wondering if all Trojans had such a high opinion of themselves, but soon the tranquility of the place had its usual calming effect, and she fell into a dreamy contemplation of the slow-circling birds.

As she watched the hawks, she imagined herself in their place, seeing the earth from their vantage, tilting a wing slightly to bank on the very air and dip down to get a better look at a hidden valley or a craggy rock shelf. She envied both their freedom and their power, but of the two, she envied their freedom more.

She didn't know exactly when she became conscious of the hoofbeats, because they came so softly at first that she could have mistaken them for the wind in the valleys below. But when she perceived them for what they were, she snapped out of her reverie and looked in the direction from which she had come.

She recognized the horse before she recognized the rider, for it was one of hers, a skittish mare that no one but she ever rode. On it was the young prince. Helen stood up and watched him approach and tried to hide her double resentment at his intrusion and his presumption in taking one of her horses.

"I've had quite a time finding you," Paris said as he dismounted. "The old lady, Eury—what's-her-name, said you sometimes come here, but her directions weren't too good. I hope you don't mind that I borrowed one of your horses."

"No, it's all right," she lied.

"The groom suggested the gelding with the white feet, but I like mares. I like this one especially; lots of spirit. Beautiful animal."

"Not too many people can ride her. I'm surprised she didn't give you trouble."

"Trouble?" He laughed and cradled the mare's head in his arm. "We Trojans have a gift. When Zeus gave the divine horses to old King Tros, he made us expert horsemen forever."

She forced a smile, but said nothing. He walked the mare a short distance away and tethered her to a tree. He took care to make sure she was within reach of sweet grass, and he stroked her neck affectionately as Helen watched. He did have a way with horses, she had to admit. He was insufferably boastful, to be sure, but his skill was genuine. She had noted how carefully he alighted. The mare tended to jerk nervously when she felt the weight on her back shift to one side, but the prince had executed the movement so quickly and smoothly that he was off before his mount could become agitated.

As she watched him now, she noticed for the first time how much he reminded her of her brothers. The dashing good looks, the perfectly tapered body, so different from her husband. Menelaus was a full-blown man, with a thick chest and waist, a deep voice, and a serious demeanor. But Paris was a youth, what she herself might look like now had she been born a male. He was reminiscent of Castor and Pollux too in his youthful energy, and even in his shameless egotism. These qualities had seemed endearing in her brothers, and she wondered why she found them so offensive in the prince.

"This is a nice spot," he said when he returned.

"Yes."

He looked in the direction of the hawks. "What eyes they must have! I've watched them at Troy. I've seen them dive into a field where the grass was a foot high and come up with a mouse, where I couldn't see my own feet."

She did not reply, and there followed an awkward silence.

Still looking out over the promontory, he said, "You probably come here to be alone, and here I am interrupting you."

"It's all right."

"But you see, I had to tell you this dream I had, and I haven't been able to get you alone for days."

"What dream?"

He finally turned to her. "Can we sit down?"

Helen resumed her place with her back to the tree. Paris seated himself cross-legged directly in front of her.

"It was the strangest dream I ever had. Sent by the gods, I'm sure of it."

"Did you have it here?"

"Oh no, back in Troy, years ago in fact. I'd nearly forgotten it, until I saw you."

"Me?"

"I dreamt I was a shepherd, and I was watching a herd of sheep up on the slope of Mt. Ida. That's a mountain outside of Troy. I was just sitting there minding my own business, with my back to a tree like you are now, when all of a sudden three goddesses appeared to me, all naked."

Helen narrowed her eyes and looked at him sternly.

"No, I mean it. They were Hera, Athena, and Aphrodite. I recognized them; don't ask me how. They were having some kind of a contest, and they wanted me to be the judge. The prize was a golden apple which was supposed to go to the fairest, and each one of them wanted it."

"Why did they pick you to decide?"

He shrugged his shoulders boyishly. "Maybe they thought I was a good judge of women. I don't know. They didn't intend it to be a fair contest anyway, because each of them offered me a bribe."

Helen smiled in spite of herself. As insufferable as he was, she found herself enjoying his story. He could have been Castor describing how he tracked a boar. He would have done it in the same cocky, self-assured manner. And even the queer, lilting Greek Paris spoke now took on an annoying charm.

"Do you want to know what they bribed me with?"

"Yes," she said, "tell me." Though Helen's face showed she didn't believe a word of it, the animosity so often present had disappeared.

"Hera promised to make me a rich and powerful king, and she showed me all the lands of Asia I'd rule over.

Now you have to understand that I'm a younger son, and in the natural course of things, I'd never get to be a king of anything. So I thought I could probably decide right then and there. But then Athena took me aside and promised to make me the world's greatest warrior, and she showed me a vision of myself coming back to Troy after a battle, and all the Trojans honoring me, even my parents and my brother Hector. That seemed even better to me. If you knew my family, you'd know why."

"And what did Aphrodite promise you?"

He hesitated. The smile faded from his lips for the first time, and he became strangely serious. "She took me up to the top of Mt. Ida, where you can see west all the way to the sea, all the way to Greece, maybe, if you had eyes like the hawks. There she said to me that if I chose her, she would give me the most beautiful woman in the world."

Helen turned away instinctively at the mention of the word.

"And she showed me a vision of her," he continued.

Helen watched the hawks circling over the distant valleys. One of them folded its wings back and dropped from sight as it plummeted to seize some unseen prey in the valley below.

"Which did you choose?" she asked.

"I chose you."

Helen stood up.

"Please don't go," he said, rising too, and catching her by the arm.

Helen might have felt many things in that moment. She might have felt anger at the egotistical young prince for presuming to seduce her. She might have felt hatred at that word "beautiful" again, still plaguing her after all these years. She might have felt fear, embarrassment, hostility. But she felt none of these things. To her amazement, she felt only the pleasure of having his hand on her arm, nor could she shrug it off, even though his grip was hardly more than a gentle touch.

"I didn't mean to offend you," he said.

"You're a foolish boy," she said, not looking at him.

"Yes, I know. That's what my father thinks too. But . . . I love you."

She had never heard the words before, not from Menelaus, not from Tyndareus or Leda, not from Hermione, not from anyone. "You're crazy," she said.

"That's what my *brother* thinks."

She turned toward him now in such a way that he did not have to drop his hand, and looked at him again. She knew that she should say something stern to him, something to put him off, but she found that she wanted to touch him. Yet if she did, a door would open, and it would all be over. She wished he were a statue so that she could feel his shoulders and his chest, the shoulders and chest she would have had if the gods had made her a man instead of a woman. She wanted to feel his arms. She nearly closed her eyes to imagine it, but she knew that would open the door, too. So many ways of opening it, but no way ever to close it again. She stood there and looked at him, motionless, stood for one endless moment between life and life. The hawks disappeared, the horses disappeared, the trees, the hill, everything disappeared, and only the two were left facing each other. Then, even by standing motionless, the door opened.

What she had withheld from her husband, what she had withheld even from herself for so many years, Helen lavished on the young man, and he paid her back in kind. Love, an airy abstraction before, became a palpable thing, something to be clawed at and pulled and wrenched for all the pleasure that could be torn from it. Like wrestlers, they attacked each other; like wrestlers they gripped and rolled and panted in the grass. And together they created a new life. Not something innocent growing inside Helen this time, but its very opposite. An insane thing, a spinning vision in rolling eyes that no sooner breathed but died. And no sooner died but was revived again, sucking life from those who made it, and neither of them knew if the monster was their creation or if they were its.

They loved as only two strangers can, from different lands and different worlds. They shared the thrill and sweet horror of their actions. Helen, used to the quiet, ceremonial duties of the marriage bed, found herself screaming to the desolate hills in a crazy mixture of pleasure and pain. She rubbed the young man's skin, feeling the ribs and muscles, and in her mindless passion felt they were her muscles, her skin. Paris, used to the silly girls of Troy, found himself locked in the embrace of a wild goddess, as likely to destroy him as love him.

Had they been able to leave it, this day might have remained just a terrible dream, remembered in years to come as a dangerous first step on a path not ventured along, but glimpsed in one frightening vision. They forged a bond, however, in the heat of their passion. No matter what their individual intentions when they returned to the palace, the bond pulled them back together. Menelaus had not said when he would return, but the two consecrated their love anew with each day that dawned in his absence.

And each day Paris, more and more deeply bound, coaxed Helen to return with him to Troy. He told her about the splendors of the city, the wide streets, the gardens, the wondrous Temple to Athena, the great palace where she would live. He told her about the magnificent horses bred in Troy, and the vistas the two would see when they rode together on Mt. Ida and in all the lands under his father's sway. Surely there were places in Ilion as fair to behold as the hills around Sparta.

But Helen was reluctant to go. It would mean leaving

all that was familiar to her. When she imagined the passion ending, however, the love only recently awakened gone, and her returning forever to her husband's bed, she felt an emptiness so complete that any alternative seemed preferable. Still, she might have remained in Sparta. Had she known that by her flight she would enlist a mighty army to follow her to Asia bent on destroying the loveliest city on earth, she would not have gone. If she thought that by clinging to her lover, her name would live on as a symbol of female perfidy, she would have given him up. But she did not know these things. She only knew that thus far in her life she had been a failure: as a daughter, as a wife, and as a mother. She thought that after a while Menelaus might be relieved that she was gone, and marry a woman more worthy of him. She imagined that eventually everyone who knew her would forget her, and she would sink into the blessed obscurity of time and the great world's many places.

So one fair morning, no different from any other in so sunny a land, the first palace servants to awake in Sparta were surprised to find the mistress riding so early. They were even more surprised to find the strange-talking foreigners already gone without waiting for the master's return. And on a ship several miles from shore a woman watched the receding coastline and bade it farewell. She saw nothing pursuing her that day, only the invisible wind that filled the sails. Yet something was following. It followed her across the sea to Asia. It followed her into the great citadel of Troy. It followed her through the war. It followed her to the grave, in fact, and after she was dead it followed her shade down the centuries. It was the word she could not flee: "beautiful."

IV

The Greeks

THE SOUNDS HEARD from the battlefield the next day were not the cries of warriors and the clash of weapons, but the steady beat of hammers and the random shouts of workers as an altar was constructed on the plain between the two armies. The Trojans had accepted the Greek offer, and a truce had been declared. All that was wanting was a suitable place for sacrifice where the Greeks and Trojans would bind themselves with vows in the sight of the gods to abide by the outcome of the duel. Epius, the Greek master carpenter, oversaw the work on the altar, and from both sides soldiers watched the progress in hopes that the war would soon be over.

Odysseus stood between Nestor and Diomedes, his fellow captains, but he ignored them as he watched the carpenter work. He admired the skill with which Epius turned living trees into boards, and then fitted the boards together into a completely new entity. The building of an altar must be an easy task, thought Odysseus, for a man who had fashioned great ships, some of which lined the shores of Troy. Odysseus was not a bad journeyman carpenter himself, but he recognized Epius as a master. The old man standing to the Ithacan's right, however, could not appreciate the aesthetics of carpentry at this time. Nestor frowned at the work.

"I don't like it," he said.

"Don't you think Menelaus will win, Lord Nestor?" asked Diomedes, youngest of the three men.

"It doesn't matter," said Nestor. "I just don't like the idea of staking the outcome of the whole damn war on a single combat."

Nestor was the king of Pylos, a sandy, coastal province on the southern shore of the Greek mainland. He had brought a large contingent of soldiers to Troy, second in size only to that brought by Agamemnon. Though over seventy years of age, Nestor was wiry and fit from an active life. In the early years of the war, he had donned his armor and ridden his chariot to the periphery of the battle, but now his fighting days were over, and he was valued chiefly for his counsel, which at the moment was being ignored.

"Besides," continued Nestor, "even if Menelaus wins, all we get is his damn bitch back, and she wasn't worth the price of a dead horse to begin with." He shook his head in disgust. "This whole thing's been one damn blunder after another."

"Losing Achilles was certainly a blunder," said Diomedes.

"Achilles can go to hell," said the older man. "That was his own damn fault. He had no business arguing with the chief."

"Agamemnon was wrong," the younger man reminded him.

"I don't care. He's the chief, and if Achilles wanted to dispute something with him, he shouldn't have done it in front of the men. He was a damn fool to put the chief in that position, and he got what was coming to him. He can pack up and go home now, for all I care. Sitting in his tent like a damn sniveling girl!"

"I still think the chief was wrong."

"Hell, of course the chief was wrong," Nestor conceded. "A man's prize is a man's prize, and the chief shouldn't have taken it away. But Achilles went about it wrong. He should've taken Agamemnon aside and talked with him in private, like I did about Philoctetes.''

"You did?''

"Of course I did. Philoctetes had the bow of Hercules, you know. We should never have left him behind, and I told the chief so.''

"What did Agamemnon say?''

Nestor waved his hand in disgust. "He's too afraid of his own men; that's his trouble. He was worried about all their bellyaching. They didn't like the smell; they didn't like hearing the poor man moan. Well too damn bad for them, I say. And these are supposed to be soldiers. Some damn fearless warriors who can't stand to hear a man in pain!''

"Everyone was afraid it was a plague.''

"Plague my ass! It was just a snakebite. I saw it myself before it festered. Nothing but a damn snakebite. The chief should've never put him off on Lemnos—a deserted island, for the love of Zeus! That was wrong, and I told him so, but I did it in private.''

"Philoctetes was a good archer,'' said Diomedes. "There's no doubt about that.''

"Philoctetes was the best archer there ever was, next to Hercules. And Hercules gave him that bow before he died. I'll tell you what I think: I think Hercules knew this war was coming, and wanted some part in it even though he'd be gone. I bet he saw it coming.'' The old man paused. "It was a damn disgrace to do that to Philoctetes; it was a slap at Hercules himself. But there was nothing I could do about it.'' Nestor shook his head. "One damn blunder after another. Times have changed, I'll tell you that, when piss-assed Trojan dandies can chase us the hell home with our tails between our legs. Times have sure as hell changed.''

He stood for a few more moments in silence; then with

a disgusted grunt he turned and headed back toward his tent.

The younger man watched him. When Nestor was out of earshot, he asked, "Do you think he really met Hercules?"

Odysseus shrugged his shoulders. "He says he did."

"To hear Nestor talk, you'd think all the great heroes died before we were born."

Odysseus smiled. "Maybe they did." The Ithacan's attention, however, was now focused on a newcomer to the plain. Drawn by the sound of hammering, a man had come from the farthest end of the Greek camp and was now standing alone some distance from the body of Greek soldiers.

Diomedes looked in the direction of Odysseus's gaze. "That's Patroclus, isn't it?"

"I believe it is."

"He hasn't been around since Achilles quit fighting."

"No." Odysseus watched him for a while, then said, "Excuse me, Diomedes. I think I'll take a walk up the shore." With that, he began a casual and seemingly aimless stroll which would carry him in the direction of the other figure.

Patroclus, like Diomedes, was younger than Odysseus, and slighter, but in his gray eyes he still had the undeniable look of a warrior. He had been sent to find out the source of the hammering, and now he had found it, but the purpose of the new structure still eluded him. As he stood there gazing at the altar, he did not perceive the other man gliding up beside him.

"He does have a gift, that Epius," Odysseus said, facing the altar and not looking at Patroclus. "The lame god Hephaestus must have blessed him."

Patroclus started briefly at the sudden intrusion, then

resumed watching the work. "Hello, Odysseus. Yes, he must have."

"I'd like to get him to build me a ship someday. They say the ships he builds are so well fitted that you can go a week without bailing."

"I hadn't heard that."

"Yes, that's what they say." Odysseus was silent for a moment as both men watched the workers. "How is Achilles?"

"Fine," said Patroclus without shifting his gaze.

"Not decided to leave yet?"

Patroclus smiled. "I never know from one day to the next."

Odysseus laughed.

"Is there going to be a sacrifice?" Patroclus asked, indicating the altar they were both watching.

"Yes, and an oath before the duel."

"What duel?"

"Didn't you hear? Menelaus challenged Paris to single combat for Helen. It's going to decide the issue of the war."

Patroclus turned to him. "What?"

"Yes. Agamemnon sent Priam the challenge yesterday, and they accepted it."

"When—"

"Tomorrow morning."

Patroclus faced the plain again, an almost dazed look in his eyes. After a moment he said, "Paris is no damn good with a sword. Why would the Trojans accept?"

The older man smiled. "I think the Trojans see it as a godsend. They get rid of Paris, Helen, and the Greeks all in one stroke."

"Then the war will be over."

"And we can all go home."

Patroclus did not respond.

"You do want to go home, don't you?"

Patroclus was looking at the altar, but he no longer saw Epius and the workers. What he saw was Phthia, his homeland, Achilles' homeland, a fertile plain in the very heart of the Greek peninsula. It didn't seem possible to him that they could actually be going home. As often as Achilles had threatened to leave, Patroclus had never quite believed it, but now if the whole Greek force departed, it really was the end, and he would see Phthia again.

"Yes," Patroclus said eventually, "I want to go home."

"And I don't suppose Achilles will mind seeing old Peleus again."

"I don't know," said Patroclus absently.

"Well," said Odysseus, patting the other man's shoulder, "I promised I'd tell Agamemnon when the work here was done, and Epius seems to be gathering up his tools. Greet Achilles for me." He walked a few paces, then turned back to Patroclus once more. "Maybe tomorrow we'll be preparing a great feast and readying our ships for the morning tide."

Patroclus smiled briefly but turned his eyes back toward the altar. As much as the prospect of leaving gave Patroclus joy, he knew it would be unwelcome news to Achilles. Achilles, for all his threats, had no desire to go home. There was nothing for him at home. Unlike most of the Greek leaders, Achilles was not a king himself. His father, Peleus, still lived and reigned in Phthia. Nor was Achilles particularly anxious to take his father's place. Government held no allure, for government was an institution of peace, and peace was merely an interruption in the single pursuit that had meaning for him.

Achilles had come to Troy at the head of the fierce Myrmidons, whose name meant "ants," the only other creatures on earth that engage in warfare. But neither Achilles nor the Myrmidons had been fighting since his

70

quarrel with Agamemnon. The quarrel had been a foolish thing over a captive woman, and Agamemnon had clearly been in the wrong to deprive Achilles of her. Withdrawing himself and his army from the fighting, Achilles might have been expected to feel some satisfaction at watching the Greeks' adversity. Instead, he fell into a black despair. The pride that nursed his resentment was in bitter conflict with an even greater pride: his need to fight and triumph in battle. Thus, his inactivity, as disastrous as it was for the Greek cause, had an even more disastrous effect on himself. Patroclus, for his part, was ashamed to let his Greek comrades fight while he remained idle, but out of loyalty to Achilles he stayed out of the combat and watched daily as his friend sank into greater and greater despondency. Now, if the fighting were truly over for good, Patroclus wondered if there were any hope for reconciliation with their allies. He also feared there could be no remedy for his friend's despair.

Patroclus knew Achilles better than anyone. He had shared his tent for nine years, but more than that he had shared with him the intimacy known only to men at war. It was an intimacy bred not of love, but of death, a more elemental and binding force. Yet it was love too, love at the very cliff edge of life, balanced between exaltation and agony. Later Greeks who were not warriors themselves formalized this love between two men and wrapped it in the peaceful garments of coyness and courtship. The playful encounter on the soft couch, however, could not hope to rival the terrifying embrace on the battlefield. Patroclus and Achilles had shed blood together, made love to the same vision of death at each other's side. No closer bond could unite them.

Neither man was married, but Achilles did have a son, Pyrrhus, on the island of Scyros, where he had lived briefly in his youth. Patroclus had only one living relative, his old father, Menoetius. At their leave taking from

Phthia, Menoetius had asked Achilles to watch over his son. Patroclus was actually a little older than Achilles, but far his inferior in battle. On that occasion Achilles' own father, Peleus, told Achilles that for his part he should heed the better counsel of his older companion. Patroclus smiled wryly at the memory, for in their nine years together, he could not remember a single instance when his friend had heeded his counsel unless it agreed with his own.

Now the war was going to be over. Could the two really go back? Patroclus tried to imagine them on shipboard laughing over their wine as they had done innumerable times around their campfire here. Could they go back to the peacefulness of life at Phthia, and see each other merely to talk over things such as livestock, and barn building, and crops? Could they, warriors together at Troy, who had felt the morbid thrill of battle, men who had nearly won the greatest city on earth, go back to being farmers? Patroclus had doubts even about himself. How much worse must it be for Achilles, for whom battle was the sole element in which he thrived. He shook his head slightly as he turned to leave. He did not look forward to telling his friend the news.

In the middle of the plain, Epius tested the smoothness of the altar with his hand one last time and nodded. He felt the intense pleasure of a craftsman who has created something fine, both in form and function. If he was conscious of the attention he was receiving from the audience on both sides, it only betrayed itself in a certain irony. He was employed to create and repair things amid vast armies bent only on destruction. He was happy his lot in life was to be a carpenter and thus make articles for peaceful use instead of for battle He was glad he was not a metalworker, forced to make swords, shields, and armor to be used in the slaughter. No, he thought, giving the altar a final, satisfied pat before following his men back toward camp, he was grateful to work in wood.

Achilles was sleeping when Patroclus returned. He had gone to the edge of the beach where the crashing waves would drown out the annoying sound of the hammers. He had stretched his tall frame out on one of the sun-warmed rocks strewn about the shore and had fallen asleep. In his sleep, he dreamt of his mother.

Achilles had never known his mother. He had been raised by his father, and Peleus told him that his mother was no earthly woman, but one of the immortals, a sea nymph named Thetis. As a boy Achilles had believed the story, for there was no one to contradict it. Besides, there were many tales of gods who had begotten earthly children. As he grew older and his strength, fighting ability, and speed of foot increased, others began to repeat the story, and even to embellish it. They pronounced him invulnerable, said his mother had dipped him in the River Styx, the boundary of the underworld, thereby making him impervious to weapons.

But that story was false, and Achilles knew it, as did all his fighting companions. He had been wounded many times and had the scars to prove it. Yet the falsity of the one story did not lead him to suspect the truth of the other. Why shouldn't his mother be a goddess? He had grown into a tall, ruggedly handsome, almost godlike man, acknowledged by all as the greatest warrior alive. Such things didn't happen by chance. So Achilles believed the story, and now his mother came to him in the way gods came to humans most often, in a dream.

She seemed to glide onto the shore like a wave. Beautiful and youthful like the other goddesses, Thetis was not adorned with silken garments, but was decked in the vegetation of the sea, and her skin took on the blue-green hue of her element. Her hair floated weightless as if supported only by the gentle eddies of the deep. She smelled of sea plants, and her breath was the sea spray. She cradled her son in her arms, and he seemed to float in a peaceful, sheltered cove. He tried to speak to her, to ask her why she was there, but when he opened his mouth, he could not form intelligible words. They seemed like the sounds made when trying to speak underwater. She paid no attention, in any case, but just stroked his face with her hand, and with each stroke, a cool, gentle wave seemed to wash over him. She did not speak either, but in the strange economy of dreams he knew she had told him something.

Then she was gone, and his face was dry from the salt breezes blowing in off the water. He shivered and opened his eyes. He saw Patroclus sitting nearby, watching him.

"Achilles, are you awake? They're building an altar for a sacrifice. Can you hear me?"

Achilles looked at his friend, but did not seem to see him.

"Are you all right?" asked Patroclus.

Reminded of something, Achilles turned and looked out toward the water, as if he might still catch a glimpse of the blue-green form floating away from him.

"What is it?" asked Patroclus.

Seeing nothing but the vacant waves rolling in to shore, the Myrmidon chief lowered his head in thought and was silent for several moments. Then, without looking up, he said, "My mother told me to go home."

"Thetis? She was here?"

"Yes, in a dream."

Patroclus sighed and rolled his eyes heavenward. He knew, of course, about Achilles' belief in his divine parentage, and though Patroclus tried to keep an open mind about such things, he could never quite believe it himself. He had, after all, lived closely with Achilles for nearly a decade. During that time, he had seen his friend's mistakes, his foibles; he had seen Achilles get angry, be unreasonable, punish a servant unjustly; he had seen him drunk, sick, and in all the stages of indignity that are a normal part of human existence. In short, he had gone through the day-to-day intimacy which inevitably wears away even the shiniest gloss that clings to the great. Others could believe his friend to be goddess-born if they wished, but Patroclus knew better.

That is not to say, however, that he thought Achilles a liar. If anything, Patroclus found his friend's almost childlike belief in his mother's divinity appealing. Besides, Patroclus got no end of fun taunting his famous friend about it. Through sarcastic repetition, he had turned the phrase, "the goddess your mother" into a joke. "What would the goddess your mother say?" he'd ask when Achilles was about to do something particularly selfish or foolish. Like a scolding parent, he would chide, "The goddess your mother wouldn't like that." Achilles for his part, though he would take such ribbing from no one else, accepted it from Patroclus, and sometimes even joined in the laughter at his own expense. However, he was not laughing now.

"Why do you think she wants you to go home?" Patroclus asked.

Achilles lifted his head and gazed at his friend, with an uncharacteristic look of perplexity on his face. "She said if I stay at Troy, I'll die."

The strange earnestness of his words sent a chill up Patroclus's spine. He looked at Achilles for a long time in silence. Then he forced a brief, snorting laugh. "Well, son of a bitch! The goddess your mother seems to have gotten it right this time. We *are* going home."

"What?"

"You didn't let me finish telling you. The war's over; or at least it's going to be. They were building an altar for a sacrifice. Tomorrow morning there's going to be a single combat between Menelaus and Paris for Helen. When it's over, we can go home."

Achilles looked at his friend for a long moment in silence, then shook his head. "No. Agamemnon would never give up Troy for the sake of that skinny whore."

"You're wrong. He already agreed to it."

"It's a ploy, that's all."

"I'm telling you, it's real," said Patroclus. "I had it from Odysseus."

His friend narrowed his eyes and stared at him. Then he shook his head again. "They wouldn't make a decision like that without me."

"They did, Achilles. You haven't exactly shown a great deal of interest in the war lately. Why should they consult you?"

"I can't believe they'd give up like this. No. How could they?"

"Maybe they decided that they just couldn't win without you."

Achilles leapt to his feet and shouted, "Then why the hell didn't the fool come and apologize to me?"

Patroclus, who remained seated, said calmly, "Probably because he's as stubborn a fool as you are."

Achilles folded his arms and walked out toward the edge of the water. His companion watched him for several minutes, then got up and ambled down to where Achilles was standing.

Patroclus was composing something encouraging to say. He was going to remind Achilles of his father, Peleus, and how happy the old man would be to see him again. He was going to describe the homecoming they would enjoy in Phthia, and the feast that would be held in their honor. But when he reached the water's edge, Patroclus was taken aback by what he saw. Tears filled his friend's eyes, and yet the look he bore was not one of sadness, but of impotent fury and despair. Patroclus turned to retreat, but Achilles was already aware of his presence.

"How could they do this?" he said, and his knuckles turned white as his hands squeezed some unseen thing.

Patroclus had no answer, so he just stood near his friend in silence. Then suddenly, Achilles looked at Patroclus with an odd, quizzical expression, as if he were posing some unspoken question.

"What is it?" asked Patroclus.

"Why did Thetis visit me?"

Patroclus shrugged his shoulders. "I don't know. To tell you the war was over?"

Achilles waved away the idea with his hand. "No. There would have been no need for that. Why should she warn me not to stay if we were all going to leave anyway?"

"You want me to explain the logic of your mother's visit when I don't even believe she exists?"

Achilles shook his head in thought, ignoring the question. "The war couldn't be over."

Patroclus saw a quickening in his friend's spirits, and so abrupt was the shift from utter despair to elation that it frightened him. "Achilles," he said, "you don't plan to stay, do you, if the others leave? I mean, we can't fight the war by ourselves."

"Don't worry," said his companion. "I'm not asking *you* to stay."

Stung, Patroclus lowered his eyes. He said softly, "There's no reason for you to say that. You know I'd stay if you and I were the only ones left on this whole damn beach."

Achilles smiled and put his arm over his friend's shoulder.

"But if your mother told you to leave," Patroclus continued, "aren't you going to obey her?"

"You mean 'the goddess my mother'? Why should I bother obeying someone who doesn't exist?"

Patroclus looked at him, and Achilles laughed. He had a great, unself-conscious, booming laugh, and it was one of the things his friend loved about him.

Patroclus shook his head resignedly and slipped his own arm around the other's waist. Feeling the warm life, he suddenly realized the horror he would experience if he ever had to feel his friend's skin chilled by death. He sent a silent prayer up to Zeus that, whatever happened, Achilles would not die before him.

After Odysseus had reported the completion of the altar to Agamemnon, the chief left to inspect the work. The two armies, whose attention had been drawn to the activity, had now returned to their camps, leaving the open space between them deserted once more, except for one large figure. Like Agamemnon, he had come out by himself. Agamemnon recognized the silhouette while still far away, for there was no one bigger than Ajax in the whole Greek army, and only one a better warrior. Ajax was the leader of a small contingent of soldiers from Salamis, an island kingdom off the coast of Athens.

Since the withdrawal of Achilles from the fighting, Ajax had become the bulwark of the army. It was partly his steadfastness that had kept the Trojans from overrunning the ships during their last foray. His reliability and fighting strength had made him a great favorite of the common soldiers, but Agamemnon didn't like him.

Ajax turned and saw the chief approaching. His great figure bowed slightly. "My lord Agamemnon," he said.

At intervals it amazed the chief that one with so imposing a frame and terrifying an aspect should be so soft-spoken and deferential. Instead of being flattered by the treatment, however, Agamemnon was annoyed by it. But it was merely one of many irksome qualities he found in Ajax's character. As fierce a warrior as Ajax was, for instance, he had a tender regard for animals, and would chastise those he saw mistreating them, including his fellow captains. He often fed his sheep and goats himself, and he kept several dogs, his favorite of which he named Capys, which meant "gulper."

Ajax also seemed to be completely humorless. He never joined in the drinking bouts or raillery engaged in by the other soldiers. On the rare occasions when he joined the captains for a repast, his grim and mirthless visage would spoil the gaiety of the occasion. The others would wait until he departed, which was invariably early, before they engaged in any boisterous behavior.

But the strangest thing of all that Ajax did, something no other Greek warrior had done, was to marry a captive woman. Tecmessa had fallen to him after a raid on one of the neighboring towns allied with the Trojans. Though it was common enough to keep concubines won in battle, Ajax formalized the connection by marriage. Were he a lesser man, he would have suffered unending ridicule for this, if not ostracism, but because of his stature in the army, his fellow captains maintained a strict silence on the matter. Many, however, the chief included, resented treating Tecmessa with the same respect they would pay to a Greek woman.

Agamemnon resigned himself to some conversation with his formidable captain.

"Will we really raise the siege tomorrow?" Ajax asked.

"We've agreed to."

Ajax nodded. "Good. We've been here too long."

The frankness of his response sent a shot of anger through Agamemnon, but he gritted his teeth and said nothing. Few of his captains would be so blunt with him. He made no further attempt at conversation. After several moments of silence, Ajax, perhaps sensing the chief's desire to be alone, bade him a polite farewell.

Of course Ajax was anxious to go home, Agamemnon thought when he was gone. All the men were, for they would leave with memories and tales to last a lifetime. Most, to be sure, had come with the hope of returning rich with loot, but even without loot they were returning rich. If not for this great expedition, most of them would have lived and died never venturing farther than the next village. Ajax, even though the son of a king, was no different. But now they were going home world travelers who could tell their grandchildren that they had seen the fabulous city of Troy and fought in the great war for Helen. But what had their chief to look forward to?

Agamemnon's gaze shifted from the altar to the city which loomed in the distance, impregnable behind its wall. Tomorrow he might leave its sight forever. What *would* he have to look forward to? Could anything else be the equal to this? He had been tasked with winning the world's greatest prize—Troy. Was he now to give up all that glory and go home to Mycenae a failure? Was he to resume a life where his most important decisions concerned disputes between peasants, where his only conflict was with neighbor chieftains over obscure frontier boundaries? The idea was intolerable. Surely the gods had not raised him up for this. He had not suffered and fought nine years, quarreled with his best captain, marooned a stricken fellow king on a deserted island, seen hundreds of his friends and kinsmen die, and sacrificed his own daughter for this. Could the inscrutable gods have offered him a seat in the lap of history only to let him slip from her skirts?

He shook his head. He had sent the challenge, and the Trojans had accepted it. His own anxious army would see to it that he kept his word. The duel would end the war, and they would go home, the men with their stories, and the chief with the responsibility for the whole doomed venture, cursed by the gods from beginning to end. He stared at the city. He stared at its wall.

V

The Trojans

HECTOR FOUND HIS wife in the great Temple to Athena in the center of Troy. His mother, Hecuba, was there too, as was his sister Cassandra. They had come with several of the other palace women to offer a gift to the goddess, a robe they had woven to adorn her statue. They hoped the goddess would be pleased by the gift and honor their prayers that the duel tomorrow would end the war. Hector took a place in the shadows of the vestibule so as not to interrupt the ceremony.

After a slow, rhythmic procession in a circle around the statue, all but two of the women knelt before it. These two carried the gift, and they stepped behind the statue and stretched the garment between them to form a backdrop. Then the whole assembly joined in a hymn.

The wooden statue had been painted once, but now retained only the dull stains of colors long since faded. Nearly the size of a human being, it wore a helmet, carried a spear in one hand and a distaff and spindle in the other, the symbols of the deity's curious dual function—war goddess and patroness of feminine crafts. It also bore the aegis of Zeus. All these accoutrements were huddled closely around the figure in the manner of ancient statues, so that the cylindrical tree trunk from which it was carved was never totally disguised.

The Trojans called the statue the Palladium, after Athena's other name, Pallas, and it had been in the city so long that no one alive could say where it came from. Legend had it that the goddess herself had given it to the city when Troy was first founded, and Troy could not be conquered as long as it remained in the city. As he watched the ceremony from where he stood in the darkness, however, Hector took no comfort in the legend. The statue seemed indifferent to the ministrations being performed in its honor. It merely looked on with a grim, blank stare.

The women now fell prostrate on the smooth stones of the temple floor and in unison chanted a prayer imploring the goddess for aid. Hector looked at his wife, who lay on the floor with the rest. Her name was Andromache. Not a native of Troy, she was the daughter of King Eetion of Thebe, and her marriage to Hector had been arranged by their fathers. She had not wanted to forsake her native land to marry a stranger and live in a foreign country, but she had not been consulted on the matter. It was merely commanded that she leave Thebe and take up residence with her new husband in the royal palace at Troy. The first time Hector saw her was on their wedding day, and he was disappointed that she was a woman of such modest looks. Furthermore, she did almost nothing to improve her plainness by dress, cosmetics, or any other means. But he was an obedient son, and it was his duty to marry her and to treat her correctly as his wife. Andromache, however, perceived his disappointment and consequently maintained an aloofness from him and treated him with the same cool correctness she received.

So they had lived together for a while, each wary and suspicious, stalking each other like two wolves, ready either to mate or to bare their teeth, depending on the other's moves. But eventually, through this ritual dance, they developed a cautious respect for each other: Hector for her intelligence, Andromache for his basic goodness.

And out of that respect, eventually, came affection. Andromache ceased to look plain to him anymore. He saw in her eyes a new beauty, the animal loyalty of a mate, a sly partner, a wolf who might have bitten his throat, but chose instead to run at his side. Their marriage became a happy one, as they themselves knew best of all.

But then the Greeks came, and it was reported to Andromache that they had raided her homeland, for Thebe was a Trojan ally. Achilles had killed both her father and her brothers. So the woman who had arrived as a stranger to Troy became yet another of its orphans. She called Hector father, brother, and husband after that, for he was all she had. Yet, at the very time she needed him most, Hector started to change. He had taken over command of his father's armies, and as he gave himself over to the war, he became less and less able to enjoy the peace and intimacy he had found in marriage. He was absent from Andromache's bed more often than not, and when he was there, his wide-eyed wakefulness would trouble her own sleep. His conversation with her, which before had been free, open, and far-ranging, became strained, formal, and trivial. The very sight of her sometimes pained him, for it brought to mind the peace and serenity he'd lost.

The birth of their first child changed things briefly. For many years it looked as though the couple would be barren, and King Priam worried that Hector would have to pass on his crown to one of his brothers instead of a son. But then, in the eighth year of the war, just two years ago, Astyanax was born. Though they were in the midst of a siege, the whole city rejoiced as if they had been liberated already. Hector seemed hopeful again too, and for a while buried the melancholy that had become so much a part of him. The new parents recaptured some of their old intimacy and spent many evenings talking well into the night about the child and the city he would inherit when the war was over. But as the rejoicing subsided and the fighting continued, Hector succumbed again to its influence, and the two wolves retreated once more to their separate lairs.

The women stood up again now, and chanted as they made another formal procession around the statue. Then, forming in front of it, they sang a final hymn to the goddess. When they were done, they proceeded out of the temple single file. Hecuba was the first to see her son, who had slipped out into the sunlight before them.

The queen was nearly sixty years of age, but like her husband, she walked erectly and with the bearing of one who had borne a royal title all her life. She approached the massive pillar beneath which Hector stood.

"The king told me," she said, "that it was you who allowed Paris to accept the Greek's challenge."

"Yes, Mother."

She looked deep into his eyes. The stern visage she presented had made Hector quake when he saw it as a boy, but now, having looked upon death for so long, Hector found gentleness in his mother's face even when she was angry at him. Over her shoulder he saw his wife and Cassandra, who, noticing where the older woman had gone, had followed and stood a respectful distance behind her.

"I don't care about Helen," Hecuba said. "You know that. She could have been sent back to the Greeks the day she arrived. But I care about my child. Everyone says Menelaus will kill him, everyone but your sister here. And they say the Greeks won't leave anyway, even when they have her back."

Hector was silent.

"If you've done this for revenge," Hecuba continued, "I pray the gods punish you for it."

She waited for a response, but Hector just looked sadly

into her face and said nothing. She gave him one last angry look and then turned her back on him and proceeded toward the palace in the same regal fashion. Cassandra, who accompanied her, cast her brother a smile over her shoulder, which he returned. Andromache remained on the temple steps and watched the women until they disappeared from view.

When the husband and wife were alone, they stood for a while in silence, avoiding each other's eyes. Finally Hector asked, "Did Cassandra really say Paris would win the duel?"

"No," answered Andromache distantly. "She just said she didn't think Menelaus would kill him."

"I don't know why he wouldn't."

"Neither do I."

They were silent again. A sea gull cried above their heads, and Hector glanced up at it, then watched as it dipped lazily over the city roofs and disappeared behind the wall.

"How is Astyanax?" Hector asked.

"Fine," she answered.

"How did the ceremony go?"

"Fine, too," said Andromache. "Athena was so pleased with the robe, she came down in the middle of our prayers and danced on her shield and promised she'd turn all the Greeks into cabbages before nightfall."

Hector laughed at the unexpected joke, but when he looked at Andromache, he saw that tears had welled up in her eyes. She had intended to be ironic, to be sure, but her silly fiction reminded her of their real situation, in a city on the edge of oblivion despite all their prayers and sacrifices to the gods. Then too, when she saw Hector laugh, something he rarely did anymore, it reminded her of the husband she had lost.

In an age when marriages were made for dynastic and economic reasons, and domestic harmony depended more on good manners and courtesy than affection, she had achieved what a few lucky souls in every age achieve—a small understanding. They had not merged or melded or fused together, for marriage cannot really do those things to people. What Andromache and Hector had done, though, was to open, slowly, tentatively, and ever so slightly, a small door between them, and through it each had glimpsed a different universe. But when the war came, Hector had closed the door again. The sight of him laughing now reminded her of this, and tears came to her eyes.

Hector was shocked by her tears, coming so unexpectedly. His first instinct was to flee the temple steps, but he overcame it and stood silently in front of her. He wanted to embrace her as of old, but was prevented by the same inner horror that had robbed him of all his other joys. Instead, he merely tried to shield her from view so that others would not see. Andromache quickly composed herself.

"Will you be spending tonight in the city?" she asked, resuming the measured, respectful tone she had come to use with him.

"Yes. That's what I came to tell you. There's no need to be in the field. Sarpedon said he'd stay out there to keep an eye on the Greeks."

She felt a quickening at the thought of sleeping beside him again this night. She looked at him. "Is it really nearly over?"

He shook his head. "I don't know. I hope so."

"I don't care if Paris dies," Andromache said. "I know it's terrible to say, but I really don't care if he dies. So many others have died."

"I don't think the queen cares if I die," Hector said.

"Don't believe it."

He shrugged his shoulders, and they fell silent again.

"Will you be home for dinner?" she asked, after a moment.

He smiled at her. "Yes. I just want to stop in to see Paris first. I want to give him some advice about fighting Menelaus. But I'll be home soon."

"Good," she said, trying, for her own pride's sake not to seem too happy. "Good. I'll tell the servants."

"You'd better tell the cook too, about the windfall we're expecting."

She looked at him, puzzled. "What windfall?"

"Of cabbages."

"I don't think you even care if I die tomorrow," said Paris, as he paced the room before her. "It'll make no difference to you which one of us you end up with, that red-haired old fool or me."

"I care if you die," said Helen. She sat on the bed, her eyes cast down.

"Yes, about as much as you care if he dies."

"I care if he dies."

"There! You see what I mean! Damn it!" he said, pounding his thigh with his fist, "God damn it all! I don't even know what I'm fighting for. Whether I win or lose, I won't have you. I've never had you, never had you really. Never."

She looked at him, confused.

"No, not in Sparta, not here, not even on our wedding day. I never had you. You always held something back."

She lowered her eyes. "You had everything. I never gave anyone more."

"You gave that damn Greek more," he said, coming to a stop in front of her. "In nine years you've never had a bad word to say about him. But about me—"

"I never gave him more."

"You gave him a child!"

She looked up at him again, her eyes suddenly filled

with rage. So unexpected and so passionate was the expression that it frightened him and he imperceptibly backed away from her. The look passed from her features, however, almost as quickly as it had come. She stared blankly at the wall.

"I don't want you to fight tomorrow," she said. "I don't want either of you to die for me. I never wanted anyone to die for me. I'd willingly die myself instead. I've offered to go back to him every year since they arrived. What more can I do?"

"Yes, you've offered to go back because you knew I wouldn't let you. But you've never been a prisoner here. You know where the gates are; you know when they're open. Why didn't you ever leave on your own if you were so willing?"

She lowered her head, but he jerked it up again with both his hands, contorting her features between them.

"Look at me," he shouted. "And tell me, Helen, why didn't you leave? Why? Why?"

She began to cry, but her tears did not deter him. "Why?" he shouted even louder. "Why didn't you leave?"

"Because," she said finally through the tears, "I thought he'd kill me. I thought he'd torture me and then kill me, and I'd deserve it."

It was not the answer he wanted. "You've never cared for me," he said, softly now, and more to himself than to her.

"Oh, why didn't you leave me in Sparta? At least Menelaus left me alone."

His eyes burned. He squeezed her chin in his left hand and drew his right hand back. Helen squinted her eyes, bracing herself for the blow, but instead of the crack, followed by the stinging pain, what she heard was a new voice.

"Shouldn't you save that for the Greek?"

Paris's wrist was caught in the grip of his elder brother.

"Stay out of this, Hector," he said, trying to wriggle free, but letting Helen go with his other hand. "What do you want?"

"I came to talk to you about your duel."

"What about it?"

"I thought you might want to know how Menelaus fights. I've seen him fight."

"I don't care how he fights."

"Then you don't care if he kills you?"

Paris glared at Hector. "He's not going to kill me, even though that's what all of you want." With that, he pried his captured hand free and stormed from the room.

The two watched him leave, and then shared an awkward silence for several moments. Helen always felt embarrassed around Hector, and guilty for the unforgivable hardships she had laid upon him, above all others.

"Thank you," she said quietly without looking up. She hesitated to look him in the eye, even though he had always been polite.

But Hector looked at her. Her slight figure, together with the size of the great bed she sat upon, made her seem very small. She was disheveled, her cheeks stained with tears, and her face bereft of both color and life. As he watched her and thought of the thousands of men who had contested with their lives for this poor creature, he had a momentary vision of a world gone mad. He had the impulse to grab her by the hair and drag her to the towers of the Scaean Gates and throw her off just to end her wretched existence.

Yes, by the hair, her hair. He looked at it. What an odd thing the gods had given human beings. No real purpose for it. It didn't keep them warm, as it did the animals. They couldn't use it to shake off flies as a horse uses its mane. Why was it there? Why should it shine like that? Why should ten thousand separate strands move as one when she shook her head? Why does it cry out to be touched?

He stared so long that she looked up at him in surprise, and of course he saw it. He bit his lip and tightened his fist trying not to see it, but he saw it. How could he blame his brother for being a fool? Could it not as easily have been himself? Paris had said to him once that the gifts of the gods cannot be refused, and Hector had scorned him. But of course it was true. Just look at her! Worth anything. Worth everything.

Helen knew what had happened. She had lived long enough with her beauty to know when it had dazzled someone. She no longer tried to deny it to herself. But it gave her courage to speak to him again.

"Do you think he has a chance tomorrow?"

Hector sighed. "I don't know. Menelaus is a better fighter, but nothing's sure in combat." He paused. "Will you go willingly if Menelaus wins?"

"Yes."

"Have you thought about what might happen to you?"

"Yes."

Hector straightened himself and turned to leave, but stopped at the doorway. "I wish to God that we had never seen you, that you'd never set foot in Troy, but I don't wish you ill if the Greeks take you back tomorrow." Then, not waiting for a response, he strode out and returned to his own apartment in the palace.

Climbing the wall bothered Antenor more and more now. His knees cracked and his calves ached as he raised himself up each of the steep steps. Before the Greeks came, it had been a walk to the beach, not a climb to the wall, that was his daily ritual. He loved the sea. In his youth, he swam and sailed in it, but as he grew old, he was satisfied just to stroll down to its edge and watch the breakers and hear the grating of the sand and pebbles on the shore. Something in the vastness of the sea and the regularity of the tides was reassuring to him. Deprived of his walks to the beach now, he satisfied himself with at least a view of it from the wall. So he would climb the battlements near the Scaean Gates on all but the most inclement days.

Antenor was one of Priam's most valued counselors, and he had earned his status not only by his words, but by the blood of his family. He had lost three of his four sons in the war, Archelochus, Pedaius, and Laodamas. The last he had watched die from the very wall he was now climbing. He sighed and pulled himself up the last step, and stood for a moment to catch his breath. That was when he noticed another figure, not quite as old as himself but nearly so, leaning over the battlements. Even from the back he recognized him, though Anchises rarely showed himself in this part of the city.

"You must have heard about the duel, Anchises," he said.

The other glanced around at him, then resumed watching the plain. "Yes, I heard about it."

Since Antenor was related by marriage to Priam, he was also related to Anchises, who headed a separate branch of the royal family. Antenor's closeness to Priam also made him fall into the orbit of Anchises' enmity, though Antenor tried his best to stay out of the feud and be friends with both sides. With difficulty he walked to the other's side and leaned over the wall next to him.

"What do you think?" Antenor asked.

"About what?"

"About the duel?"

Anchises made a dismissive gesture with his hand, but said nothing.

"My son, Laocoön, thinks we never should have agreed to it," said Antenor. "He thinks we should keep on fighting." He paused. "It's strange. The loss of my other sons made me want to see the war end, but the loss of his brothers only makes him want to continue it."

"That's because he's a priest and never had to fight."

Antenor nodded his head and took no offence at the blunt statement. "Yes, that's probably it. Your son certainly knows what it's really like."

Anchises lapsed once more into silence. It was well known that he didn't approve of his son's participation in the war. Nevertheless, Aeneas had fought side by side with Priam's and Antenor's sons throughout the conflict. There may have been some tension between Aeneas and the royal family because of the age-old quarrel, but there was never any question of his loyalty. Antenor had a particularly high regard for Aeneas.

The two men stood together now without speaking for a while, each lost in his own thoughts. Finally, Anchises broke the silence: "He had no right to do this, you know. Priam had no right to get us involved in this."

Antenor waved away the notion. "Don't blame Priam. We all wanted to fight in the beginning."

"Not me. I never wanted to fight. Zeus the Cloud Squatter! I wanted them to ship the Greek slut the hell home."

"Yes, you did, Anchises, you and a few others, a very few. And it's turned out you were right. But it's done now."

"Yes, it's done now, and it may be the end of this city."

Antenor shook his head. "It won't be the end of the city. They can't get inside the wall, just as we can't push them off the shore. It's a stalemate."

Anchises sneered, unconvinced.

Antenor continued, "The Greeks just have to be made to understand it. They're an intelligent people. We know we can't win. They must be made to see that they can't win either."

"Who the hell is going to tell them?"

Antenor paused. "Well, if this duel hadn't been proposed, I was ready to do it myself."

Anchises looked at him. "Do what?"

"Talk to them. I was willing to go and speak with them about a settlement. Given half a chance, I think I could have come to an understanding with them."

"Did you suggest that to Priam?"

"No, to the queen, to my sister."

"What did she say?"

"She forbade me to mention it to Priam."

Anchises turned back to the plain. "She was probably afraid he'd like the idea."

"Maybe. But it didn't matter. I was ready to meet with the Greeks whether they approved or not."

"They would have called you a traitor."

"Not if I could have ended the war."

"Well," said Anchises, sighing and pushing himself away from the wall, "let's hope your duel ends it once and for all." Then, without a farewell, he proceeded down the steps that Antenor had so recently climbed with such difficulty.

When he was alone, Antenor turned back to the field again and looked at the tents of the Greek camp, which separated him from the great blue expanse beyond. He missed the sea more than ever now. He nodded his head slightly to himself. "Yes, let's hope so indeed."

As the sun began to set in the Aegean that evening, it lit the pediment of the great Temple to Athena a fiery gold. Inside the temple, a young woman danced. To strains of a music unheard, played by a musician unseen, she whirled in dizzying circles around the ancient statue of the goddess, as if lost in a dreamy landscape she alone could see. Earlier in the day, she had taken part in the ceremony with the other palace women, but now she had the sanctuary to herself. The temple faced west, so at this hour the nearly horizontal rays of the sun illuminated the dark interior, and shone through the young woman's flowing gown, revealing her swaying figure underneath as she reeled and spun around the floor.

Cassandra loved the temple, and spent more time there than in the palace. She liked its cool shadows during the day, and the quiet at night, but no time was more beautiful to her than sunset, when the golden light entered the doorway and fell upon the statue itself. She was a pretty young woman, and in the normal course of events, she would have been married by now and raising children of her own. But it was universally recognized in Troy that her mind was tainted. She believed she had a gift of prophesy, and though people accepted the powers of genuine prophets, in Cassandra's case they attributed her belief to madness.

She had been only twelve when the Greeks arrived. She was a happy, lively girl, fascinated by the gods and all the legends about them. She would beg her parents, and anyone else who had patience, to tell her the familiar stories over and over again. And she was always brimming with questions. Where did Poseidon get his trident? How did Hephaestus become lame? What became of Zeus's father? But then, one day, during one of the numerous truces in the early days of the war, she had wandered out the Ilian Gates on the south side of the city, and something had happened.

It was her brother Hector who found her, lying by the banks of the Scamander, her dress torn and a wild look in her eyes. He carried her back to the city, where her family pressed her to reveal what had happened to her. She spoke incoherently for a long time, but when lucidity returned to her, she said she had been visited by the god Apollo. He had come to her as she as picking flowers by the river. What happened then, she could not explain, for the encounter was outside her experience and past her understanding, but she did say it ended with the god spitting in her mouth. She could describe it no other way, but she believed she had been blessed thereby, and had been given the ability to speak the future.

Her family, however, took no comfort from the divine visitation, and grieved that the impressionable girl's wits had been lost. At one time they had hoped to form a valuable alliance by marrying her to a neighboring prince, but they now gave up the idea, and, like many a royal family in ages to come, were forced to harbor madness in their bosom.

The mad were not shunned in those days, though, nor put away out of sight. They might be pitied for being denied the ordinary joys of life, but people also stood in awe of their sublimity, for they had been touched by the gods. They saw through different eyes, heard through different ears, perceived a different world. Thus the daughter of Priam and Hecuba achieved by her madness freedom of action, of movement, and of speech denied other women of her time.

Although Cassandra's encounter had been with Apollo, she formed a strong attachment to Athena after that, and considered the great virgin war goddess a special protectress. She would spend hours in the temple improvising dances around the Palladium, or just wandering among the inner columns. She felt no fear when she was in the temple. It was as if the great aegis the goddess wore was thrown around her too.

Lightheaded and nearly faint with the spinning movements, Cassandra finally came to a stop in front of the grim-faced statue while she caught her breath.

"Has the goddess told you if the war's going to end?" asked a voice behind her.

She turned around, but the images before her eyes were still shivering after her whirling. There was a man standing in the doorway, his figure backlit by the declining sun. She stared for a moment until he came into focus. Then she smiled. It was her cousin, Aeneas. She liked Aeneas. He sometimes stopped in the temple on his way home when he spent the night in the city. Related as he was to the royal family, he might have lived with the rest of them in the palace, but the lingering effects of the feud and a certain loyalty to his father induced him to make his home in the suburbs instead. He lived with his wife, his son, and old Anchises in the easternmost part of the city, near the Dardanian Gates. It was an older section of town, on the inland side, and the farthest away from the field of battle.

"What does Athena say?" Aeneas asked.

Cassandra glanced over her shoulder at the statue, which still wore the robe placed on it earlier in the day. "The lady Athena never speaks to me," she said.

Aeneas strode into the temple now and came to a stop by her side. "I thought all the gods spoke to you."

"Oh, no. Not all of them. They're a lot like people. Some talk a great deal, some only a little, and some not at all. The ones that talk the most you have to watch out for, because they tell the most lies."

"Really?"

"Oh, yes."

"Who lies?"

"Hermes does. Hermes tells the most outrageous fibs. He told me once that Mother had turned into a great spider, and we were all to start collecting flies for her to eat. So I got a jar and went out to find some, but it was very hard to catch them alive, so I went to Mother to ask if dead flies would be all right."

"And what happened?"

"Well, she hadn't changed into a spider at all. Another time Hermes told me that the cows had sprouted wings and were flying over the barn and shitting on the roof. So I went out to see."

Aeneas laughed. "Were they?"

"Of course not. Cows can't fly, so I knew Hermes was lying again."

"How about Zeus?" asked Aeneas. "Does he ever lie?"

Her face darkened. "I hope so."

"Why?"

She turned and began to walk in a slow, aimless path around the temple. "Zeus sends me dreams of a burning city, our city."

Aeneas watched her in silence.

"It's always the same. People running and screaming, and the city on fire. And everyone dead, Father and all my brothers; and Mother on her knees crying."

"I hope it is a lie, then," said Aeneas softly.

Cassandra came to a stop in front of the statue, and reached out to touch it. It was an odd, tentative gesture, something between an adult's need to caress and a child's need to feel what it sees.

"She's very beautiful, isn't she?" Cassandra said.

Aeneas smiled. "They say the goddess herself is. I don't know if the Palladium is a good likeness."

"You're never there," Cassandra said, still gazing at the statue.

"I'm never where?"

"In the dream, in the city. I've seen just about everyone else in it, but never you."

Aeneas looked at her tenderly. "Maybe the gods aren't very reliable, Cassandra, if some lie to you and others send you bad dreams."

Cassandra dropped her hand from the statue but continued to stare at it. Aeneas looked around the temple floor, then walked over to where she had dropped her cloak. He lifted it, held it for a moment, and then stepped up behind her and placed it on her shoulders.

"It'll be dark soon. You should keep this on so you don't get chilled."

She nodded, and he squeezed her shoulders lightly before he let them go.

"I promised Creusa I'd be home before nightfall. Do you want me to walk you back to the palace before I leave?"

She faced him now and smiled at him. "No. I'll be all right."

He hesitated a moment longer, then turned and strode out of the temple. Cassandra watched him go, and as she did, she prayed an impossible prayer. She prayed that the great father of the gods, the immortal and almighty Zeus, the all-knowing king of Olympus, had sent the terrible vision of a city in flames merely to trouble a poor girl's sleep.

In the field that evening, a balding, fat man sharpened the point of one of his arrows as he spoke to his countryman. Pandarus's age and physical condition might have prevented him from combat were his weapon anything other than the bow. He was an archer like Paris, and his skill, like the prince's, had earned him a protected place in the ranks where he could let his arrows fly without endangering himself.

"My lord Sarpedon," he said. His voice wheezed, and his eyes did not stray from the work he held in his hands. "Are you content to give up our advantage after the duel tomorrow?"

"I'm not particularly content, but it *is* the Trojans' war. If they want to decide it by single combat, it's up to them."

"Indeed. But it seems to me that any number of things could happen that might start the fighting again."

"What things?"

"The truce might be broken; it doesn't matter how. Truces are commonly broken. Anything could cause it. A spear thrown, a bow shot, maybe even an angry word. Who knows?"

"It won't be broken by me."

"Of course not, Lord Sarpedon. But if it should be broken—"

"If it should be broken, what?"

"You'll withdraw the army and head home anyway, leaving the Greek loot to the Trojans?"

Sarpedon narrowed his eyes at him. "I gave my word to Hector that I wouldn't break the truce."

"I understand," wheezed Pandarus.

The Lycian leader was silent for a moment, then said, "But if some fool does break it, Sarpedon is not going to go home empty-handed."

Pandarus smiled. "Of course not."

VI

The Duel

WHEN THE SUN reached the peak of Mt. Ida the next morning, the two vast armies were already arrayed on the field. From a distance, it looked like they had formed a great, uninterrupted circle around the altar and dueling ground, and such a circle might have served as an emblem for the unity of hope in the common soldiers' minds. Perhaps the armor they now wore might be put off for good at the end of this day. Perhaps they might feast with their fellows before nightfall, perhaps even with their erstwhile enemies. And tomorrow, all thoughts would be of peace.

But it was not really a complete circle. Rather, it was two large semicircles, for each side had left a portion of barren ground between them. Thus, a line thirty paces broad bisected their circle, Greeks on one side, Trojans on the other. Had one of the gods viewed the curious geometric figure below, he might have named that margin the "xenophobic line" for the fearful thirty paces that have always separated the different peoples of the earth.

The Greek leaders arrived before their Trojan counterparts, and all but Achilles were there. Yet even he was represented, for Patroclus had ventured out their morning to wish Menelaus luck and to join the others to see the outcome of the duel.

Agamemnon stood well out in front of his men. Beside

him stood Odysseus, who had agreed to act as Menelaus's second. The two now watched as the great Scaean Gates opened far up the field and the royal chariot emerged, followed by several others.

Agamemnon had assumed that it would be Hector who officiated for the Trojans at the sacrifice, for it had been Hector all along who spoke and acted on behalf of his city. But as the principal chariot approached, he saw another figure standing beside Hector, a tall, regal-looking, white-haired man. The royal chariot passed through the Trojan line and came to a halt near the altar. Hector and Priam stepped off, and while Hector quieted the horses, Priam walked slowly up to Agamemnon.

In the nine long years of the war, the two had never met. Now they stood facing each other in a long, eerie silence before their two armies. Both were kings, but one was a vigorous commander-in-chief who had killed many Trojans with his own hand, while the other was an old man, his fighting days over, enduring the bitterest conflict of his long life. Agamemnon looked deeply into the eyes which were looking deeply into his own. He saw a face made haggard by both time and care, yet he saw a dignity that caused him a strange embarrassment. He wanted to shift his gaze, but found that the penetrating stare leveled at him held him fast. He found it easier to speak than to turn away.

"Lord Priam."

"I am Priam."

"You have accepted my brother's challenge to your son?" As he said the words, the Greek commander had the oddest sensation of settling some family dispute rather than one between two nations.

"I have," said Priam. Neither his voice nor his visage altered.

"Will you perform the sacrifice yourself, or —"

"I will," said Priam. He turned now and motioned to

Hector, who in turn signaled another in the ranks of the army. Agamemnon did the same, and shortly two large, white rams emerged from the semicircles into the open field between.

The Greek leader and the Trojan leader then made their vows and performed their ritual sacrifices on the altar, each slaughtering his animal in God's name so that Zeus would hear his words and hold the speaker to his promise. When the ritual was concluded, Priam, without another word, remounted his chariot, this time without Hector, and was driven back to the city. Then Agamemnon retired to the line of his army, while Hector and Odysseus paced out the area for combat. At the appropriate time, two others emerged from the line of spectators and entered the magic circle formed with so much ceremony and anticipation. Once the seconds were content that all was fair and equal, they also retired to their respective lines, leaving the field empty save for the two combatants.

The last time Menelaus and Paris had seen each other, a decade ago now, neither had been wearing armor. Their relationship then had been as host and guest, one of the most honored and sacred of all bonds. Menelaus had fulfilled his part in that bond, for he had shown the young Trojan prince hospitality and unfeigned good will. But no one present this morning, on either side of the broad field, would deny that Paris had broken the covenant. Scorning his own duties as guest, he had corrupted his host's wife and then stolen away with her.

When he sailed from Sparta that day, no doubt Paris thought he would never see the red-haired man again, given the difficulty of travel, and the strength of his own city. Yet, within a year the Spartan king was on his very shores, with the flower of Greece behind him. And so they had fought one another on their respective sides,

Menelaus in the front lines, and Paris, as an archer, in the rear.

The man Paris remembered had an easy disposition. Not a clever man, and not sophisticated, but quick to laugh. He had enjoyed playing the host, enjoyed filling the prince's cup, enjoyed showing him the rustic beauties of Sparta. Paris, out of politeness, had kept from laughing when Menelaus pointed out a prize riding horse for the prince's commendation, a horse which might be used in Troy to pull a wagon. But the man who faced him now, grim in his armor, grim in his aspect, seemed no longer the buffoon, the foolish cuckold. There was in his eyes a kind of insanity, born not so much from bestial anger, as from that uniquely human wrath that can come only from betrayal.

Paris had rarely wielded a spear or a sword before this. The absence of Philoctetes from the Greek host left the Trojan prince the greatest bowman on the field, and many, many Greeks and fallen to his arrows. Now, however, he was to cross swords with a swordsman, and he had neither right nor might on his side.

For all that, he was not reluctant to face Menelaus. In some ways the Greek was easier to face than the young prince's brother, or his father and his wife watching at this moment from the walls of the city. For years he had felt their scorn. For years he had heard their accusation, spoken or unspoken, just or unjust, that he was allowing others to fight a battle that was essentially his. Now he was to fight that battle himself, and he did not fear death.

As arranged, each man was armed with a sword, a shield, and a throwing spear. They circled each other at first, each hunched over and weighing his spear in his right hand, feinting with his shield in the left. Paris had a good eye, and he hoped it would guide his spear so that he might wound his much more powerful Greek antagonist before they came into close quarters. But Menelaus was closing the gap between them, rapidly erasing whatever advantage Paris might have had. Deciding instantaneously that the moment had come, Paris heaved his spear. Almost at once, however, he realized that the trajectory was wrong. Menelaus shifted only slightly, and the spear stuck into the ground next to him. It made a low-pitched, twanging sound as it quivered momentarily in the air.

Paris now had no choice but to draw his sword and close the gap between them. He knew that Menelaus would have to throw his spear quickly or risk opposing its thin, light shaft to the heavy sword which Paris would now wield. Menelaus aimed at Paris's head, and cast his spear high into the air. The Spartan did not have much hope of actually hitting his target. He knew, however, that the high arc would force Paris to look up, giving Menelaus the time to draw his own sword and attack.

Paris successfully dodged the spear, which fell many feet from him, but he was almost immediately caught by a blow from Menelaus's sword. He staggered back, and only brought his shield up a second before another blow, aimed at his neck, fell. As it was, the Greek's sword knocked the shield against his body, and he staggered again.

The prince had barely recovered from the second blow before he received a third, and this one he did not sufficiently deflect. Menelaus had made a long, downward slice with his sword, and though it did not fall on Paris's side where he had intended, it glanced off the shield and caught him in the upper thigh. The prince did not know at first that he had been hit. He thought he'd merely knocked his leg with the bottom of his shield. It was the wetness that first told him he was wounded. He glanced down and to his horror saw the black-red gash in his own flesh. He felt a sudden sickening.

Menelaus, taking advantage of Paris's momentary

lapse, came at him again. Paris looked up in time to see the next blow coming, but not in time to counter it. The sword clanged against his helmet, and he was sent reeling to the ground. Had his death immediately followed, Paris would have been spared the ultimate pain of it, for the blow had knocked him unconscious. But Menelaus, even as he lifted his sword to give the final thrust, felt a sting where the arrow hit him.

Hector was the first to realize what had happened. He saw the shaft protruding from Menelaus's shoulder, and he knew that Pandarus was to blame. There were only two bowmen in all Troy who could have made such a shot from that distance, and one was lying unconscious on the ground. He ran out onto the open field in an attempt to keep order and maintain the truce, but the Greeks, seeing Menelaus crumple to the ground, began to shout and shake their weapons in the air. Agamemnon ran out toward his brother, as did the leaders near him, and their armies followed. But no one rushed out with such violence as Patroclus.

Perhaps it was a certain fondness he harbored for Menelaus that motivated him, or it might have been the feelings of guilt for being absent so long from the fighting. Whatever the cause, when he saw Menelaus treacherously struck down and the Trojan leader running onto the field, something snapped within him. Patroclus grabbed his own weapon and rushed directly at Hector.

By now the Trojans, seeing what looked like an attack, started to follow Hector with their own weapons out. Hearing their battle cries, he turned to stop them, but then whirled around again when he perceived the rush of someone behind him. He raised his hand to try to stop the other, but Patroclus's sword was already in motion, and Hector took the blow squarely on his shield. It made him stagger.

Hector might at this point have cried out to Patroclus

that he was only trying to maintain the truce and keep his men back. The Hector of nine years ago, Hector the farmer, Hector the horse tamer might have been able to do this, might even have been able to convince the maddened Patroclus that the act of treachery was an individual one, not planned by the Trojan leaders. He might have been able to quell the anger and maintain the truce until the culprit could be produced.

But Hector did not cry out, for this was Hector the warrior. Feeling the blow on his shield, being made to stagger at the other's hands, he forgot about the truce, he forgot about the men he was trying to stop, he forgot even the city he was trying to save. The anger rose up in him once more, the primitive, elemental wrath that came from a well as old as the earth. For the sake of this feeling he had given up his wife, his child, his parents, all that he had and all that he was. For the sake of this feeling and what it allowed him to do, what it indeed forced him to do, he had given up everything. He lowered his head, and from beneath his brow he looked at Patroclus out of grim, black, lifeless eyes. He drew his sword.

Patroclus was a skillful fighter. After all, he had been trained by the best warrior of all, but he was no match for Hector. His next blow was deflected by the Trojan, and by a deft sideward movement of Hector's shield, his sword was knocked from his hand. He bent to reach for it again, holding his own shield before him, but the Trojan kicked him off balance, and as Patroclus raised his shield arm to right himself, Hector thrust his sword deep into his now unprotected lower abdomen. Patroclus screeched hideously, and then fell at Hector's feet, his blood splattering the other's sandals.

The Trojan soldiers, who had waited to see what their chief would do, raised an insane cheer. The same men who had hoped to be feasting with their enemies by nightfall, now, with the sight of blood, were ready to leap into the slaughter again. The broken circle collapsed as the two armies poured into the center. The battle was joined, and the xenophobic line disappeared, breached once more by blood and the broken bodies of men.

Seated outside his tent far up the beach, Achilles could hear the noise of the fighting and was anxious for Patroclus to return with the news of what happened. He knew by the sound of the battle cries that one or the other side must have violated the truce. This proved to him that his interpretation of the dream he'd had the previous day was correct: The war was not going to end. He was planning with some pleasure how he would taunt Patroclus with this new evidence of his mother's divinity and prescience. To his surprise, however, instead of seeing his friend walking along the path, he saw a horse and rider galloping toward him.

Achilles stood up and recognized the commander-in-chief's herald. His first thought was that Agamemnon had chosen this moment of distress to send his apology finally and to beg Achilles to return to the fighting, but Achilles was angered that the chief would choose to do it by proxy.

When the winded man arrived and had dismounted, Achilles offered him no greeting but said only, "If Agamemnon has anything to say to me, he can say it in person."

"Pardon me, Prince Achilles," said Talthybius between breaths, "but Lord Agamemnon is tending to Lord Menelaus, who's been wounded."

"Menelaus?" Achilles snorted. "Did the Trojan boy get the better of him?"

"No, my lord. Paris was nearly dead, but Menelaus was hit by a Trojan arrow. We don't know if they intended this all along or not, but then both sides attacked."

"Well, what's that to me? What does Agamemnon want to say to me?"

"Two things, my lord," said Talthybius. Even in his breathless state he uncoiled the string of words he had hastily committed to memory. "First, he sends his apology, which must needs be brief in the present crisis, but he hopes you will allow him in the future to make restitution for the harm he did you—"

Achilles, his eyes narrowed at the messenger, broke in, "I know the value of the chief's promises." Then he turned to walk away.

Talthybius, undeterred, continued, "And second, he sends you the sincerest expression of his sorrow."

The other man spun around. "His sorrow? Sorrow for what?"

Talthybius, putting aside his text, lowered his eyes. "My lord, Patroclus is dead."

"What?"

"He joined in the fighting, my lord, trying to save Menelaus, and he was struck down by Hector."

Achilles looked stupidly at him. "Patroclus?"

"Yes, my lord."

The Myrmidon chief instinctively looked for his friend over the herald's shoulder on the path, as if to refute the words he had heard spoken. Why shouldn't his expectation of his friend's return be more solid evidence for his life than this breathless man's words were for his death? If he were to just sit down and dismiss the man, would not his friend be seen strolling back as he had a hundred times? Patroclus dead? No. Patroclus and Achilles, *they* were the killers. Side by side they had killed scores, and saved each other's lives too, when necessary, though it was Achilles who did more of that. Patroclus was better at talking than fighting.

Achilles smiled a faint, half-smile as he thought of what he had planned to say to Patroclus. "Well, what do you think of 'the goddess my mother' now?" The herald, staring at Achilles and seeing the smile, wondered if the gods were stealing away the Myrmidon captain's wits, and Talthybius began to fear for his own life. But the smile stayed only briefly, and Achilles' eyes returned from the path to the herald once more, although his focus seemed to fall far behind Talthybius.

"His body—"

"Recovered, my lord, by Ajax. It's safely by Agamemnon's ship right now."

"Hector, you say."

Talthybius hesitated, not following for a moment the other man's erratic train of thought. "Yes, my lord."

Achilles was silent, continuing to look at or perhaps through the herald. Then all of a sudden he shook his head, as if to disrupt a pesky fly. He turned and walked a few steps away. He looked at his tent, then at the beach and his ships, then at the camp where his men were congregated, some of them playing catch with a disk. Talthybius got the impression he was taking a mental inventory of some kind. When Achilles spoke next, it was in his familiar offhanded, sardonic voice again, but he did not turn around to face the herald.

"You can tell Agamemnon I accept his apology, and I will expect his promised restitution. You can also tell him to have"— he paused, then did the small headshake again—"to have the body brought here. My people will see to it."

"Yes, my lord. My lord, will you be—"

"My men and I will be joining the battle. Go and tell him."

Talthybius remounted and was off, happier with the news he was bringing to his chief than what he had been forced to take to Achilles. The Myrmidon captain, meanwhile, turned around again and watched him ride down the path toward the central encampment. He watched intently the figure he knew was there so that he would not see the one he wished were there.

The Trojan citizens on the wall did not know for some time exactly what had happened. The distance was too great for them to have seen the arrow. They only knew that both combatants had fallen, and then they saw the two armies move against one another. Most had, at one time or another, watched the progress of the war from this vantage point, but today all had come to the ramparts hoping to see its conclusion. When they heard the clash of arms yet again, however, a profound silence descended upon the group. They looked on in mute wonder at the mightiness of fate, which tantalized them with escape, and then sped them on irresistibly to destruction.

The royal family had a special place on the wall to the right of the Scaean Gates, and they, like the other citizens, were ignorant of what had touched off the fighting again. Priam stood immobile next to his wife. Their daughter Cassandra stood with them, as did their youngest son, Polites. Helen, as usual, stood apart from the rest. Andromache, who rarely came to the walls, was also there today, with her two-year-old son, Astyanax. She usually avoided watching the battle, because she had a superstitious fear that her eyes upon her husband might hinder his strength. But now, like everyone else, she stood transfixed. She had picked out Hector earlier, before the duel, but then she lost sight of him in the general melee. The battle had been raging for nearly an hour when she noticed the dust cloud at the north end of the shoreline.

Everyone was used to the dust by now, whenever there was a battle. The Trojan plain, its crops gone and its wild vegetation trampled, turned to dust shortly after the fighting season began each year. But this cloud was coming from the furthest Greek encampment, and there had been no activity from that quarter for some time. She grasped the hand of her son and led him further along the wall to where she would have a better view. The cloud was moving down from the beach now toward the field. Andromache tried to imagine that it was being caused merely by a gust of wind, or perhaps it had been raised by an unusually large group of spectators coming to watch the battle. But then from out of the obscurity of dust she saw the unmistakable outline of war chariots and the glint of bronze in the morning sun. She whispered, "Myrmidons."

Hector had remained in the center of the battle line and had been having some success making the Greeks retreat. He was not aware of the Myrmidons' entry into the battle until he began to sense the intense pressure on the Trojan right flank. Being on the ground, and in the midst of a dust cloud himself, he did not have the view which the citizens on the wall had. Gradually, however, he realized that his own forces in the middle were being crowded on their right-hand side. Achilles' men, long rested and suffering none of the low morale of their allies, were having a devastating effect on the Trojans. Hector saw the men around him yielding way and stumbling over each other as they were pushed backward. The Greeks at the center, who had themselves been retreating and were still as unaware as he of what was happening far to their left, became heartened by the Trojan predicament, and pressed their own attack.

Faced with this situation, Hector tried to call an orderly retreat, but his center forces were evaporating, and he began to see men dropping their shields and running toward the city gates. He retired to the rear to find someone who knew what was going on.

Once out of the dust, he saw his brother, Deiphobus,

the second in command, with a small squadron he was organizing behind the lines.

"Deiphobus, what happened?" he shouted.

"Myrmidons on the right flank," his brother called to him. "They decimated the Lycians. Sarpedon's dead. Pandarus's dead. I'm trying to get my men back into the city before they cut us off."

Hector gathered whoever was in his immediate vicinity and joined his brother's retreat toward the Scaean Gates. The Trojans' only ally in this disorderly flight was the dust, which obscured their movement and slowed down the Greek pursuit.

The townspeople, who had been watching the rout in horror, opened the gates wide to admit the fleeing soldiers, and Hector was within sight of the portal when he saw a small group of Trojans under the city walls some distance away who seemed to be nearly surrounded by the Myrmidons.

Leaving his troops in Deiphobus's care, he ran toward the beleaguered knot of fighters. He had misjudged the situation, however, for before he reached the group, they had already made good their retreat to the Thymbraean Gates in the northern section of the wall. He turned around to look for his brother and his men, but the Myrmidons, in complete control now of the main approach to the city, had blocked his way back. Then he heard the thud of the Scaean Gates as they were swung closed. He had heard the sound a thousand times, and each time before it had meant safety, security, a rest from toil. But now it gave him a sickening feeling in the pit of his stomach.

An odd silence descended on the battlefield. In the distance, Hector could still hear the Greeks exalting as they picked up Trojan armor left behind, and he could faintly hear the groans of the dying, those whom the Greeks had not yet mercifully dispatched. But here before the wall, everything was still. He did not realize at first that the Myrmidons knew of his presence. When he wasn't attacked or even approached, he thought he had not been seen, even though there was little dust this close to the city. He looked up at the walls and could see clearly the townspeople looking down at him. But it took him a while to sense the other pair of eyes watching him from the ground. He turned again to the spot where he had left Deiphobus, and his brother was not there, but now another man was.

Hector had of course seen Achilles before; they had never consciously avoided each other. They may even, in a general encounter, have crossed swords before. But now it was the two of them alone, and in sight of the whole town. Achilles' men, by some unspoken command, had sheathed their weapons and were keeping apart from the two commanders.

Hector looked into the eyes of the other man as the Myrmidon captain approached him. "Prince Achilles," he said, "my parents will pay you a large ransom for my safe return."

"Did you kill Patroclus?" asked the other. His voice was measured, calm, and without emotion.

"In the normal course of battle, I did."

"Then in the normal course of battle, I will kill you," said Achilles in the same flat monotone.

The words seemed strange. Kill me, Hector thought, kill me? Hector, who had been fighting continuously for nine years, who was the very pillar of his city, the prop on which his father leaned, was he meant to die this day? Could it be that he wouldn't see the inside of Troy again, he wouldn't see the oak tree inside the Scaean Gates? He was no more than a hundred yards from it right now. If they opened the gates, he could see it from here. Could it be that he would never sit beneath its cool branches again?

Hector had killed and been nearly killed himself so many times that he had long lost count. Death may have been there by his side all along, but he had not been aware of its presence. Now, however, it was standing before him, in the form of a greater man. He wished he'd thought to say good-bye to his wife. Now he could offer her no consolation, except the rites she would perform for his corpse.

"Prince Achilles," he said, "if one of us should fall, will you make an agreement with me not to dishonor the body, but give it back to his people?"

"Yes," said the other, who never took his eyes off him. "I'll make such an agreement with you when I see a wolf make one with a sheep."

Hector watched as the other man now assumed his battle stance, his feet spread apart, his knees bent slightly, his left arm slowly rotating his shield in mesmerizing circles, and his right hand, palm up, weighing the balance point of his spear. The Trojan glanced up at the wall again. His wife, he knew, was watching, as were his father and his mother and all his people. If he were to die, they would mourn for him and would remember this hour until the very last of theirs. He knew he must show courage, even though it would sharpen their grief. The memory of his fall should remind them of Troy's grandeur and the extent of their loss. He should inspire them by his final actions to preserve their city with bravery and determination.

He looked back at the Greek, and the grim face he saw, inhuman beneath the metal brow of his helmet, excited a visceral fear in him that he had never known before. No longer did Hector feel like a man, a human being who had tamed horses, tilled fields, learned government, planned with his wife their child's future. What he felt like now was prey, a thing to be killed, something to be stuck with a great shaft of bronze until the blood and the life spilled out of it.

Still moving his shield in small rings, Achilles drew his spear back so that his right hand was well behind his body. Hector knew it was the moment to prepare his defense, to enact before his countrymen the drama which would end his life. His instinct as a warrior caused him to raise his shield automatically. But then, as he watched the eyes of the other and saw the sudden glare that meant the spear was going to fly, another instinct took over. It was an instinct that abides in all living creatures, but which in Hector, perhaps, lay buried deeper than in other men. In front of his family, in front of his town, surrounded by the enemy and with no possible refuge available to him, Hector ran.

He ran like the prey that he was, with mindless, reckless speed, and Achilles followed. The way to the city blocked, the way to the shore filled with Greeks, he ran a course parallel to the city walls. The Myrmidons, through a circling action, might have stopped his flight, but instead they merely guarded the paths to the various gates, and made way for their chief, who alone chased him. The citizens on the walls watched in stricken silence. No one could hurl abuse on Hector, for no one could say with surety that he would act otherwise.

Hector ran and ran. Place disappeared, time disappeared, only speed was left. His body, which had served him in myriad ways since birth, now served only as a moving vehicle to carry him away. If he were conscious of anything, it was only of the wind, the wind he was causing to rush by his face, the wind sucked into his lungs, no sooner in but expelled again, the wind that was his life. He was competing with a born runner, though, who might have overtaken him, but Achilles merely pressed him from behind, stayed at his heels, and waited for him to tire so that he could strike him from the front.

This terrible pageant went on longer than anyone thought it could. As tired as Hector became, as much as his legs and chest ached with the exertion, he went on running, for it was death to stop. Before he was through, he made a complete circuit of the walled town. When he had come around to the front of the city again, however, he was almost relieved to see the mass of Greek warriors who, impatient with the long delay, had formed a line to block his path. No place left to go, and exhausted besides, he stopped, turned, and faced his pursuer. Achilles was winded now too, and for a moment both stood hunched over with hands on their hips, replenishing their overtaxed lungs. They might have been two boys who, for amusement, had raced each other around the city, and now were resting before another lark. But Achilles quickly revived and, not waiting for Hector, assumed his battle stance again, and let fly his spear.

It was probably due more to the Greek's tired aim than Hector's ability to dodge that the spear fell harmlessly to the ground. So Achilles drew his sword, and the two began to circle each other.

Achilles struck first, and his weapon, aimed at Hector's left thigh, landed with a clang on the Trojan's shield. The blow deflected, Hector leapt back. When he did so, the fear left him, and he no longer wanted to run. The familiar war wrath welled up in him again, and though it meant his death this time, he wanted to strike the man who had struck him, strike the man in front of him and beat him senseless.

He lunged at Achilles and rained a half dozen blows on his shield while the other retired in amazement. The citizens on the wall gave up a shout for their doomed champion. But Achilles was not daunted for long. He merely accepted his adversary's new posture and went back to work. He allowed Hector so spend himself on fruitless blows and waited for his own chance. The two circled and clashed and retired in a strange rhythmic dance, with death waiting to claim one partner.

The end came for Hector when he held his shield a hand's breadth too low as he aimed a blow at Achilles' side. The Greek, seeing the opening, made a quick downward slice with his sword that severed Hector's spinal column and the arteries in his neck.

Hector felt the blow, but did not feel himself collapse on the ground, nor did he hear the Myrmidons cheer, nor his own people on the wall send up a dismal cry of woe. He would not feel it later when Achilles pierced his ankles with a sword and then threaded the gash with rope so he could drag Hector's body in triumph behind his chariot. He would not hear himself reviled or feel his body desecrated in the Greek camp, nor would he feel the sun beat upon him as he lay long unburied. And finally, many days later, he would not feel the gentle rocking of the wagon as his father took him back to the city once more, having ransomed his body from the man who killed him.

Though his skin was still warm and his legs twitched for several moments on the ground, all that had been Hector was gone. All, that is, but the memory, a memory that might have died too with his wife, or with his son, or with the last of his people—an old, old man in a foreign land, who had been just a boy that day in Troy when he watched the great hero fall. But if there were such an old man, he was not content to let the memory die with himself. He told another boy the story, one who, in his old age, told another, and so on, until one old man in this tenuous chain told the story to an unfortunate boy, blind from birth. And though that boy could neither wield a sword, nor sail a ship, nor plow a field, he could sing. When he became a man, he sang of Ilion, and in his song, he made of Hector's death the death of Troy, and he made the death of Troy the death of all that is good in us when faced with all that is evil.

VII

The Shield

WEEKS PASSED, AND Troy knew a desolation it had not known since the war began. The citizens, whether they had harbored illusions to the contrary or not, now saw that victory was impossible. A truce of ten days had been called to bury the dead, but when the truce expired, the army did not venture outside the walls. And the town, though still inhabited by living souls, anticipated in its quiet and deserted streets the feel of a city long dead, unearthed a thousand years later for another generation to wonder at.

The king and queen of this strange metropolis had remained secluded in the palace since Hector's funeral. Priam had appointed his next eldest son, Deiphobus, to the command of the armies, but he had done so perfunctorily, and Deiphobus had accepted the post without enthusiasm. Aeneas took on the difficult task of convincing the various allies, either through gifts or promised rewards, not to desert the city. Many allies had already done so under cover of night. Daily Aeneas reported his progress to Priam, and daily Priam thanked him, but no news, either good or bad, seemed to encourage the old man.

Andromache, too, was little seen outside the palace walls except to accompany Cassandra to the temple. Though Andromache had little hope of the gods' succor, she found an odd comfort in her sister-in-law's presence. Cassandra did not attempt to console her, did not try to convince her that the pain would pass or lessen. She never mentioned Andromache's grief at all. Instead, she prattled about anything and everything, gaily, as the mad have license to do. She told Andromache the familiar stories of the Gorgons, of the Harpies, of the great flying horse, Pegasus, but in her own crazy versions, and sometimes Andromache would smile in spite of herself, and forget for a moment or two that she had seen her husband's corpse dragged through the dust.

There was one in Troy, however, who still did not know that Hector was dead. After the fighting began on the day of the duel, Paris was carried back to the city and brought to his apartment in the palace. The wound in his thigh was deep and mended slowly, but even more severe was the blow to the head which he had suffered. In the days that followed, he alternated between periods of unconsciousness and delirium, and no one could say if he would live or die.

During this time, Helen took it upon herself to be his physician and his nurse. She dressed his wound, she cleaned his bedding, she forced him to eat in his fitful intervals of wakefulness, she sat with him during the day and lay in a corner near him at night. The rest of the royal family visited only rarely. Were they not so preoccupied with their own loss, they might have felt a grudging respect for Helen. She had, after all, watched both her husbands fall at once that day, and now one of them lay near death, while the fate of the other was unknown to her. Still, she complained to no one. She merely went about her work.

And through her ministrations, Paris did recover. After one particularly bad night, during which Helen changed his sweat-soaked bedding several times, Paris woke and saw her staring down at him.

"Helen?" he said feebly.

"It's me."

"You're alive!"

"*I'm* alive?"

"I dreamed you were dead."

She smiled. "I'm not."

With an effort he tried to lift himself up so he could take hold of her. She leaned down to make it easy for him, and then he clasped her to him in a grip that might have hurt her if he had his full strength. .

"You're still alive," he said, more to himself than to her. "You're still alive."

Helen could not tell if it were the delirium again, even though this was the first time he had recognized her. The desperate grip with which he held her made her fear that this would be his last effort on earth. But at length he relaxed it and let her up so he could look into her face again.

"The old redhead beat me, didn't he?" Paris said.

"Yes."

He smiled weakly and shrugged his shoulders. "I'm sorry I couldn't win for you. What happened? Why didn't you go with him?"

"Someone hit him with an arrow. The fighting started again."

"Menelaus was hit?"

"Yes."

"Is he dead?"

"I don't know."

He was thoughtful for a moment. "So we're at war again."

"Yes."

"What did the king say? Was he disappointed with me?"

"He hasn't said much about it," she answered briefly. "Would you like something to eat?"

Paris nodded absently. "What about Hector. What did he say?"

She looked away. "Nothing. I'll call for one of the servants to bring you something."

"He didn't say anything?"

"No."

"He must be furious with me. I can't blame him. But I did try. I was willing to die out there."

"I'm sure he knows that. You nearly did die."

Helen went to the door and instructed a servant outside to bring Paris some food.

"You know," he said when she returned, "I thought I'd be thinking about you during the duel, but I wasn't. I kept thinking of him, Hector, standing behind me and watching me. I must have looked pretty bad."

"I couldn't tell. I was so far away."

"Where is he? Out with the army?"

"No. Everyone's in the city."

He looked up at her, surprised. "Everyone?"

"Yes."

"What happened? We were camped all the way down the field. We had the Greeks trapped around their ships."

"Achilles came back with the Myrmidons."

"Oh," he sighed, closing his eyes. "Did I bring that on too?"

"No, you had nothing to do with it."

He fell silent. A servant arrived with bread, cheese, fruit, and wine. Helen helped Paris sit up, and watched with a small joy as he fed himself without her aid for the first time.

"How long have I been here?" he asked after several mouthfuls.

"Weeks. It's been a long time."

"Has anyone been in to see me?"

"Of course."

"The king and queen?"

"Yes. Everyone's come."

"Hector too?"

She lowered her eyes. "No, not Hector."

Paris's face clouded over. "He must be hoping I'll die."

"No, he isn't."

"I don't blame him. Menelaus beat me in a fair fight. I should be dead. The war should be over, and you should be on your way back to Sparta. Hector's right. I should be dead."

"No you shouldn't. You said yourself once that the gifts of the gods cannot be refused. One of them saved you. It was a gift."

Suddenly a throbbing pain gripped Paris behind his eyes, clouding his vision. He grimaced as the image of his wife blurred in front of him. Helen, who had been seated by the bedside, leapt up horrified and bent over him once again and called his name. But as quickly as the pain came, it passed, and Paris reached feebly for her hand when it came into focus again.

"It's all right," he said. "I'm all right." He smiled up at her to reassure her, but she still looked at him dubiously. That's when he saw it in her eyes, something he had never seen before. It was not disdain or fear, feelings he had read there all too often, nor was it pity, a feeling he might have expected to see. What he saw now was caring and unfeigned affection.

"You really didn't want me to die, did you?" he said.

"I told you I didn't."

With another effort he clasped her to him again, and this time she did not fear the tightness of his grip. She had been the woman whom no one would hold, no one would console. But now, they held each other in a long, desperate, timeless embrace. In a mad world of chance and death, they had been granted a reprieve, no matter how brief, and each repeated silently the elemental refrain, You're still alive. You're still alive.

It was Paris who broke the silence many minutes later. "I've got to see Hector. I've got to talk with him."

Helen loosened her embrace. The look in her eyes had changed.

"What's the matter?" Paris asked.

She looked away and shook her head.

He was silent for a moment while he watched her. "What's happened to him?"

She closed her eyes.

"My God," he said, grasping her arm, "is Hector dead?"

She nodded without looking at him. "Achilles killed him," she said. "We all saw it from the wall, after you and Menelaus fell."

He released her arm and lay back on the bed with the realization of it. "He died for me," Paris said, almost under his breath, and for a moment he felt one final spark of anger at his older brother. The rivalry of a lifetime was over, and Hector had won it once and for all. In an ultimate triumph, Hector had even died for him. A faint smile appeared and then disappeared on Paris's lips as he acknowledged the irony of it. He shook his head. The contest was over.

"It wasn't your fault," Helen said. "Achilles singled him out."

When the anger passed from Paris, a new feeling took its place. "I'll make it up to him," he said with a calmness and a seriousness that Helen had never heard from his lips before.

"It wasn't your fault," Helen repeated. "There's nothing you can do to Achilles."

"I didn't want him to die, even if he hated me."

"I know."

"I'll make it up to him."

Laocoön gazed at the shield. The elaborately carved bronze disk had been hung above the altar to Apollo in the palace as a memorial, and so it became the priest's job to care for it. This shield did not have a nick in its ridge where Achilles' sword bit into it, nor did it show the imprint of any other blows it might have sustained from Greek weapons. Too good for use, this shield had been made for Hector as a rich treasure, given to him years ago by a grateful city. Now it hung silently in the dim, smoky light of this interior chamber.

The last of Antenor's living sons, Laocoön was a priest of Apollo, the god of prophecy. Unlike his father, who had become less and less warlike over the years, Laocoön maintained a fierce hostility toward the Greeks. Furthermore, his attitude was reinforced by the strange testimony he found in his divinations before the god. He couldn't understand the conciliatory tone that his father was now taking, and the two had had violent arguments about it. Laocoön would remind his father of the three sons the old man had lost in the war, and then Antenor would warn Laocoön that all their family would be lost if a peace couldn't be concluded. But the priest knew that no peace was possible, because no Greek could be trusted. The only things the Trojans should trust in were their strong wall and the strength of their arms.

What was foremost in the priest's mind right now, however, was the message he had received from Paris. He had been surprised when one of the palace servants arrived and told him that the prince wanted to meet him here. Paris, who had lingered so long at death's door, had only been out of bed for a few days, and Laocoön had no idea why he should want to see him. So he sat and waited and looked at the shield.

He'd never thought about it before, but now, forced to contemplate the great circle of bronze hanging before him, Laocoön wondered why it was the shield, the *defensive* weapon, that artisans lavished the most care on. In the manner of those who do no fighting themselves, he saw the offensive weapon, the sword, as the more fitting symbol of manly virtue, and therefore the more logical piece of military equipment to display artistic ingenuity. The hilt of the sword should be encrusted with jewels, he thought, carved with wonderful beasts, and the blade should be etched with pictures of deep meaning. Instead, the sword in those days was actually very plain, with just a simple crossbar above the straight, unadorned handle. It was the shield on which the armorers practiced their highest art.

Shields were made of several layers of material, usually metal alternating with animal hides, which were bonded together. Armorers had found through experience that such construction was nearly as strong as a solid metal disk, but considerably lighter. It was the top layer, the outside, which was used as a bronze canvas for the craftsman's talent and cunning. The shields used in battle often had simple geometric designs, or rude pictures of the gods and heroes etched upon them. But one such as this, designed as a gift, would be a tapestry for the artist's most elaborate fancy. Using a series of concentric rings and pictures, he could tell a story or celebrate an event as clearly in symbols as a poet could do in words. The finished product would then be a possession of great value. It represented the only currency in an age before the use of money.

The finest practitioner in the city had been commissioned to make this particular shield, and it was to be a fitting tribute to Hector, the defender of Troy. On the outside rim of the disk, the armorer carved the great city wall itself, broken in four places corresponding to the four gates, the Thymbraean, the Dardanian, the Ilian, and, at the top, the Scaean. Arrayed in a ring just inside the wall, he pictured the gods Trojans worshipped as their particular benefactors: Athena, Apollo, Zeus, Poseidon, and Aphrodite, all in their characteristic poses and with the accompanying artifacts that identified them. Then he pictured the line of Trojan kings, from Dardanus through Hector's father, Priam, along with small representations of some of the most prominent buildings of Troy.

Then he carved a ring of ships, and within that ring horrible scenes of war. He showed battle chariots with broken bodies underneath their wheels. He showed Hector slaying a Greek captain, while Ares, the god of war, looked on, pleased.

Then he pictured a ring of fire, and inside it a lone ship sailing away and setting down in the harbor of another great city, which dominated all the earth around it. He showed legions of soldiers issuing forth in strange garb. Then he showed a great sword stuck in the ground, and people around the sword groveling before it. He showed more war, and crowded cities, and pestilence. He showed new, inexplicable war engines, and great dust clouds smothering whole cities.

And in the very center of the shield, completing the elaborate design, the skilled artist carved a grand and stately horse. This final emblem was to honor Hector, who was known throughout Troy as "the horse tamer."

Laocoön's contemplation of the shield was interrupted by a stumbling noise behind him. Paris had entered the chamber, and was steadying himself by clutching a table next to the wall. Laocoön leapt up.

"My lord, are you all right?"

Paris waved away assistance. "Yes. Yes. Sit down." The priest did as commanded, and the prince made his way slowly and carefully to a second chair and drew it up directly in front of Laocoön. When Paris was seated, the priest scanned his face in the dim light. He was thin and pale, but there was a look of nervous energy in his eyes.

Paris, to halt the intensive scrutiny by the other, began speaking quickly. "I need to get into the Greek camp."

"But my Lord, there's been no fighting now since—"

"It's not a battle I want. I just want you to get me into their camp."

Laocoön stared at him. "Me, my lord? How?"

"I don't know how. You're a priest. Think of a way."

"But—"

Paris raised his hand. "Listen to me: I need three things. First I need to get within thirty paces of Achilles—"

"Bow-shot range," said Laocoön quietly.

"That's right. Second, I need a place concealed enough to get off one good shot from. And third, it's got to be broad daylight."

Laocoön looked puzzled.

Paris smiled and tapped the left side of his head. "Menelaus's sword seems to have clouded my eyes a little. I don't see very well in the dark anymore. So it's got to be daylight."

The priest would have spoken again, but the prince abruptly stood up, and again very carefully and slowly made his way to the door. Laocoön followed.

"My lord, even if you're able to make the shot, how do you get back into the city?"

Paris turned. "Getting back would be a fourth thing." The bewilderment and fear in Laocoön's eyes prompted Paris to smile again. "It's not often that a priest gets a hand in killing someone like Achilles. I thought you'd be pleased, considering how you feel about the Greeks." The prince laughed a brief, sardonic laugh. Then he patted Laocoön on the shoulder. "Figure out a way to get back if you want to, but make sure you get me the three things I asked for."

When Paris was gone, Laocoön staggered back to his chair. Whether or not he was a coward had always been a moot point. Being a priest and thus a noncombatant, he never had to face it before. He faced it now, and realized he was a coward. He looked up again at the picture of Hector plunging his sword into the belly of a Greek captain, and he wondered what it would feel like to have a sword stuck in his own belly. Yet his cowardice was now a moot point. He had no choice but to do his prince's bidding, and he began to think of the last thing Paris had said, about having a part in the killing of Achilles. His hatred of the Greeks nearly matched his cowardice. If they could really do it, it might mean that the Greeks would leave at last. Why should the loss of their greatest warrior not have as devastating an effect on the Greeks as it had had on the Trojans?

But how to get into the Greek camp, and how to lure Achilles to a meeting? How? Laocoön gazed at the shield. All along the Greeks had granted truces, usually to bury the dead, so contacting them was not difficult. And he could probably concoct some story that would allow a couple of Trojans outside the walls. But inducing Achilles to come: that would be the hard part. What was Achilles interested in? What could be bribe him with? Gold? But could he come up with enough gold to interest someone like Achilles? Maybe he could offer him a woman. Laocoön shook his head. No, it wasn't sure enough. Why should Achilles be interested in still another slave girl? He stared at the shield. He needed something better, something Achilles couldn't turn down. What could be offer him?

Slowly, imperceptibly, a thin smile began to appear on the priest's lips.

The Temple to Thymbraean Apollo was a small, gemlike edifice, which stood some distance north of the city outside the walls. In the days of peace, its setting in the midst of a shady grove of fir made it a pleasant destination for religious devotees during the day and for young lovers at night. During the nine years of the war, however, it had been all but abandoned, except for an occasional Greek who used its confines as a convenient place to nap out of the sun in summer, or as a shelter against the wind in winter.

Since their return to the fighting, the Myrmidons had formed a temporary camp in the vicinity of the temple, and it was to their camp that a messenger had been dispatched from the Trojan priest Laocoön. He asked permission from Achilles to come with an assistant to the temple for the purpose of sacrificing to Apollo. The god was angry with them, the messenger said, because his Thymbraean shrine had been ignored in Hector's obsequies. Achilles, who had kept much to himself since the death of Patroclus, would have denied the request had the priest not offered him, in exchange for the privilege, the ceremonial shield of Hector. Achilles already possessed Hector's battle armor, but this piece, described in all its splendor by the messenger, promised to be much finer. So he granted the request.

Consequently, on the appointed day, a wagon emerged from the Thymbraean Gates, so named because they faced north toward the temple. Seated in the wagon were Laocoön and his assistant, who was muffled against the sun. Tied in the back was a large, white ram, standing next to a tall jar of grain for an altar offering. Laocoön's assistant held Hector's great shield in front of him.

The Myrmidons they passed took only a cursory look at the passengers and cargo, and none of them noted that two excellent riding horses were hitched to the wagon. What they mainly noticed was the shield. Few had ever beheld one of such fine workmanship, and they envied their captain, who would soon be the possessor of it.

They let the wagon pass into the shadowed confines of the temple, where the two men got out and took the jar and the ram inside.

Once inside, Paris threw off his robe and, having pulled his bow from the jar, began stripping away the grain which still adhered to it. Laocoön, meanwhile, returned to the wagon to retrieve the shield, and while pretending to pat the horses, he severed two leather straps which bound them to the wagon. Then he hefted the shield and started walking away from the temple to a clearing which Paris had chosen beforehand. When he reached the center of the clearing, he stopped.

The greatest unknown in their plan was whether or not they could get Achilles to accept the shield in person. If the Myrmidon leader sent a lieutenant to fetch it, Laocoön was to claim that he could only deliver it directly to Achilles, but the priest recognized that he had little negotiating strength in such a situation, standing as he was at the edge of the enemy's camp, completely in their power. If the lieutenant refused to get his leader, Laocoön would have no choice but to surrender the shield, perform the useless sacrifice, and go back to Troy. So the priest stood in the windy clearing and waited.

Achilles was in his tent when a servant told him the Trojans had arrived and one of them had the shield. Achilles had been thinking of Patroclus and welcomed the distraction. He emerged from the tent and saw the lone figure with the bright object standing some distance from the temple. He suspected no treachery, nor did he fear any. He was, after all, the greatest warrior alive, and were a foe to approach him with sword in hand, it would be the foe who should tremble, not himself. Without a word, he strode toward the priest, and several of his men accompanied him.

Laocoön did not know from where in the camp Achilles might emerge, but when he saw a party making for him, he recognized the leader among them immediately. With that recognition came a leap inside him that made his body shudder. Perhaps at the back of his mind he had hoped that Achilles would not come. Their mission would fail, to be sure, but at least Laocoön would get home safely. He would sleep in his bed tonight and live to see another morning. But now he realized that the plan would go forward. Paris would take his shot, and the priest himself might die in the aftermath of it. But there was nothing to be done. He closed his eyes momentarily and resigned himself to whatever would happen. Then he opened them and stood stock still, lest any shaking betray him.

Thirty paces behind him, unseen in the darkness of the temple, Paris too recognized Achilles. He had already positioned himself and flexed his bow. Now he gauged the range. On the battlefield, he had always been able to get his trajectory first by sending off a few arrows into the crowd of enemies. But now, although he had taken several arrows, he could only be sure of getting off one. From the experience of a thousand shots on the field, in every wind and covering every distance, he had to judge this one. He drew back the string.

Achilles stopped a few feet from Laocoön, but did not look at the priest. He was admiring the shield of his fallen enemy. It was a fine piece of work; there was no denying it. He understood many of the emblems on it, for the Greeks shared with the Trojans a common iconography. But some of the devices were obscure, a license allowed artists of every age. He was pleased with it nevertheless, and happy to number it among his possessions.

Laocoön had practiced a speech to deliver to the Myrmidon captain, but when the moment came, all he could say was, "My lord Achilles," and handed him the shield. Then with no more ado, he turned and walked back toward the temple. He walked consciously and

132

purposefully, as if walking away from a bear, resisting the nearly overpowering urge to break into a run and thereby transform himself into prey.

Paris had instructed Laocoön to stay slightly to the side as he returned to the temple so that he would not be directly in front of Achilles. But the priest in his anxiety had forgotten, and so Paris was forced to wait several moments before he had a completely unobstructed view. He could see, however, that Achilles was holding the shield out in front of him, still looking at it, but luckily he had turned to his left, so the bronze was not in a position to protect him. Paris was going to aim for the center of his chest. That way if he shot high, there was a chance the arrow would still pierce his neck or head, and if he shot low, his abdomen. Any hit in those areas could still prove fatal.

The two fingers with which Paris hooked the string were all the way back next to his right ear, and his left arm was fully extended as he waited for the priest to get out of the way. Paris had a good eye; even from this distance he could see the pleased look on the Myrmidon's face as he admired his new acquisition. The prince held his breath. Laocoön made three more steps, and then Achilles' torso, like the sun at the end of an eclipse, finally slid out from behind the priest's shadow.

Yet at the same moment, even as Paris allowed the string to roll off his two fingers, the ache behind his eyes returned, his vision clouded, and Achilles, whose sharp image just a second before could even be discerned smiling, faded into the substance of a ghost. But the arrow was gone.

Achilles was examining the strange dust clouds pictured on the shield when he was hit. He thought at first that he'd been bitten by a snake. What else is likely to sting you in the foot? He was amazed to look down and see the arrow stuck in his heel. He looked up bewildered, for there were no enemies about. The men near Achilles, however, when they saw what happened, crowded around their chief so that he could not be shot again.

In those brief moments of consternation, Laocoön ran into the temple and hurried Paris out the other side to their horses. Paris was cursing himself for his faulty shot, but his temporary blindness and the quickness of the Myrmidons in shielding their chief kept him from getting off another. The two mounted their horses and gallopped toward the Thymbraean Gates.

Most of the Myrmidons they passed did not know yet what had occurred. Those that did were forced to pursue the Trojans on foot, since their own horses were corralled some distance away. But the Trojans had chosen swift-running steeds, and once they had passed the last knot of surprised Greeks and dodged a few hastily aimed spears, their way was clear. Paris and Laocoön gained the safety of the city moments later, and were ushered through the Thymbraean Gates to the cheers of the guards stationed there. Achilles' companions, meanwhile, labored to remove their chief to his tent, but their way was impeded by their own fellows who clamored loudly around them to know what had happened.

And in the small, gem-like temple the white ram, its life prolonged by the vicissitudes of human fortune, nibbled at the grain fallen from the overturned jar.

It was the laughter that shocked Agamemnon the most, the laughter at the end. Not that he would have expected the great hero to cry out in pain, or gnash his teeth, or curse his fate. He may have hated Achilles once, but Achilles had never been a coward. The laughter, though, had cut right through the chief. What did it mean? That fate was unpredictable, that it took twists and turns that no one could foresee? They all knew that. They had been raised on stories of heroes who had been victims of it. But did Hercules laugh? Did Oedipus?

Of course no one had expected the wound on his foot to be serious. Agamemnon's own brother had taken an arrow in the shoulder during the duel, and it had healed completely. Their best surgeon, Machaon, had examined Achilles and pronounced that he would be walking without a limp in a week or two. The wound did seem to heal, too, at least on the outside, and Achilles was able to get around on it. But the color was never quite right, and the pain continued to get worse and began traveling up his leg. Then, to everyone's horror, bubbles began to appear under the surface of his skin. Machaon opened up the wound again to remove the poison, but Achilles' condition did not improve. The leg became so infected that he could no longer walk on it and had to be carried around on a stretcher. In time he didn't want to move at all, and when the infection reached his trunk, everyone knew the end was near.

It was on that final night that he laughed. They had all gathered around him, Agamemnon, Menelaus, Odysseus, Ajax, Diomedes, Nestor. He babbled first about his mother and about Patroclus, and then he let out with a wild, insane laugh, as if he had a glimpse of some cosmic joke, one played on himself: the greatest warrior alive felled by a misshot arrow wound in the heel. Men so used to the horrors of war might have been expected to understand the strange effects of pain and delirium on a fellow warrior and pay it no mind, but the sound of the laughter seemed to mortify them. They stood around looking at each other confused, consternated. Even old Nestor, who had seen and heard everything, was moved and had to leave the tent.

The funeral rites were performed, and when they were done, the great pyre was lit. The flames could be seen as far away as the island of Tenedos. And when the fire was out, they gathered his bones in a jar and buried them next to those of Patroclus in a mound near the Hellespont.

Agamemnon sat alone now in his tent. Maybe there really was little wonder in the laughter. Perhaps they were all unconscious participants in a great farce designed in heaven and played out on earth. Surely no sense of fairness could be discerned in the events Agamemnon had witnessed. Menelaus had lost Helen through Trojan duplicity in the first place, and now through duplicity again they had all lost Achilles. The Greeks could defeat the enemy on the field, but the Trojans remained unbeaten in the war and safe behind their wall. Agamemnon wondered why fate should so often favor the devious over the straightforward, the deceitful over the true.

But the chief's reverie was interrupted by a balding head stuck through his tent flap.

"Lord Agamemnon?"

"Come in, Odysseus. Pour yourself some wine," said the chief, indicating a pitcher set on the table in front of him.

The Ithacan availed himself of this, and sat down across from Agamemnon.

"Well, what does he say?" asked Agamemnon disgustedly. Faced with his army's discouragement over Achilles' death, the chief had bowed to their desire to have another divination performed by Calchas. He had once placed great faith in the prophet's ability, for it was Calchas who told him many years ago that he would take the city of Troy. Indeed, it was on the prophet's word that he had sacrificed his daughter at Aulis. But as the war dragged on and they got no closer to their goal, he lost faith in Calchas, and the sacrifice at Aulis seemed like just another cruel joke.

Odysseus smiled. "Calchas seems to want to play

136

Eurystheus. He's imposed some labors of Hercules on us, but not as many.''

"Labors of Hercules? What are they?''

"There are three of them. The first is to recover Philoctetes' bow.''

"What? Philoctetes' bow? Did Nestor have something to do with this?''

Odysseus laughed. "I don't know, but his lordship is telling the whole camp that he was right all along.''

"How in hell are we supposed to find Philoctetes' bow? The man's dead, for God's sake. Who knows where his bow is now? Why didn't that damn prophet tell us this before we left Lemnos ten years ago?'' Agamemnon breathed a disgusted sigh. "What else?''

"We're supposed to bring Achilles' son here to help us take the city.''

"His son's a child.''

"I think he's eighteen now, or nineteen.''

"And the third?''

"The third is the most interesting. We're supposed to steal the Palladium.''

"The statue in Troy?''

Odysseus nodded.

Agamemnon fumed for a few moments in silence, then asked, "What do *you* think?''

The Ithacan took a sip of wine. "It's good sailing weather. The spring storms are past. We might be able to get to Scyros and back in a week. That's if Pyrrhus is willing to come. But I don't hold out much hope for finding the bow. And as for the Palladium—''

"The Palladium's impossible,'' said the chief. "Do you think Calchas is lying?''

Odysseus smiled. "I think Calchas is smart. He wins either way. If we don't get the items, he can say that's the reason we didn't take the city.''

Agamemnon scowled. "Let's let it pass for a while. I

won't give a decision one way or the other. Maybe the men will forget about it."

Odysseus nodded his assent and took another sip from his cup. "My lord," he said after a moment, "will you be distributing Achilles' treasure?"

"Yes. I've been looking it over and trying to decide how to divide it up equitably. I've picked out some nice things for you."

"Thank you, but there's only one piece that I want."

"You deserve more than one."

"Then you can give me the one all the more easily."

"Name it."

"I want Hector's shield."

Agamemnon's face clouded over. "Ajax has asked for that."

"Oh? Have you given it to him yet?"

"I haven't given anything to anyone."

The Ithacan fell silent, and the chief understood by his silence that he was not withdrawing his request in favor of Ajax.

Agamemnon was perplexed. With Achilles gone, Ajax was uncontested as the greatest fighter. He had a right to claim the prize for that reason alone. But there was another. He had once fought Hector, and though the approach of night had left their combat undecided, those who witnessed it said he had the better of the Trojan, and they would agree that Ajax deserved the shield.

Odysseus, on the other hand, though a decent fighter himself, had a rather different value to the Greeks, a higher value in Agamemnon's opinion. Odysseus possessed a wily intelligence, which had served the Greeks well in the past, and might still be the only route to victory. The chief did not want to disappoint Odysseus. Besides, Agamemnon didn't like Ajax, didn't like his bluntness, his somberness, his foreign wife. Yet, the greater part of the army would consider Ajax's claim superior.

"Well, thank you for the wine, my lord," said Odysseus as he stood up to leave.

"Stay and have another cup."

Odysseus refused, blaming several pesky but unenumerated duties that called him back to the Ithacan camp.

Alone once more, Agamemnon recalled momentarily the deep musing he had been engaged in when Odysseus arrived. He had been pondering the mystery of fate and the predicament of humanity. Such cosmic concerns, however, now faded to insignificance when compared to his new problems. Now, instead of trying to decipher the mind of God, he had to find some way to divert his army from demanding a useless sea voyage to search for a magic bow; and more important, he had to decide how to give a shiny hunk of bronze to one of his captains without insulting the other. He recognized the irony of it. To be always distracted by such things, he thought, was the fate, and perhaps the salvation, of the living.

Tecmessa had been born a princess in Teuthrania, and had never expected to be milking goats. Nevertheless, she had gotten quite good at it. She could fill the most narrow-necked jar with hardly a spill, even now, in the failing light of dusk.

Situated south of Troy, Teuthrania was an allied province that the Greeks had attacked early in the war. Tecmessa was one of the spoils that had fallen to Ajax. She knew the fate of young women captured in battle, and she resigned herself to it, though she maintained her dignity. There was shame in being a slave, to be sure, yet the shame was lessened by the universal cognizance that only fortune and the chance of war determined who was a slave and who was not.

So Tecmessa had accepted her bondage and hoped that

the gods would eventually see fit to reverse her fortune once more and set her free. In the meantime she cooked for the great, fierce-looking Greek, she served his food, poured his wine, took care of his garments, and in the evening submitted to his lovemaking. She thanked the good gods that he was at least kindly with her, despite his appearance.

It never occurred to Tecmessa that Ajax might begin to love her. It was an age before romantic love as we know it. Ajax already had possession of her in every way possible, so there was no need or reason for him to desire wedlock. That first time he watched her at length while she milked the goats she feared he was displeased with her work, but instead he praised her gentleness with the beasts. Then he began asking her about Teuthrania, and he told her about Salamis, where she would eventually live. When she first heard of it, she dreaded going there. She'd never lived on an island, and she feared it would make her captivity complete, to be bounded on all sides by the sea. But as she became more accustomed to the idea, her fear subsided. Even Ajax's fierce demeanor softened in her eyes, though she was never entirely comfortable around him. For his part, he ceased treating her like a servant, and he relieved her of the heavier duties. Yet it still came as a surprise to her when he told her he wanted to marry her.

Of course, she did not really have much choice in the matter, if indeed she ever had a choice, even when she was a free woman. Were she still living at home and Ajax had approached her father, the king might have given her to him anyway without consulting her wishes. But now, the only person who could bestow her hand was the very one asking for it, so her fate was sealed. Yet she did not mind greatly. Though she may not have loved the man, at least she knew him fairly well and did not need to fear that he might beat her, or that his lovemaking might be rough or crude. The worst thing she could say about Ajax, in fact, was that he rarely smiled, and never laughed at all. This was a singular quality, however, and because of it he remained for her a strange and forbidding presence, even after she had lived with him for years.

When she was still his slave, she would not have presumed to try to make him merry, and by the time she became his wife, she knew it was impossible. Yet she did not know from whence arose this somber attitude toward life. She thought at first that it was the war, the daily fighting, from which he would come home to her covered with other men's blood. Yet battle, for all its horrors, did not seem to have that effect on the other soldiers. She would often hear soldiers laughing and singing well into the night, but never her own lord. The only time he seemed happy, really, was when he was with his animals. She would see a look of the most placid contentment in his face when he was feeding the sheep, or when he was petting his dog Capys and talking gently to him.

Tecmessa would have liked to ask Ajax why he found life such a serious travail, but even if she could have articulated the question, she knew he could not answer it. If Ajax were given to deep thoughts as Odysseus was, or Agamemnon, he never revealed it. So the princess-turned-slave-turned-wife accepted this, and like many a consort after her she sought out the one joy her husband had and made it her own, too. She shared with him the love and careful husbandry of his animals.

Lifting the jar to her shoulder, she gave the goat a last pat with her free hand and then started back on the path from the paddock. The sun was nearly down, but even from this distance she could see Talthybius, the commander-in-chief's herald, leaving their tent. Her heart leapt a little in anticipation, because she hoped he had come to deliver the shield. She did not, of course, want Hector's shield for her own sake. Despite its intrinsic value, she had seen enough military equipment to last a lifetime and didn't need still another piece around. But she wanted it for Ajax. It seemed to be something he really desired, and he seldom coveted anything. Though he would not have been able to communicate it to her, she guessed that to him the shield was recognition, late but finally rendered, for the service he had done the army. It was the first thing he had ever asked from Agamemnon, and the chief could not deny it to him.

She hurried the rest of the way to the tent, heedless of the milk sloshing out of the jar on her shoulder. But when she gained the entranceway, she did not see the shiny bronze disk within. She saw only the dog Capys and her husband, who gazed at her with a strange, vacant stare.

"He's denied me the shield," Ajax said, and though the words were spoken to her, she felt he was saying them to someone else, an unseen judge, perhaps, in a high, celestial court.

She put down the jar and went to him, kneeling by his side. "Oh, my lord, I'm sorry."

"He's given it to Odysseus."

"He's wrong to have done that. Did he say why?"

"He said he wants me to have Hector's battle armor instead. He said it means more." Ajax gritted his teeth, and she could feel his muscles tighten. "Hector's battle armor is hacked to pieces!"

She put her head on his knee. "I'm sorry, my lord."

Ajax said no more, and the two remained in this position for some time, Tecmessa caressing the great legs she leaned on, but sensing all the while the staring, unseeing eyes wide open above her head. Finally, abruptly, Ajax rose, dislodging her.

"Where are you going, my lord?"

He did not answer, but left the tent, Capys following. Thinking he might be planning revenge on the chief, she rushed out of the tent after him. Once outside, however, she could see that he was not heading toward the center of the camp where Agamemnon lay. He was going in the opposite direction, probably just to be alone. He needed to be alone, she thought, and she resisted the urge to pursue him.

It seemed too easy that they should all be gathered here before him, all in one place, waiting, as it were, for him to come. Yet there they were. Agamemnon, his stupid brother Menelaus, the false-hearted Odysseus, doddering old Nestor, foolish young Diomedes, all standing here waiting for him. No matter. He'd show them now. He didn't care if they outnumbered him. He was the best of them, and now he'd show them once and for all.

His sword went up, fell, and down went the chief in a great splash of blood. "Give the shield to Odysseus? You won't give away my prizes any longer." He slashed with his sword again, and down went Nestor. "Take that, you old fool. That's for looking down your nose at my wife. I know you did when my back was turned, but my back isn't turned now." He saw Menelaus standing in a corner. "This whole business was your fault, because you couldn't keep your whore. Well, I'll make sure you'll be of no use to her even if you get her back." He stabbed Menelaus in the groin, and the other recoiled in agony. Then more Greek captains appeared, but it didn't matter. He hacked and slashed until every one of them lay bleeding at his feet. "All of you hated me. You used to wait for me to leave the banquet so you could laugh at me. Go ahead and laugh now!"

But someone was missing. He looked around. Odysseus had scurried behind him hoping to get away. Discovered now, he stood shaking and cowering. "Did you think I would forget about you? Did you really think I was that stupid?'' He raised his sword, but then paused. "No. You don't deserve to die like a man. You deserve to die like a snake.'' He sheathed his bloody sword and picked up a large stone with both hands. He raised it over his head and with all his might plunged it down again, crushing Odysseus's skull. Odysseus crumpled before him. "Squirm your way out from under that, if you're so smart!''

He took one more look around, and then, satisfied with his work, he stepped out and closed the gate. Now he and his wife could go home and forget all this. He would have to explain it to his father, of course, but his father would understand, once he told him the shame he had suffered. It was odd, though, he thought, that they had all gathered so conveniently for him, and that none of them had drawn a sword. But they were cowards; that was the only explanation. Something about Odysseus's face, too, was disturbing. Something strange about it, that he couldn't quite put his finger on. Well, it doesn't matter. It was done now, finished, and he was glad. Tomorrow, home! It was the damnedest thing, though, that they should all be herded there in his—

He stopped. He turned around.

The army from Tiryns, Diomedes' city, was stationed next to Ajax's army, which occupied the southern end of the Greek encampment. Thus, it was the young leader Diomedes who first came running when he heard the screams the next morning. He feared the Trojans had staged another ambush, and his fears seemed confirmed when he saw Tecmessa leaning over the fence of the paddock, covered with blood and yelling incoherently. Around her stood Ajax's people, silent, transfixed. But the blood staining the Teuthranian woman was not her own, nor was it human.

Diomedes was no stranger to carnage. Though still a

144

relatively young man, he had fought at Troy for nine years and had seen the worst that war can produce. The first time he saw a man's brains dashed out, the sight had sickened him, but it sickened him no longer. He was steeled now to anything, he thought. But as he walked, slowly now, up to the paddock, he beheld a sight that made him turn away in horror.

Animals have always been killed by human beings, usually for food, sometimes in religious rituals, and occasionally, in the most barbarous lands, for sport and entertainment. Diomedes himself had killed many animals with his own hands, but he had done so without anger, without malice, and he caused as little suffering as possible. A beast's innocence and simplicity usually protects it from the antagonism we lavish so abundantly on our own kind. But no such protection shielded the animals here.

Sheep, goats, and dogs were strewn in a gruesome disorder throughout the yard. Some had their heads severed, some their limbs, some had been hacked repeatedly, the spine treated like a chopping block. The body of an old ram lay several feet from where its intestines had tumbled out of a two-foot gash in its belly. One goat had been stabbed through the neck with a knife and pinioned to a fence post. At Tecmessa's feet was Capys, killed by a stone, his head now merely a concave caricature of a dog's features. And all over blood, soaking the rich wool of the sheep, matting the dogs' coarse hair. Blood everywhere.

"Who did this?" shouted Diomedes, still turned away from both Tecmessa and the slaughter. But the Teuthranian woman continued to rave, and the rest stood mute.

Diomedes looked around and saw that the person who had shed so much blood left a distinct trail of the same element leading away from the paddock. He drew his sword and followed the red stains on the ground.

145

They went far, past the camp and inland toward the forest, and they became fainter. So faint did they become, in fact, that Diomedes feared he would lose them entirely, but just when they seemed like they would disappear behind the next tree, the small droplets of blood joined a new, rich reservoir. Diomedes sheathed his sword.

The great hulk of a man lay stretched under the tree, his left hand over his head and the sword protruding from under his arm where he had fallen on it. For a second time, Diomedes spared his eyes the cruel sight before them.

"You're going to take that voyage," said the chief, "and you'd better leave before nightfall."

"What voyage?" asked Odysseus.

"To get Achilles' son and the bow."

"But there is no damned bow!"

"It doesn't matter. Just go and get Pyrrhus, stay away a couple of weeks, and come back with a bow, any bow. The men blame you for Ajax's death, and you've got to let them cool off."

A brief, hardly discernible look of anger flashed across the Ithacan's face. If Agamemnon had not known Odysseus so well, he might have missed it, so skillfully was it disguised. But no sooner did it appear than it was gone, and the Ithacan resumed the knowing smile he so often bore.

"All right. I'll take the voyage."

Agamemnon was visibly relieved. "Can you leave today?"

"Yes," said Odysseus, rising from his seat in Agamemnon's tent, "I can get a ship out today."

"Good," said the chief, rising too. "While you're gone, I'll try to calm things down."

Odysseus nodded.

"One other thing," said Agamemnon before the other passed out of the tent.

Odysseus turned.

"You'd better get rid of that damned shield."

VIII

The Bow

THE ISLAND OF Scyros lay twenty miles to the east of the Greek coast, close enough for its residents to see the broad outline of the mainland most days of the year. It was not toward Greece, however, that the young man usually cast his eyes when he climbed the tallest hill on the island. It was in the opposite direction toward the open sea, toward Asia.

Pyrrhus had seen his father only once. Achilles had stopped at the island on his way to Aulis before the war. Pyrrhus was only nine years old at the time, but that single meeting was burned into his memory. He was impressed most by the size and grandeur of his father. Deidameia, his mother, had told him a great deal about Achilles by then, but the man in the flesh was even more impressive than the stories about him. Pyrrhus had never seen a more handsome or godlike figure. The boy had bowed his head when first introduced to Achilles, and he remembered the great booming laugh above him.

"Look at me," said the voice. "Achilles' son doesn't have to bow."

Then the great man had reached under the boy's arms and lifted him into the air so that the two could look at each other on the same level. The scowling face so close to his own, scrutinizing his features, immobilized the boy. He feared the giant might drop him in disgust, finding him a pitiful excuse for a son. In those moments of panic, he remembered smelling the strange earthiness of his father's breath and the manly scent of his body. Presently, however, the frowning face before him broke, like the sun emerging from behind a cloud, into a beaming smile of pleasure and satisfaction.

"I've brought you something," Achilles said when he set him down on the earth again.

One of the Myrmidons accompanying his father handed Achilles a bronze dagger, and Achilles handed the weapon to the boy. Pyrrhus was surprised by how heavy it was, much heavier than the sharp sticks he had played with, pretending they were daggers. He couldn't keep his eyes off the shiny blade.

"When I come back from Troy," his father said, "I'll bring you a sword, a fine Trojan sword."

Then Achilles left him, taking Deidameia into the palace to pay his respects to her father, King Lycomedes. The boy ran into the woods to play with his dagger, and when he returned, the great man was gone. All he could see was the sail as the ship headed west toward Aulis.

That had been ten years ago. Since then, Pyrrhus had grown into a tall, strong young man, not unlike his famous father. Against his mother's wishes, he had also learned war craft from old soldiers living on the island. He would spend hours every day practicing with spear, sword, and shield. His secret hope was that someday he could fight by his father's side. He had heard only scattered news of the Trojan War since Achilles' departure, usually from merchant vessels traveling between Asia Minor and Greece. Some would report Greek victories, some Trojan, and all told of the great feats of his father.

The sail Pyrrhus spied on the horizon this morning, though, was not a merchant ship; it was a warship. He could tell that from very far away. Long before it docked he knew it wasn't a Myrmidon vessel, though he could not tell precisely where it hailed from. With his mother and grandfather, he went down to the beach to meet it.

A balding, short-legged man was the first to step ashore, and while his men saw to the mooring, he strode up to where the three were standing together. He scanned them, his eyes lingering longest on Pyrrhus, and then he bowed deferentially to the king.

"My lord Lycomedes?" he said.

"Yes?"

"I bring you greetings from Lord Agamemnon. My name is Odysseus, from Ithaca."

The three stared at the newcomer. "I've heard of you, Odysseus," said the king. "You're welcome here. This is my daughter, Deidameia, and her son, Pyrrhus."

Odysseus bowed politely to the others.

"Is the war over?" asked the king.

Odysseus bent his head shyly. "Regrettably no, sir, though it is, perhaps, nearing conclusion."

"How is Achilles?" asked Deidameia.

The Ithacan's eyes darted at Pyrrhus, and then focused on his mother. "My lady, it is partly because of Achilles that I'm here." He took a breath. "After slaying the great Hector of Troy, the lord Achilles himself was slain. Please accept the sorrow I bring you from Agamemnon on behalf of us all."

Deidameia lowered her eyes but did not cry. Achilles' death could not help but send a pang through her, for she had lain in his arms and borne his child, but severe or prolonged grief was spared her. She had known his company only briefly, and had learned to live without him long ago.

Pyrrhus, however, was moved, though he endeavored to hide it, and Odysseus watched him as he stared out to sea, not daring to alter his facial expression lest it betray his emotion.

"Have you been to Phthia?" asked the king, unperturbed. "Peleus should know of this."

"He should, my lord," said Odysseus, "but this voyage has taken longer than we expected, and we must return. I was hoping I might prevail upon you, sir, to send the message yourself to King Peleus."

Lycomedes looked suspicious. "We can dispatch a ship to Peleus, but if you had so little time, why did you come here instead of going directly to Phthia?"

Odysseus paused, then said, "My lord, I've come to ask your permission to take Pyrrhus back to Troy with me." The young man's eyes now snapped back to Odysseus, but the Ithacan continued to address the king. "The lord Agamemnon would like to honor your grandson with a high place in the army and the command of the Myrmidons."

Deidameia looked up and would have spoken, but Lycomedes put his hand on her shoulder.

"Are things so bad for the Greeks that they're recruiting boys now?" asked the king.

"Pyrrhus is surely young, my lord," said the Ithacan, "but a boy no longer. Perhaps he would like to take his father's place."

The king eyed Odysseus. "It was nearly twenty years ago that Achilles was first a guest here. I welcomed him for King Peleus's sake. But Achilles betrayed me, his host, as much as Paris betrayed Menelaus. Never asking for my daughter's hand, he got her with child, which was only discovered after he'd gone. We were a small kingdom, we are still, compared to Phthia, with no great army like the Myrmidons, so to keep peace we swallowed the insult done our house, even though I could no longer contract an honorable marriage for my daughter. I even welcomed Achilles back a second time when he was on his way to Aulis. At that late date he might still have righted the wrong he'd done us by marrying Deidameia, but he did not. In the meantime, my daughter and I have raised his son. Now you tell me he's dead, and you want Pyrrhus to take his place. Why should I consent to that?"

Odysseus looked at the king solemnly. "You have told the story accurately, my lord. I can't deny it. Many could blame Achilles for his actions, but—"

"If they do," the young man interrupted, speaking now for the first time and glaring at Odysseus, "they had better say it to me."

The Ithacan looked at Pyrrhus, and when he saw the anger in the young man's eyes, a barely discernible smile passed over Odysseus's lips, but he quickly squelched it and assumed his solemn demeanor once more. This time, however, he directed his speech to Pyrrhus.

"You're quite right to say so. You are your father's heir now, and all men should address their words to you."

The king looked at his grandson. "Pyrrhus, you're of age to do as you please. If you want to accompany Odysseus to Troy, you're free to go. I can only give you advice, and my advice would be to stay out of it. Many have died at Troy. Your father died there, and he was the best of them."

"I'm not afraid."

The king shook his head. "I know you're not, but fear has nothing to do with it. You should consider the cause of the war before you risk your life. It does not involve you."

Pyrrhus hesitated and looked out to sea again, weighing his grandfather's words.

"Excuse me, my lord," interrupted Odysseus, "but I must correct you. You are quite right in saying that the original cause of the war didn't concern Pyrrhus. But

152

now," he said, turning again toward the young man, "his father having been killed by the Trojans, he has the best cause in the world for going."

Pyrrhus looked at the Ithacan.

Odysseus continued: "In fact, I was so sure that you would want to come with me, that I brought the gift your father intended for you if you came to Troy."

He gestured to his men, who had stayed behind him. Now they approached, bearing before them a great, shiny bronze disk. The young man's eyes widened as he beheld it. Almost inaudibly Pyrrhus said, "He only promised me a sword."

"The sword is back in Troy," said Odysseus quietly, watching the other's face, "but this is great Hector's shield."

Pyrrhus was dazzled by the workmanship and the lustre. He reached for it, but Odysseus put his hand gently on the face of it, right over the image of the horse in the center. His men understood the gesture and held it back from the young man. The Ithacan then leveled a strangely sinister gaze at Pyrrhus. "Your father didn't will you this so it could hang on a wall in Scyros."

Anger flashed in Pyrrhus's face again. He reached for the shield a second time, but Odysseus persisted, never removing his eyes from the young man. Slowly, then, Pyrrhus turned until he faced the Ithacan squarely. His eyes showed a menace that neither his mother nor grandfather had ever seen there before. "I'll take the shield, Odysseus," he said calmly. "If this is my father's last gift to me, don't think you can keep it from me whether I go with you or not."

Odysseus raised his chin slightly; otherwise he did not move, and he continued to stare at the other.

"But I am going to Troy," said Pyrrhus.

The Ithacan smiled and dropped his hand from the disk.

*   *   *

The distance between the island of Scyros and the island of Lemnos is about seventy miles over the open seas, a day's voyage with favorable winds, but ancient sailors rarely traveled over the open sea if they could avoid it. The customary method of navigation was to stay within sight of the coastline and look for landmarks along the way to a destination. Consequently, Odysseus and Pyrrhus sailed for several days in the northern Aegean before they finally spied Lemnos in the distance off their starboard bow. Once they sighted it, they wheeled around to the seaward side of the island where Odysseus remembered the magnificent, nearly enclosed bay. Here it was that they rowed ashore.

During their voyage, Odysseus told Pyrrhus about their mission to retrieve the bow on their way back to Troy. Though fascinated at first with the prospect of beholding the weapon of Hercules, Pyrrhus began to lose hope of ever really seeing it as he learned more and more of Philoctetes' story. Odysseus told Pyrrhus about the snakebite and the running sore that developed from it. He told him how the surgeons had tried to cure Philoctetes, but to no effect, and how his cries and the stench of his wound began to alarm and demoralize the army. Finally Odysseus told him how the men had petitioned Agamemnon to leave Philoctetes at Lemnos, even though the island was unpopulated. Thus, by the time Pyrrhus stood with Odysseus on the deserted beach, which showed no sign of human life, the youth had given up whatever lingering hope he had of seeing the bow or its owner.

"I don't see why you didn't just kill the man outright rather than leaving him here to die," said Pyrrhus.

"You're probably right," said Odysseus, nodding his head. "It would have been kinder, but none of us could do it. So we left him his bow. We figured if the gods wanted to preserve him, they'd send him game he could kill with it."

"What about water?"

"We left him a skin."

"But is there water on the island?"

Odysseus shrugged his shoulders.

"He must be long dead now," said Pyrrhus, shaking his head, "and his bow rotted, or lost."

"Very likely," said Odysseus, as he scanned the line of trees up from the shore, "but I suppose—"

Suddenly he stopped, and his eyes, which had been sweeping back and forth along the tree line, became fixed on one particular point. Pyrrhus, following his gaze, saw it too.

"What is that?" asked the young man. "It looks like a line of stones."

"Two lines of stones," said Odysseus, "leading into the woods."

Leaving the rest of the men behind, they made their way up to the edge of the forest and to the strange configuration they had seen from the shore. What they found when they got there were two parallel rows of stones that formed a sort of decorative border to a path, some twelve or fifteen feet long. It connected the sandy beach with another path, similarly bordered, that disappeared into the woods.

"Well, someone's been here," said Pyrrhus, "that's for sure, but who would bother to do something like this?"

Odysseus looked up the path as far as he could see into the forest. "Evidently, someone who has a great deal of time on his hands."

"There's no other ship," said Pyrrhus. "We would have seen it. We sailed around most of the island."

Odysseus nodded. "If there were another ship, it would be in this bay."

They were silent for a moment, and then Pyrrhus noticed his companion shaking his head and smiling. "What's the matter?" the younger man asked.

"I'll bet he's still alive," said Odysseus. "The cunning old dog, I'll bet he survived. This is just the sort of thing he'd do to keep busy."

Pyrrhus was silent for a moment. "If he did survive, what will we do about the bow? He won't want to give it up."

"He won't have to give it up. We'll take him to Troy with us, bow and all."

"You think he'll go, after what you did to him?"

"Of course he'll go."

"What makes you think so?"

Odysseus smiled and patted the younger man on the shoulder. "Wait here. I've got to get some things from the ship. And while you're waiting, imagine what you would do if you hadn't seen another human being in nine years. Would you want to stay here, even to a nurse a grudge?"

The bordered path was well trodden, and the small party Odysseus selected had little trouble following it several hundred paces to a large, natural clearing in the woods. When the men stepped into the open area, they marveled at what they saw. The clearing was the terminus of several paths, each more or less as well trodden as the one they had taken and each carefully bordered by rocks. Rocks ringed the entire clearing, and in the center, delineated a round, smoking fire. Here could be seen rudely made implements for the spitting and cooking of game. Other artifacts for hunting or dressing or building, of similar manufacture, lay in a neat arrangement on the ground. On the trees hung carved effigies of the gods. But what attracted their attention most was the structure at the opposite end of the clearing.

Using four living trees as supports, the ingenious builder had fashioned a dwelling. The walls were constructed of wood gathered from the forest floor and attached to the trees and to each other by woven grass and pegs. The pitched roof was covered with more grass, tightly bound to keep out the rain, and the doorway was covered by animal skins sewn together. It would be a tolerable home anywhere, but here, on a deserted island, it excited their wonder and admiration.

Perhaps no one marveled at the sight more than Odysseus, who appreciated ingenuity wherever he found it. He motioned for the small group to advance toward the hut, when suddenly their progress was arrested by the appearance of a figure in the doorway. The party froze, but the man, oblivious to their presence, stepped outside and strode with a slight limp toward the fire pit. He was a grizzled, wiry man, dressed in skins, his gray hair and beard cut roughly. But there was no mistaking his identity.

"Philoctetes!" said Odysseus, the word coming forth as an exclamation more than a greeting.

The man stopped. It had been so long since he had heard a voice other than his own that for a moment he stood perplexed. Then he turned and looked at the group of men, but still did not show any sign that he saw them or understood what their presence meant.

"Philoctetes, don't you recognize me? I know it's been a long time, but I recognize you."

What the man was beginning to recognize, however, was spoken Greek, which for him had been reduced to a few phrases mumbled to himself. He thought in Greek, of course, and when he stubbed his toe or missed a shot at a bird, he cursed in Greek, and in prayer he sent his silent pleas to the gods in Greek, but for nine years he had heard Greek from no other lips. He had forgotten the pleasure of hearing his mother tongue spoken, hearing how others put the familiar words together in unfamiliar ways. He continued to look at the party, and especially at the speaker.

"Yes," he said finally, "I recognize you."

"May we . . . join you?" asked Odysseus.

Philoctetes again took a moment to respond, and when he did, it was merely to gesture with his palm that they might come into the center of the clearing.

Odysseus and Pyrrhus advanced, and the others followed. When they were still several paces away, Odysseus stopped and spoke again. "Philoctetes, this is Pyrrhus, Achilles' son."

The youth nodded to the man, but Philoctetes did not acknowledge it. He kept staring at Odysseus.

"You left me here to die," he said. "Why have you come back?"

"To take you to Troy, if you want to go."

Philoctetes did not alter his features. Though the party might have expected to see anger in his face, or perhaps relief and joy at his rescue, all he showed was a blank frown, an expression that had become as much a part of his face as his nose or his eyes. If any emotion was at all visible, it was perhaps a hint of sternness in his gaze. Finally, he said, "Don't tell me the war's still on."

"It is, sadly," answered Odysseus.

"Serves you right, then," he said, almost to himself. "Serves all of you right."

"How is your leg?" asked Odysseus, ignoring the last comment. "It seems to have healed."

"It's healed," said Philoctetes briefly. Then the archer scanned the group, lingering a long moment on each, as if recalling their identities. The members of the party were abashed by such close scrutiny, and averted their eyes when his fell upon them. Finally, after several moments of this inspection, Philoctetes looked at their leader again. "Do you have any wine?" he asked.

Without looking around, Odysseus reached behind and one of his men handed over a skin, which he passed to the great archer. Philoctetes closed his eyes as he inhaled the aroma he had been denied so long; then he put the skin to his lips and took a long draft. So long was the draft, in fact, that the members of Odysseus's party grinned at each other, but they became serious again when the archer lowered the skin and revealed his customary frown. He looked at Odysseus as if he might speak once more, but instead, he raised the skin to his lips a second time and took another long draft. It was only when he was about to raise the skin to his lips a third time that he stopped, as if remembering a social grace long buried. He looked around at them. "You may as well sit down," he said.

Philoctetes sat too, took another long draft of wine, and then passed it back to Odysseus for the others to partake. "Why does Agamemnon want me back now?" he asked, after wiping his mouth on his arm.

"He can't win the war without you. One of the gods must be punishing him for his treatment of you."

The archer deepened his frown.

"But Philoctetes," said Odysseus, "how did you live all these years?"

"You thought I'd be dead, didn't you?" he said, and for the first time a hint of a sardonic smile appeared on his lips.

"We feared it."

"I lived by my bow," he said offhandedly. "The island's filled with game."

"Then you still have the bow of Hercules?" asked Pyrrhus.

He turned to the young man. "You've heard of the bow? Yes, I still have it."

"I'm impressed by the home you made yourself," said Odysseus.

Philoctetes glanced over his shoulder at it. "It would have been easier to build if you'd left me an axe." He looked back at the Ithacan. "Why has the war lasted so long?"

Odysseus then recounted to him the main events of the nine-year siege, ending with the death of Achilles.

"What about Deipyrus?" asked Philoctetes. "Is he still alive."

Odysseus shook his head. "No, dead."

"Hypsenor?"

"Dead."

"Amphimachus? Opheltius?"

The Ithacan shook his head sadly.

"Ajax?"

Odysseus sighed. "Dead too."

"Ajax too? Who could have killed Ajax?"

Odysseus's men shifted uneasily, but Odysseus did not hesitate in his answer. "He went mad, they say; made war on his livestock, then killed himself."

"His livestock!" Philoctetes shook his head in disbelief. "What about Nestor?"

"Oh, Lord Nestor's still alive, and anxious to see you again."

"But many of my friends are dead."

"The list of dead on the Trojan side is equally long, probably longer," said Odysseus.

"And now Agamemnon wants me."

"Everyone does, Philoctetes."

"Who's been leading my people?" the archer asked.

"Medon, but he's as anxious as anyone for you to come back and take your rightful place."

Philoctetes was silent for a moment, then looked at Odysseus sternly. "The chief better realize that the score between him and me isn't settled just because he sent you here."

"He knows that, Philoctetes. He's collected a large-treasure for you, which he hopes you'll accept for the wrong he did you.''

The archer frowned but nodded. It was the only bloodless way scores could be settled in those days, and there was no honor lost if the treasure was large enough. Philoctetes was indicating by his demeanor that he would reserve judgment until he saw the size of the restitution he was being offered. There was silence as the party waited for the archer's decision.

He stood up, and Odysseus's men would have stood too, but the Ithacan motioned for them to remain seated. Philoctetes walked around the clearing, looking at the surroundings which had been so familiar for the past nine years. He glanced down the various paths: One led to a favorite hunting spot, another to the tallest hill on the island, where he had gone often to look for ships. He looked at the implements he'd made, some after much trial and error as he learned the strength of materials and of bindings. Then he looked at his hut, which he had built and rebuilt and improved over many years. He gazed at it for several moments.

Few human beings would choose a life apart from their fellows. Philoctetes surely would not have. As much as anyone he had been a man of his times, a man of his society. He had not assumed the life of a hermit willingly, and over those nine years of solitude not a day had gone by when he had not wished to be rescued. Yet he had passed the test, the trial by fire that solitude imposes. In its own way it is a more severe test than war, or pain, or hardship of any other kind. Only a few souls in history have been put to such a test; fewer still have passed it, but Philoctetes was one. And he'd done it by killing his food, by building his home, by carving gods, and by arranging stones.

The Trojans on the wall who kept watch on their besieging enemies noted both the departure of Odysseus's ship and its return two weeks later. They reported these events to the king. Earlier they had reported Achilles' magnificent funeral, followed quickly by the less grand funeral of Ajax. But none of their reports induced Priam to resume the fighting. It was Paris who did that.

The king had not approved of the ambush on Achilles, nor had he known about it until it had already taken place. Though he hated the Myrmidon chief as the slayer of his son, he had also found him to be honest in his dealings. Achilles had released Hector's body for a proper ransom, and he had scrupulously maintained a truce during the period of the funeral. Priam could not condone his treacherous murder, and he was disgusted with Paris for perpetrating it. But the king's feelings were not shared by the Trojan populace. When it became known that the prince had wounded Achilles and the wound proved fatal, he became a hero. Even Queen Hecuba seemed pleased.

What surprised Priam, though, was not the cowardly ambush. That was typical of Paris. It was the gradual change that took place in the prince afterward. He seemed to think he had inherited a mantle from his fallen brother. It was ill-fitting, to be sure, and much too big for him, but he was determined to wear it as best he could and continue the war. He began to ask the king's permission to lead the army out into battle. He said the Greeks were as sick of the war as the Trojans, and this was the time to attack them. Priam discounted his requests as mere bravado, but in time, when his pleas did not cease and it became obvious that he was sincere, Priam began to feel a growing respect for his son.

The king called a meeting of his council, the first since Hector's death, to determine the matter. The council was much diminished in size now by the absence of many former allies, and there was a prevailing gloom among those who remained. But Deiphobus, to whom the king had entrusted the army, seemed to think it was a good idea to give Paris a chance. A surprise attack, he argued, might be just the demoralizing blow that would finally induce the Greeks to go home. Most of the council was swayed by his opinion, even though Antenor spoke against it. So they decided to let Paris lead a late afternoon attack, when the Greeks would least expect it.

On the appointed day, therefore, the king mounted the steps of the wall and prepared once more to observe his people enter the slaughter.

For a moment Agamemnon didn't know what he was hearing in the distance. It had been over two months since the Trojans had ventured outside their wall, and the chief had even begun to wonder if he would ever encounter them in the field again. But when he looked in their direction, he saw men and battle chariots streaming out of the Scaean Gates, already attacking his forward line.

The Greeks, preparing their evening meal, were taken completely by surprise. Although they kept a continual watch on the city, they had been lulled by the long idleness. The only soldiers armed were those at the very front, and from here, Agamemnon could see that the Trojans were hacking them to pieces.

He sent Talthybius in one direction to spread the alarm, and went in the other himself. Most of his captains, however, had heard the battle cries, and were already arming and rushing to the field lest their camps be overrun. When Agamemnon reached the Thessalian tents, he saw Philoctetes, bow in hand, ranging behind his army, looking for a place to position himself. During the weeks of Odysseus's absence, Agamemnon had never dreamt that the great archer still lived and would fight at Troy. When Philoctetes arrived with Pyrrhus, however, to the cheers of the whole army, the chief had given him an enormous treasure as recompense for his ordeal on the island. Agamemnon was relieved that Philoctetes accepted the gifts and buried his animosity.

"Philoctetes," Agamemnon shouted, "follow me."

They passed behind several contingents entering the fray, and Agamemnon led the archer to a small rise that commanded a view of the line of conflict. From that position, the chief could see the extent to which his army had been caught off guard. The Trojan armies had attacked on a broad front, so broad that an encircling movement on their part was possible if the Greeks did not guard their flanks. What alarmed him even more than the Trojan position, though, was the aggressiveness with which they now fought. He had not seen such ferocity since the time Achilles retired from the battle.

Philoctetes, comprehending the situation quickly, dropped to one knee, drew his bow, and began letting arrows fly at the Trojan line. He did not shoot like so many of the other archers, who merely shot into the crowd, knowing that the arrows would find some mark. Philoctetes aimed each shaft carefully to make a kill. His favorite target was the neck, since it was usually unprotected, but he also would shoot at the breast if he thought the angle and velocity would allow him to pierce the armor.

Agamemnon stood by him and watched with fascination as one arrow after another found its mark. He had seen the great archer demonstrate his skill at Aulis years before. Then he had used wooden blocks as his targets, but now he aimed at the most capable Trojan warriors in the front ranks, and he felled them with astonishing consistency. The chief also marveled at the bow itself. It was a smooth, beautifully carved weapon, of rich, polished wood. Agamemnon coveted it, and yet he knew that for him it could never be more than an ornament, like a beautiful lyre he could not play. In Philoctetes' hands, however, the instrument was employed with the grace and skill of a master. Philoctetes would pull an arrow from the quiver over his shoulder, draw it across the bow as he raised the weapon to take aim, then release the string all in one smooth motion. Perhaps most remarkable, however, was the calmness with which he went about his work. Amidst the chaos of the battle, and facing the prospect that at any moment the Greek lines might break down completely, the archer maintained a perfect serenity.

But Agamemnon could not long admire his companion's skill. For all the men downed by Philoctetes' bow, the Trojan advance continued. The enemy was pushing the Greek forces back even in the sector closest to where the two stood. Rather than risk being overrun, they abandoned their position and retreated to another part of the field. Using an overturned wagon for cover, Philoctetes resumed shooting.

From the new position, the chief could see that they had happened upon what appeared to be the very heart of the battle, where the impetus for the attack seemed to come. There at the center, both fighting and directing the movement of his men, was Paris.

The chief was surprised. The only time previously that he had seen Paris with a sword in his hand was during the duel with Menelaus. He had considered Paris a coward; the whole army had. And yet there he was in hand-to-hand combat like a hardened veteran.

"Philoctetes," Agamemnon whispered to his companion, without taking his eyes from the Trojan prince, "do you see the one in the center there?"

The archer looked in the direction of the chief's gaze. "The one with the large plume?"

"Yes. That's Paris."

"That's Paris?"

Agamemnon nodded.

Philoctetes wordlessly drew another arrow across his bow.

"You can't get him in the neck," said Agamemnon. "He holds his shield too high."

"No," said Philoctetes calmly, squinting his eyes in his customary way as he looked down the shaft of the arrow, "I can't get him in the neck." He said it as a skilled craftsman might to an apprentice who had just presumed to comment on his art. "No, not in the neck," he said as he released the string.

The Trojan helmet was well designed to protect the head from missiles and from the glancing strokes of swords. It covered the whole cranium and forehead, and in the back it went as far down the neck as possible without restricting movement. In the front, two cheek pieces covered the sides of the jaws under the eyes, and a long, thin nose piece came down from above. The only parts of the face unprotected were the eyes, which, of course, could not be covered. But even the eyes were somewhat shielded by being recessed behind the nose and cheek pieces. These were close enough together to keep out the broad edge of a sword. There was more than enough room, however, for an arrow to pass through.

Agamemnon had watched the arrow. He'd seen it first in the magnificent bow, lost it for a moment in the air, and then saw it once again emerging from Paris's helmet, stuck in the socket where his eye had been a second ago, the point now lodged in his brain. Agamemnon watched the prince totter for a moment, as a jet of blood shot from his face and onto his armor. Then he saw him fall to the ground, the sword still gripped tightly in his hand.

No sane person is immune to a natural horror when witnessing outrages to the human body, no matter how accustomed to them. Agamemnon had every reason to rejoice that the man who had stolen Helen, who had started the whole bloody war and had kept it going by his own selfishness, the man who had ambushed and killed Achilles had finally gotten his desserts. But what he felt at that moment, with the terrifying image he'd just seen still before him, was a strange sympathy for the young prince, whose last feeling on earth was of a shaft of wood stuck where the glorious light of day should have shone.

The men around Paris were dumbstruck by the death of their prince, and especially by the manner of it, and some fell back as they dragged his body to safety. But the mass of Trojan warriors were unaware of what had occurred and continued the battle. They had pushed the Greek line far down the field, nearly to the ramshackle barricade, and had even broken that in several places. They did not have sufficient numbers to capitalize on the advantage, however, and the Greeks were always able to knit up the breach. So when nightfall ended the fighting, the Trojans sought the safety of their wall once more.

Each side, when it was over, felt they'd had the worse of it. The Greeks were demoralized because they had been taken so completely by surprise and driven down the field. The Trojans, though elated at first by their initial success, were appalled when they realized the number of casualties they had sustained, a loss they could not afford. And the city mourned anew for the most famous among the slain, the young prince, so recently a hero, and now dead.

But this battle had the effect of convincing at least one Trojan that the war *must* end. Antenor had stood next to his old friend, his king, on the wall. He had watched Priam as they carried Paris through the gates, the arrow still waving hideously in the air from the prince's face.

He had heard Hecuba's screams, seen Cassandra run to the sanctuary of her temple, felt Paris's youngest brother, Polites, tremble by his side. He had watched the soldiers count the dead, and had seen the triumphant joy on their faces turn to anguish and despair. He had heard his son, Laocoön, curse the Greeks yet again and urge still more fighting as the answer. But Antenor knew the real answer, the only answer.

IX

The Statue

DIOMEDES WAS WAITING outside Agamemnon's tent just before sunset the next day. The incessant wind from the north, so bitter during the winter months, was now a welcome breeze, blowing his hair in front of his eyes. He thought of home. The crops would already be growing in Tiryns. Diomedes remembered the smell of the earth this time of year, and felt homesick.

The tent flap parted and a balding head emerged. Odysseus bid the chief farewell, and started on the path back to the Ithacan camp. Diomedes fell in step beside him.

"Are we going home?" asked the younger man.

Odysseus glanced at his companion and then returned his eyes to the ground in front of him. "Apparently, unless we can steal the Palladium."

"What? You mean the statue in Troy?"

"Yes. Got any ideas how to do it?"

"The chief thinks the Palladium will win the war for us?"

Odysseus smiled and shook his head. "The chief's at his wit's end. The men told him unless he can get the Palladium, as Calchas said he should, they want to leave."

"But the whole thing's ridiculous. The only way to steal the statue is to get into the city, and if we could get

169

into the city, what the hell would we need the statue for?"

"Yes. Clever one, that Calchas," Odysseus chuckled.

"And even if we could get it, what good would it do us? A hunk of wood can't win the war for us," said Diomedes.

Odysseus shrugged, and the two proceeded along the path in silence.

"They caught us off guard, though, yesterday," said Diomedes after a few moments. "I never expected it."

Odysseus nodded. "Did you see Pyrrhus fight?"

"Yes."

"How is he?"

"Oh, he's his father's son all right."

"Good?"

"He's fast, he's reckless," said Diomedes, "and he gets that look in his eyes like Achilles used to get, like he was smiling when he really wasn't."

"How did the Myrmidons take to him?"

"Like he was his father, especially after they saw him fight."

"Good," said Odysseus. "Good."

"He was carrying Hector's shield too."

Odysseus frowned.

They had reached the vicinity of the Ithacan camp. Here Diomedes stopped.

"Do you ever wonder," the younger man said, before taking the branching path that led to his own tents, "if the gods really intend for us to take the city?"

Odysseus looked at him.

"I mean, after what happened to Achilles, and then what happened to Ajax."

Odysseus smiled, then patted the other's arm. "Good night, Diomedes."

The two parted, and Odysseus proceeded the rest of

the way alone. As he reached his tent, however, one of his men was there to meet him.

"Sir, there's a Trojan here to see you."

"A Trojan?"

"A graybeard, sir, unattended and unarmed. He's waiting inside."

Odysseus threw open the flap.

"Lord Odysseus," said the old man within, "it's good to see you again."

"Lord Antenor," said Odysseus, stepping in. "Sit down. I'll pour you some wine."

"Thank you," said the other, "thank you," and with difficulty he lowered himself into a chair.

Odysseus poured out two cups and handed one to his visitor. "It's been many years since I've seen you, Antenor."

"Nearly ten years," said the other. "You came at the beginning of the war to try to negotiate a peaceful settlement."

"Yes, I remember. You offered me your hospitality while I stayed in Troy. How is Theano?"

"She is well, under the circumstances."

"And your sons?"

"My sons, except for Laocoön, are all gone."

"I'm sorry to hear that, Antenor. I knew of one that was killed."

"Three were killed," the old man said without emotion.

"I'm sorry."

Antenor shook his head, rejecting the condolences. "I'm on a mission today similar to the one you were on ten years ago, and I pray the gods I'm more successful."

Odysseus took a sip of wine. "As I remember, you were quite against a settlement back then."

"Well, I've changed. Three sons are too many to lose."

Odysseus nodded. "We've all suffered loss."

"Yes, we've all suffered loss. And yesterday one of your men killed Paris. Did you know that?"

"Yes. Agamemnon saw it."

"Well, I don't mourn for Paris. It was Paris who was responsible for the ambush on Achilles."

Odysseus narrowed his eyes.

"Yes, it's true," said the older man. "Priam didn't know anything about it, and I want you to know that."

"I believe you, Antenor."

"So far as I'm concerned, Paris only got what he deserved, but I do grieve for his father's sake."

"Of course."

"More than that, though, I grieve for the utter futility of this war, Odysseus. The battle yesterday decided nothing. The only thing it accomplished was more bloodshed on both sides."

"I agree, Antenor, I agree. But what settlement can there be? Are you here to offer Helen, now that Paris is dead?"

The old man shook his head disgustedly. "I wish I could, but the people credit her for bringing Paris back to health, and now the prince has died a hero. Even the queen has softened toward her. They'll never give her up."

Antenor took a long draft of the wine and then leveled his gaze at the Ithacan.

"You have a reputation, Odysseus, as an intelligent man."

The Ithacan smiled. "So do you, Antenor."

Antenor waved away the compliment. "That's the reason I came to you. I'm going to put the situation to you as I see it, and I want you to tell me frankly if you disagree with me."

"All right."

"We in Troy know that we can't win the war. Our

172

armies aren't strong enough or numerous enough to drive you from our shore."

Odysseus nodded.

"But by the same token, you can't take the city. Because of our wall and because of the tenacity of our people, we've weathered the siege nearly ten years now. If necessary we could do so for another ten. As far as I'm concerned, it's a standoff. We could shed more blood over it, but it would be pointless. Do you agree?"

"Yes I do, Antenor. Enough blood's been shed."

"So we're left with this: We want you to go home, and you in all likelihood want to *go* home. Your men might even be capable of mutiny if the war drags on much longer. Is that a fair way of putting it?"

"I think it's safe to say most of the men would like to go home," said Odysseus, "but a mutiny—"

Antenor shook his head vigorously to forestall the other's denial. "Then the question comes down to this," he continued. "If it's obvious that you can't take the city and you can't get Helen back, and furthermore your men want to go home, why do you remain here? I've asked myself this question, and the only answer I come up with is that your leaders are afraid to go home looking like they've been defeated. Is there truth in what I say?"

"There's truth in what you say."

"Then our job, Odysseus," said the old man, "if you want to join with me in this, is to find a way you can leave honorably, without looking like you've been defeated."

Odysseus smiled. "You've stated the situation very well, and you've gotten right to the crux of the matter. But is there a way of solving that dilemma, Antenor?"

"I think so. Why not choose the simplest solution of all? We've called numerous truces in the past. Why not just call a permanent truce and declare peace between us? Neither side a victor, neither side a loser. Conduct a sacrifice, exchange gifts, and part amicably.''

"Yes," said Odysseus, nodding, "and peace would be restored, and everyone fighting here would appreciate it. But what about those at home when we return? They'll remember why we came to Troy. They'll look for fathers, husbands, sons among us. Many of them will be dead, and it'll look like they died for nothing.''

"We've lost many dead in Troy also.''

"Yes, Antenor, of course, of course, but don't you see, any peace we declare will look like a victory for you. We'd go home having failed in our purpose. You, on the other hand, by defending your city and keeping Helen, would have succeeded.''

Antenor looked down for several moments in thought, then narrowed his eyes at his companion. "All right. What you say is true, Odysseus. In the sense in which you speak, you have failed, and we have succeeded. In blunt terms, that's the situation. You're an intelligent man, and so you see it for what it is. You can't get the things you came here for, and I'm not here to give them to you. I'm here to try to help you find a way to leave with some self-respect. If you don't want to search for that with me, I'll go home, and we'll wait until your own men force you to leave with no self-respect at all.''

With that the old man began to rise, but Odysseus reached out a hand and patted his arm. "Please don't leave, Antenor. I just wanted to make sure we understood each other. In fact, something you said even now gave me an idea that might get around the problem.''

"What's that?''

"The exchange of gifts,'' said Odysseus, stroking his beard in thought. "The right gift, given by your people to ours, would show that the peace we declared was mutual and that we left out of our own free will.''

"What do you mean? What kind of gift? It can't be a large treasure. That would look like tribute."

Odysseus took another sip of wine. "And on our side it would look like a bribe. No, a treasure wasn't what I had in mind. The gift should have no material value at all, or at most very little, but it should be something important to your people, something that symbolizes your city. It should be something famous, too, that everyone has heard of. If you gave us a gift like that, it would show the people at home that you respected our power, even if we didn't succeed in conquering you."

Antenor looked dubious. "What gift do you have in mind?"

"You have a statue in Troy, in the Temple to Athena."

"The Palladium?"

"The Palladium, that's right. All the men have heard of it. Many of us had even heard about it back in Greece. If we could take that statue home with us, no one would think we had been defeated."

"No, I couldn't give you the Palladium. The statue's been in the city as long as anyone can remember. Some say it was a gift of the goddess herself. I'm not saying I believe that, but many people do. There's even a legend that it protects the city." Antenor shook his head. "No, it's much too highly valued. You'd have to choose something else."

"But that's just the point, Antenor: The more highly valued it is, the more balanced the peace will seem. No one would believe you gave it to us unless we posed a serious threat to you."

Antenor continued to shake his head. "What you say is true, but it's out of the question. You'll have to choose something else."

Odysseus was silent for several moments while he eyed the old man. The he sipped his wine again. "It seems, Antenor, that you're not as serious about negotiating as I thought you were. Maybe you're right about a mutiny among our men. It could happen. It could happen soon. But then again, it may not happen for another year, and in the meantime we might see more destruction and more bloodshed in your homeland. I should think that peace, in exchange for an old wooden statue, would be a good bargain."

"But you don't understand how revered the statue is in Troy. It's sacred to the goddess. If it were gone, what would we put in its place in the temple?"

"I'm sure you could substitute another statue. Or maybe our gift to you could be the replacement. That would be fair."

"Your gift?" asked Antenor.

"Why not? Another statue, perhaps, dedicated to the goddess."

"Do you have such a statue?"

"No, but I'm sure we could make something as good as the old wooden one that you have, perhaps even better. We have a number of fine artisans here."

Antenor sat in thought for a while, his face grave. Without looking up at Odysseus, he said, "It wouldn't be such a bad idea to have a statue of yours in the city. It might serve as a reminder in the future of what we suffered through our own folly."

"Then it would serve a double purpose," said Odysseus. "It would end the war and perhaps even ensure the peace in the future."

"But the people are superstitious. There is the prophesy that the Palladium protects the city."

"Yes, Antenor, but you know how prophesies so often come true in unexpected ways. If the war ended because you gave us the statue, then wouldn't the statue still be responsible for protecting the city?"

"Perhaps," the old man nodded, "perhaps." Then he sat for several long moments in thought, presiding over another dialogue taking place within him. Finally he said quietly, "It might work."

"Of course it will work," said Odysseus. "We could make a great ceremony of the exchange."

"No," said Antenor, looking up again, "there can be no ceremony. Priam would never agree to let the Palladium go. He'd sooner give you Helen. I'd have to get the Palladium out of the city after dark, and you'd have to leave your statue on the shore when you sailed. There could be no public exchange. But it still might work. Once you were gone, I could proclaim the peace I concluded with you. When Priam and the council see that you're gone, I don't think they'll mind the price."

"You'd want us to leave our gift on the shore?"

"Yes," said Antenor, and then he saw the oddest expression on Odysseus's face, an expression he had never seen there before. Perhaps no one had seen it before. It was a look of surprise, touched by wonder, unusual in itself for so self-possessed a man, but all the more unusual coming as it did after a none-too-surprising statement by Antenor. The most remarkable thing about the expression was the absolute nakedness of it. Over his long life, the king of Ithaca had developed to a fine art the skill of masking his true feelings, but for a moment, just one moment, his guard fell.

Antenor smiled. "I know what you're thinking. Once I give you the Palladium, I'm trusting you to keep your end of the bargain and leave. You're thinking you might just keep the statue and never raise the siege. Well, that's right. You could do that. It would be dishonorable, but you could do it, and then we would have lost an old wooden statue, as you say. But you'd lose something more important than that. You'd lose your last chance to conclude any kind of a peace with us. We both know that a mutiny of your men is possible. You'd be risking your reputations, your safe homecoming, and maybe your lives. So I don't think it's a bad deal on our side."

But Odysseus was not thinking of the Palladium at all. Somewhere in the labyrinthine corridors of his brain, an idea had fluttered. It was the merest ghost as yet, born of nothingness, still without form, needing nurture before it could take shape, but it was alive, and the consciousness of it shocked him to his very soul.

"Well, what do you think, Odysseus?"

"Why, yes, of course, Antenor," the Ithacan stuttered, his face now returning to normal as he tried to concentrate on the old man's words again. "No, there'd be no question of our reneging. You're right. Of course. We'd lose more than you."

"Do you think Agamemnon will go along with the idea?"

"Yes. I think so. I think he will."

"All right. I'll send my messenger to you tomorrow. If your chief agrees to it, I'll get you the Palladium within a few days. And you can tell my messenger when you plan to leave."

"I will, Antenor."

With difficulty again, the old man rose to go. Odysseus rose too. Before parting at the entrance, they faced each other once more. Antenor smiled. "It will be strange, won't it, if you and I, by putting our heads together like this, were able to accomplish what all the fighting failed to accomplish in ten years?"

Odysseus smiled too. "Yes, very strange."

Antenor nodded and then passed through the entranceway. Before the tent flap was fully closed, however, Odysseus had already turned around to face the inside, and in his eyes was a look of such wildness that had the old man seen it, he might have thought he'd just made a pact with a madman.

*   *   *

Helen was surprised to hear her name spoken. She was standing by her window alone, gazing into the darkness. For a moment she did not recognize the voice. Andromache had not uttered her name for years, and she had ceased speaking to Helen entirely since Hector died. She turned from the window and faced her.

"Helen, I wanted to tell you," said Andromache hesitantly, "I'm sorry about Paris."

Helen bowed her head slightly in acknowledgement. It had not occurred to her that members of the royal household might come and pay their respects, least of all Hector's widow. But she might have known that Andromache would do the decent thing, despite her feelings. Of all the women she had met since she had come to Troy, she admired Andromache most. She admired her strength, her intelligence, her happy marriage to Hector. Badly in need of companionship during the days when she first arrived, Helen had hoped that she and Andromache would become friends. Even though Andromache was a few years older, they had much in common, both coming as they did from other lands, both marrying into the royal family. But Andromache took an instant dislike to her, and though she was civil and courteous when they met, she never sought Helen out or revealed her thoughts to her the way Helen had hoped. When the war began and Hector took command of the armies, Andromache grew even more cool and distant. Helen became ashamed in her presence, and would lower her eyes when the two met. But now, emboldened perhaps by the redness that ringed her eyes after so many hours of crying, Helen did not lower them.

The two stood silent for a moment and looked at each other. Andromache admired the still-beautiful face of her younger companion. Helen's skin was dryer now, her hair not so lustrous, and tiny lines had appeared at the corners of her eyes. The years at Troy had taken away

179

her youthfulness, to be sure, but they had only deepened and enriched her beauty. Andromache realized, in spite of herself, that she envied Helen.

It would have surprised anyone who knew Andromache. It even surprised her. She was a person who, above all, seemed to value what was truly important in life: peace, her family, her home. She disdained the superficial and the ephemeral in favor of the real and the permanent. She was no stranger to adversity; she accepted as a corollary of existence the random mix of good and evil that comes to human beings. It was this equanimity, this philosophical acceptance, this rock-hard practicality that Hector had admired in her. To Andromache, Helen represented the opposite pole, one who had sacrificed all to a selfish whim, who had abandoned her child, who allowed others to suffer on her behalf, who had let an arbitrary and transient gift of the gods, her beauty, dominate her life and ruin all who came into contact with her. Yet, even as she believed these things fervently, Andromache envied Helen her godlike loveliness.

For it was indeed a gift of the gods, a favor, something one could not strive for, could not attain through work and diligence. Surely there were women who strove to look like Helen, using either fine clothing or paint, but those attempts were doomed to failure. Helen herself was careless of her looks, downplayed her beauty if anything, dressed without ostentation, painted herself not at all. Yet, her natural beauty was always there. Andromache was too intelligent to strive for beauty through artificial means. She knew that the very nature of a gift is that it cannot be earned. Yet she was sorry the gods had seen fit to grant it to Helen and not to her.

Perhaps it was the realization of this envy, after so many years of denying it to herself, that made her disinclined to leave now, though her duty to the other woman was now discharged.

Hesitantly again, and averting her gaze, Andromache said, "They say Paris was quite brave at the end."

The very awkwardness with which it was uttered moved Helen. She turned back to the window. "He was a foolish boy," she began to say, but even as she said it, an uncontrollable spasm in the muscles around her mouth pulled the corners of her lips down, and her eyes filled with tears.

Andromache's first instinct was to go to her, to offer comfort, and she took a step toward Helen, but a decade-long aversion held her back. She stood and watched the other sob.

"Oh, he *was* a foolish boy," Helen said, wiping her eyes. "He was a stupid, foolish boy, trying to be Hector, and now he's dead. I know none of you thought much of him. He didn't think much of himself. The only prize he ever thought he got was me. Maybe that's why he wouldn't give me up. He wasn't as bad as you thought. I know he was a coward. But so was I. I couldn't condemn him for that. And he was lazy and childish. But he was all right for me. I wouldn't have deserved someone like Hector. I didn't even deserve Menelaus, but I felt I deserved Paris. He was like me."

"You did love him, then," said Andromache.

Helen turned around, a puzzled expression on her face. "You doubted it too," she said. "There's no reason why I should be surprised. He doubted it himself." She faced the window again. "Of course I loved him. He was all I had."

Andromache suddenly felt ashamed of herself. For the first time she saw in the other woman's grief the pattern of her own.

"He told me in Sparta," Helen said, almost absently, "that we'd ride together in the hills around Troy for the rest of our lives. Within the year the Greeks came, and I haven't been outside the walls since. Now we'll never ride together again.''

Andromache was silent for a while, then lowered her eyes and said, ''I remember how envious I was of you when you arrived here, because you could ride.''

''You were?'' Helen said, turning and looking at her.

''Yes. You know how crazy they are about horses here. Hector wanted me to be able to ride with him too, but I was hopeless. I could never get control of the horse. I've always been afraid of horses. What an embarrassment I must have been to him. He never said anything, though.''

''I would have taught you. You should have asked me.''

Andromache smiled.

''Hector was always good to me,'' said Helen. ''He had no reason to be, but he was.''

''He had no reason to treat you badly,'' said Andromache, sighing. ''And neither did I.''

Their eyes met briefly, and then both averted their gaze.

''How is your son?'' Helen asked after a moment.

''I've told Astyanax about his father,'' said Andromache, ''but he doesn't understand.''

''He's very young.''

''Yes,'' said Andromache, ''he's very young, and I know it's not his fault, but sometimes I hate him for not hurting like I do.'' She paused. ''Do you ever think about your child back in Sparta?''

''I do, sometimes. She can't be a child anymore. She ought to be nearly of marriageable age by now. There was talk in those days of marrying her to Agamemnon's son. I wonder sometimes what she thinks about me, what they've told her. I wasn't much of a mother to her. I never felt much like a mother. It amazes me sometimes when I realize I am one. I don't deserve to be. Hera never blessed me as she did you."

"Aphrodite blessed you."

Helen shook her head. "Aphrodite didn't bless me."

They fell silent now. The moment had come for Andromache to leave, for Helen to thank her for her visit. Andromache hesitated, then held out her hand to the other. Helen took it in both of hers. When they had been two wives, connected by a royal tie, they had remained strangers. But now the two widows, connected only by their grief, were reluctant to leave each other's side.

Agamemnon gave up trying to sleep. He left his tent and walked to a spot where he could see the city. There was no moon tonight, but Troy provided its own light. The walls were outlined in a red glow from funeral pyres burning all over the city. Warriors slain in the previous day's battle were now being consigned to the flames. Agamemnon looked at the wall. The idea was crazy, he thought. The Trojans would never be fooled.

At first the chief had been happy with Odysseus's news. Somehow Odysseus had talked Antenor, Priam's counsellor, into giving the Greeks the Palladium. It seemed too good to be true, but then Odysseus told the chief to forget about the Palladium. The Palladium was nothing, nothing compared to what the Greeks were going to give the Trojans in return.

"A horse!" Odysseus had cried with almost demonic glee. "Oh, I had a time thinking of the shape of the thing. I thought of all kinds of things, even a great statue of Athena, but how many men could you fit in that? And you had to have enough men in case you met resistance once inside the city. So it had to be a good-sized thing, and the right shape. Then it came to me. A horse. Don't you see? A horse for the people who pride themselves on their horses. A horse for the horse tamers. Oh, it'll be irresistible! They'll *have* to take it in; the bloody fools will have to! Oh, it will be the gift to end all gifts!''

Agamemnon had never seen Odysseus in such a state, and it took a long time to get him to calm down enough to relate his conversation with Antenor and the plan the two had hatched. But it was the horse that he kept coming back to, the strategem that would get them into the city. Agamemnon couldn't believe Odysseus was serious; the idea was preposterous.

"They'll never drag it in," the chief had said. "They'll burn it where it stands."

"Then they'll burn me too, because I'll be inside. But they won't burn it, for all that. Take my word for it."

Agamemnon could only get Odysseus to leave by agreeing to think it over. The chief watched now the play of the flames on the distant walls, the walls he had not surmounted in ten years of fighting. It couldn't work, he said to himself again. And yet, what did he have to lose? He might lose Odysseus, to be sure, and anyone else reckless enough to go along with him. But the Greeks could not conquer Troy in the legitimate way, on the field of battle, the way he thought they would when he had been promised victory long ago. Perhaps it was the will of the gods that Troy should be taken by means of a hollow, wooden contrivance. Why shouldn't the gods condone Greek trickery? Had they not condoned Trojan trickery all along?

He gazed at the wall. A wooden horse, though? Could that really be what the gods had intended all along? A wooden horse?

The scream could be heard all the way to the palace. It had been many days since the battle, so it could no longer be a grieving wife or mother. Besides, it didn't sound like a cry of grief, but one of terror.

Andromache, who had been late in following her sis-

184

ter-in-law this morning, knew the source of the scream immediately and ran into the temple. She found Cassandra huddled under one of the inner columns, shivering and hysterical, a wild frenzy in her eyes. Andromache knelt by her, enfolded her in her arms, and gently rocked her.

"Oh, Cassandra, what's the matter? It's all right, Cassandra," she soothed. "What happened?"

The girl shook as if she had been drawn from an icy pond, and the only sounds she made were the whimpering cries that accompanied her breaths.

"What is it, Cassandra? What happened?"

Unable to speak, she lifted one hand and pointed to the center of the temple. Andromache looked in that direction and saw the vacant pedestal where the Palladium had stood, the statue that had been in Troy as long as anyone alive could remember.

X

The Horse

To Epius, the Greek master carpenter, it was a problem of engineering. A horse, the live animal, supported a thousand pounds of its own weight on four legs that tapered down to shafts little bigger than a man's wrist. The living bone, the tensile strength of the muscle, and the horse's own sense of balance all combined to make such support possible. A wooden horse, however, many times larger and heavier than a living one, and carrying within it the weight of men besides, could never stand upon such narrow footings. No, the legs would have to be stylized and come down to much larger bases than a real horse actually had, and then these four bases in turn would have to be attached securely to a strong, stout platform upon which the whole horse would stand. That was the only way to prevent the thing from toppling under its own weight.

Epius had protested at first that his ability was not equal to so colossal an undertaking. Secretly, he disliked the whole idea of turning his creative skills to the making of a war engine. But Odysseus insisted, and Agamemnon backed him up. To be doubly sure that the carpenter did a good job, Odysseus informed him that Epius himself would be one of the horse's occupants in the assault, the only one who would not be a volunteer. Since there was no choice, Epius did not resist, and set about his task.

Odysseus need not have worried, however. Though the purpose of the engine may have been repugnant to the carpenter, and though an innate cowardliness made him fear for his life once inside, he eventually forgot these concerns as he became engrossed in the building of the horse. Epius was, first and last, a craftsman, and he had been commissioned to create his finest work.

For his wood, Epius chose the fir trees that grew around the small temple to Thymbraean Apollo. They would provide both the strength and the flexibility he needed. He had his men fell almost the entire grove, for he needed wood not only for the horse itself and the platform, but also several round, straight trunks to function as rollers so that the horse could be moved.

It was the felling of the trees that the Trojan sentries first noticed from the wall. They were puzzled by the action, and wondered if it was connected in some way with the ambush on Achilles, which had happened so near the grove. In the weeks that followed, however, they began to see a great form take shape before the Greek camp. When the tower-like legs were completed, and the whole platform could be seen sitting upon rollers, few of the lookouts doubted its purpose. This was to be a siege engine, a moveable, protected tower probably, that could carry the Greeks over the wall and into the city.

Yet the Trojans did not greatly fear such an engine. Even if it were tall enough to deliver Greek soldiers to the top of the wall, it was but a single tower and could be used in only one place at a time. Its movement would be slow and ponderous at best, thus giving the Trojans plenty of advance warning. They could easily mass their forces at its intended point of assault long before the engine was actually hauled into place. And even if a battle was joined at the top of the wall, by fastening torches to poles or arrows, the Trojans could burn the thing where it stood.

As spring deepened into summer, the lookouts watched its construction, and only began to question their siege engine theory when they saw the figure emerge on top of the four pillars. It was a horse, there was no doubt of it: a great, wooden horse. When word spread around the town, everyone in Troy who could make the climb went to the battlements to see the apparition, and when they saw it, they were amazed. Why would the Greeks be building such a thing? To be sure, it might still be a war engine of some kind, but they knew the Greeks were not given to frivolity. If it were merely a protected stairway for assault troops, they would hardly have bothered to put a head and a tail on it. What could they be up to?

Even as the Trojans speculated, however, they felt a strange attraction toward it. They were, after all, a people devoted to horses, and the image of one, forty feet high and standing on their shore, appealed to their lively Asian fancy. It was something they might have done to honor their city's heritage, but it was so unlike the Greeks.

Agamemnon, for his part, remained aloof from the project, almost indifferent. Though he had given his consent to go ahead, at no time during the construction did he really think the ruse would work. In fact, he never quite believed the crazy scheme would even be tried. He kept hoping something would intervene: a decisive battle, a capitulation, an earthquake that would tear the wall asunder, anything. Consequently, he left all the details of the plan to Odysseus. But no battle, no divine intervention occurred. And after six weeks, the sound of the hammers ceased, and the work was completed.

Odysseus directed the men to begin stowing their belongings in the ships and to separate what they would leave behind. The amount of loot, armor, weapons, tools, livestock, cooking utensils, pottery, and debris accumulated over the course of the siege was staggering, and Odysseus wisely told the men to select only what they needed or valued most to take with them. Still, the ships groaned under the load. But the work progressed in a carnival atmosphere, the men happy, almost giddy with anticipation. Soldiers bartered with each other as they filled precious cargo space; some had to throw away artifacts that could not fit, artifacts which a month before had seemed priceless. But they did everything in the spirit of lightheartedness. Agamemnon had not seen them in such good humor since the war began. He knew the reason for their joy, and it merely intensified his gloom.

The armies had been told, of course, that this was supposed to be a pretended departure. They would wait until nightfall so their movements could not be seen from the wall. Then, except for the men designated to enter the horse, the soldiers would proceed to burn whatever was left of the camp, board the ships, and leave the Trojan shore. They would anchor on the seaward side of the island of Tenedos, less than five miles off the coast of Troy. There they would remain for the following day, returning at nightfall to see what had become of the horse. If it had been brought into the city, they would beach their ships in the darkness and await the opening of the gates by their comrades within.

But what would happen if they came back to find the horse still on the shore, surrounded by Trojans? Or worse, what if they found the horse in flames? Would they row up on shore, establish a beachhead again, and resume the siege? No, even Agamemnon knew that was impossible. Once in their ships with all their belongings aboard, and seeing the failure of this, their last hope, his army would never consent to it. Their pretended departure would become real, and the struggle of a decade would finally be over. The Trojans would have won;

Agamemnon would have to admit defeat, turn his sails west, and head home.

So Agamemnon stood now with his army, on what might well prove to be his last night at Troy, forming a huge circle around the horse. An unnatural quiet reigned. It was all the more strange, coming as it did after the raucousness that had characterized the loading of the ships all day. Now the soldiers stood motionless, admiring the great form looming before them, and they marveled at the power of the gods. They had built the horse themselves, of course, many of them felling the trees and fashioning the boards with their own hands, but now that it was done, their creation seemed a thing apart. It was too grand for their own mean powers. With a curious blend of humility and intuitive wisdom, they gave credit to the immortals. In some dim chamber of their consciousness, they recognized that their collective achievements were truly godlike.

Near Agamemnon stood the men who would climb the ladder and enter the trap door on the flank of the horse. Along with Epius, there were nine others: Odysseus, Menelaus, Diomedes, Pyrrhus, Philoctetes, Antilochus, Sthenelus, Idomeneus, and Machaon. All but the builder had volunteered, and all had their own private reasons for wanting to go. Years later, Greeks of another age would consider it the purest of pedigrees to be descended from one of these men, but on that day in 1184 B.C. the ten men standing beneath the colossal legs were not thinking of their progeny, nor of their place in history. Nervously shifting from one foot to another, some stood, wondering if they would still be alive by the next day's sunset.

Agamemnon had hoped to say something eloquent and inspiring, but when the moment came and the ladder was put in place, words failed him. Instead, he embraced each one individually. He took leave of young Pyrrhus

190

first, looking one last time for his more famous father in his face. As the youth climbed up, the chief embraced the physician, Machaon, whose services would be sorely missed. Then he clasped Diomedes and Diomedes' charioteer, Sthenelus, who would not desert his commander even in this venture. Agamemnon took leave of Antilochus, old Nestor's son, then Idomeneus, his captain from the ancient, storied isle of Crete. For a long moment he clasped Philoctetes, resurrected from the dead so recently, and now entering what might be another tomb. Then he embraced Odysseus, who alone among them wore a smile. Agamemnon pulled back slightly, and stared into the sparkling but unfathomable eyes. The chief wondered if his skilled tactician, the mastermind of this plan, had played his last trick. He squeezed Odysseus and let him go.

Longest of all, the chief hugged his brother, Menelaus, the redness of his hair undetectable in the moonlight. For many days Agamemnon had tried to talk him out of going, but Menelaus had insisted. He said he couldn't let the others take the risk without him. Besides, he said, if this truly were the end of the war, he didn't want to survive it to go home empty-handed. So Agamemnon embraced his younger brother one final time.

Last came Epius, who carried with him the rope ladder they would use to descend if the ruse worked. Agamemnon clasped him briefly too and then watched him enter the womb of the great wooden beast. An assistant followed Epius up the ladder to help from the outside as the carpenter put the trap door in place. Epius had contrived a very small, irregularly shaped hatch that could be opened only from within, and was invisible from without. Agamemnon tried to get a last glimpse of the occupants, but the blackness was too deep. The hatch slid into place, and once more the horse presented a smooth flank.

The armies dispersed to their respective camps to

begin the fires, but the chief remained, gazing at the great form, wondering what god had brought him to this pass, him, the Lord of Mycenae, King of Kings. He had been told many years ago that Zeus promised him victory over Troy, and he had been made commander-in-chief to that end. Yet over the course of the war, his control of events had never been more than minimal. Now he stood beneath this great, wooden monstrosity and was forced to stake his reputation, the only thing that would live after him, on one crazy strategem. He looked at the walled city only a few hundred yards away. It was not a long journey by chariot. A real horse would cover the ground in a few minutes. But for this horse, how long a journey, how very, very long.

Agamemnon shook his head and said a silent good-bye to his ten comrades sealed within, whom he did not expect to see again. He looked up at the grim, wooden face blotting out the stars overhead, and wondered at the feebleness of human will. The glory he had hoped for, which would make him famous throughout history, was wholly and absolutely dependent on a crackbrained scheme even a child could see through, yet there was nothing he could do about it. Feeling very old suddenly, with the weight of many years' suffering upon him, he turned and made his way back to his tent. The horse with its strange cargo, about to embark on a journey into the timeless realm of legend, stood alone now and silent on that Asian shore and gathered dew in the cool night air.

The lookouts on the wall watched the conflagrations in the Greek camp all night long. Even after a battle, when funeral pyres lined the shore, there had never been so many fires, nor of such magnitude. Some of the Trojans guessed that the Greeks were burning their camp and leaving, but they could not be sure until daylight. The sun rose early over Mt. Ida the next morning. It was the eighteenth day after the summer solstice—July 9, by our reckoning—and in the dim light of dawn, the sharpest-eyed among the sentries above the Scaean Gates reported to his fellows that the Greek ships were gone.

When the sun rose higher and a second lookout confirmed this, and then a third, a cheer went up, the likes of which had not been heard in Troy for ten years. One of the guards ran to the palace to tell the king, but the noise from the wall had roused the population, and Priam was already making his way to the battlements. As he reached the stairs, those at the top shouted down to him that the Greeks were gone. He paused; then, instead of proceeding up, called for his chariot and ordered the Scaean Gates opened. There was a momentary silence as the guards stared open-mouthed at the king. Then, with a shout of joy and triumph they obeyed his command, and the great doors creaked on their hinges as they swung wide.

The people crowded behind the king and stared through the gates. It was the same littered field, to be sure, now adorned by the huge horse in the distance, but this morning the great Trojan plain lay free of soldiers, free of enemies. The beach was no longer spiny with warships, and beyond, the blue Aegean rolled freely to their shore. The quality of light was different too. The morning sun seemed to burn away with the night vapors all that had sullied their land. Even the air smelled new and fresh. A mighty cheer went up again, and those nearest Priam heard the king utter to himself, "They're gone. Damn them to hell, they're finally gone."

Deiphobus appeared, and Aeneas, and several of the other captains with their chariots, and once the king was mounted on his own, the ground before the city rumbled with hoofbeats and the clatter of wheels. The citizenry stayed back at first and let the soldiers precede them, lest they be caught in a trap. Armed men fanned out in every direction to make sure no contingent of Greeks had been left behind. But when all was pronounced clear, the unarmed population, all those who could walk or ride, poured out of the gates and onto the field. Some had not set foot on this ground since it had been farmland, and they looked for old landmarks of the life before: a well, a tree, a path.

The soldiers in chariots reached the shore first, and some, even before they inspected the remains of the camp, ran down to the water's edge to wade in the sea. They laughed and splashed each other. Others inspected the ramshackle wall the Greeks had built. Whatever was made of wood in it had been burned, but the stones and waste metal that had been used were still there, thrown down to the ground now. Many of the fires that had consumed the camp were still smoking, and charred pieces of furniture could be seen smoldering among the ashes. Some soldiers looked for treasure, but whatever was of value had been taken. Scattered on the ground were merely pot shards, the tattered remnants of clothing and tents, animal bones, and ruined armor, much of it Trojan. It might have been a depressing sight, were it not for the joyousness of the occasion. Priam alighted from his chariot, and in the presence of his army gave thanks to Zeus, Athena, and Apollo, the special protectors of the city.

When the soldiers and the citizens had satisfied their curiosity about the camp, inevitably, they made their way back to the horse, whose long, early morning shadow reached nearly to the water's edge. The Trojans formed a great circle around it, similar to the one made by the Greeks the night before. They stood, and they stared, and they asked each other, What was it? Why did the Greeks build it? Why did they leave it here?

Priam stood with them, and his counsellors gravitated

194

to him, each speculating about it. Deiphobus and Aeneas reported to the king that, after a thorough search, no Greeks had been found anywhere in the area, and then they too fell in by his side and watched the great wooden form. Many thought it was a divine offering to insure a safe trip home. Poseidon, the god of the sea, upon whose back the Greeks must make their way, was also, oddly enough, the god of horses. So it was a logical premise that the departing armies created such a wooden effigy to placate the god most responsible for their safe return.

Others thought it was sort of a battle monument. After any significant combat in those days, it was customary for the winning side to set up a trophy to commemorate the victory. The Greeks, perhaps, by this act were proclaiming themselves the victors in the war, even if the ultimate prize eluded them. Those who discounted that theory claimed the Greeks would not be so foolish as to build a monument that could so easily be destroyed by fire. But the theory's adherents said that was the reason the Greeks made it in the shape of a horse, an animal sacred to Troy. They counted on Trojan totemism to save the monument from the flames.

Still others could not give up the idea that it was originally designed as a siege engine, and when the plan was scrapped midway through, the Greeks converted the half-finished tower into a horse statue either to disguise their failed attempt, or simply to mock the city they had decided to desert. The one thing nearly all agreed upon, however, was the impressiveness of it. The horse looked even more colossal up close than it had from afar. And though the Trojans could not explain why the Greeks had built it, they now considered it their own.

By mid-morning virtually the whole city had joined the circle, and the sound of their voices, exclaiming, speculating, uttering theories and counter-theories, might have sounded to the horse, if it were alive and its tall wooden

195

ears could hear, like the buzzing of a great swarm of insects. But amidst the incessant hum all at once came a sound that chilled the blood of all who heard it and struck the crowd dumb. It was a shriek, as if from the earth itself, expressing in one, inarticulate, mindless howl all the pain and fear and hopelessness of life.

Immediately a clearing widened around a young woman. Wild-eyed she looked at the horse, but then she lowered her gaze. She seemed to look at nothing at all, or at something unseen, and muttered in a dazed, flat voice, "Burn it." When the only response was astonished stares, she threw her head back and screamed, "*Burn it!*" She stretched the words, making them grate hideously on her vocal chords, and the awful sound mortified the crowd.

Andromache pushed her way into the magic circle and caught the girl in her arms. "*Burn it!*" Cassandra screeched again. "Oh, my lady, my goddess, Athena, please. *Burn it!*" Then she collapsed, sobbing, into her sister-in-law's arms. Andromache held the girl tightly and tried to soothe her, pushing the hair, wet with tears, from Cassandra's face; but she would not be quieted in the presence of the horse. Finally, with the help of some servants, Andromache carried her back toward the city. The crowd opened a path for them as they passed.

When Cassandra was gone, the silence that had descended on the people continued for some time. But then the priest, Laocoön, with determined step strode to where Priam was standing.

"My lord," he said, in a voice loud enough for all to hear. "Your daughter, despite her infirmity, is right. The horse should be destroyed."

There was an audible gasp from those who saw the horse as a prize and something to be kept as a spoil of the war.

196

Priam frowned. He cared little about the horse, but he didn't like Laocoön. "What is your reason?" he asked.

Laocoön looked around at the crowd. "My reason is," he said in the same booming voice, "that I haven't forgotten the Greeks, as everyone else here apparently has. I don't trust them."

Deiphobus broke in. "I have no love for the Greeks, but I have found them to be trustworthy when we've made truces with them. In fact, on the last two occasions, we were the ones who broke the truce. You should know that best of all, Laocoön, since you took part in the ambush on Achilles."

"Yes, your brother and I ambushed Achilles," shot back Laocoön, "and if we hadn't, none of us would be standing here now. If we had depended on you to rid us of him, we'd all still be cowering behind our wall."

Deiphobus started for him, but Priam raised his hand, and those around Deiphobus held him back.

"You have not told us yet, Laocoön," said Priam, "why we should destroy the horse. What harm does it pose us?"

The priest looked from Deiphobus's face back to Priam's. He could not articulate his fears. He had but an airy sentence and his own vague apprehensions to go on. He wanted to say that he didn't like the size of the thing, or the grim face it had, or the strange, tower-like legs that supported it. He wanted to say he didn't like the fact that it was constructed on rollers. But he couldn't say these things without sounding foolish. He turned back to Priam. "I don't know what harm it poses for us, but I believe what Apollo tells me."

Again there was a reaction from the citizens. Laocoön was a priest of Apollo, and his word about the god was not to be taken lightly.

"Did Apollo say there was some harm in it?" asked Priam calmly.

197

Laocoön bit his lip to keep it from quivering. The god had not told him this precisely, and he believed enough in Apollo's power to fear retribution if he lied about the god's words. No, Apollo's message had been vague, as intelligence from the gods often is. At the time he received the warning, he had no idea what it referred to, but now he knew; he knew beyond a doubt. Yet, it wasn't enough to know; he needed to be able to convince the king. His mind raced through all the auguries he had performed to find any evidence that might substantiate the warning, but he could come up with nothing.

"Well?" said Priam.

The priest glanced around. The people were no longer looking at the horse, but at him, waiting for his answer. Even those who did not like him, Deiphobus, Aeneas, the king himself, wanted to hear his reason. His person they might despise, but that he had an insight into the god's mind they all respected.

He wet his lips and turned back to Priam. "Apollo told me to beware of gifts borne by Greeks."

There was a murmur and a small ripple of laughter from the crowd.

Priam narrowed his eyes at the priest. " 'Beware of gifts borne by Greeks'? That is what the god said?"

"Yes."

"This is *all* he said?"

"Yes."

"When did Apollo give you this message?"

"Years ago. He put it in my mind once while I was praying."

The king was silent for a moment as he continued to stare at Laocoön. "This is an ambiguous saying," he said finally. "Does it mean all gifts or just some gifts? And what is a gift? Maybe Helen was the gift he was referring to. How do we know that the horse is a gift?"

"It could not be Helen, my lord," said Laocoön.

198

"Helen was not given freely, as a gift is. It must be the horse. The horse is the only gift they've given us during the war. I'm sure Apollo was trying to warn us, and I believe we should heed the warning and burn it."

His earnestness seemed to move some of Priam's counsellors who were standing by, and the king was about to ask them to speak their opinions openly when suddenly a new voice was heard, that of Antenor, Laocoön's father.

"My lord, it is a gift, but not to us. We must not destroy it."

Priam turned to him. "What do you know about this, Antenor?"

To everyone's astonishment, the old man dropped to his knees before the king. "Please forgive me, my lord."

"Forgive you for what? Get up, Antenor."

Not moving, the old man continued. "The horse is a gift to the goddess Athena, to replace the Palladium. We can't destroy it or we'll anger the goddess." Antenor shook his head uncontrollably and began talking more to himself than to the amazed people around him. "I expected a small statue. I never thought they would build something like this. This won't even fit in the temple."

"What are you talking about?" said Priam. "Please get up!" He gestured to his son Deiphobus, who forced the old man to his feet again. "Now tell me, Antenor, what is this all about?"

"You must forgive me, my lord," he began again. "It is because the Greeks have been honest with us, as Prince Deiphobus says, that I trusted them to keep their word in this bargain. And they have kept it. You see it yourself: they're gone, just as they promised, and they've left us this magnificent tribute."

"What bargain?"

"For the Palladium. They wanted the Palladium." Antenor lowered his eyes and shook his head. "They wanted something to take home to show that they hadn't lost entirely. It was the only way they'd leave."

"You gave them the Palladium?" asked Priam incredulously. He took the old man by the sleeve and waited until he raised his eyes again. "*You* stole it, Antenor?" he said, nearly in a whisper.

With an oddly childlike look on his wrinkled face, and even the faintest hint of a sheepish smile, the old man nodded his head. "So you see, my lord, we can't destroy it. It's the goddess's new statue. I promised it to her in exchange for the old. We've got to bring it into the city and place it before her temple."

"Never!" shouted Laocoön, who had stood mute during the exchange between his father and the king. "Are you crazy, old man? Isn't it enough that you admit you're a traitor? Do you really expect us to turn around now and take this monster into our city?" He turned to one of the soldiers and snatched the spear from his hand. The crowd gasped, thinking that he was going to kill his own father, but instead he ran into the center of the circle. "Let the thing be burned first! Destroy it!" With that, he heaved the spear at the horse, and it stuck with a reverberating thud in the broad wooden side of the beast.

Earlier, the crowd might have been persuaded to follow Laocoön and consign the horse to the flames, but now the mood had changed. Seeing the spear still vibrating in the great form, the people were stunned into silence. If this truly were a gift to the goddess (and Antenor had no reason to lie about it, since he had incriminated himself by admitting it), then Laocoön had just committed a greater sin against the city than his father had, for he had desecrated the divine gift with a spear.

Laocoön stood in the center alone, waiting, and the

people looked to their king for a decision. Priam shifted his eyes from son to father.

Antenor said, "He's right about me. I am a traitor. I made a deal with the Greeks without your permission, my lord. I only did it to get them to leave, but it was wrong, and I'm ready to die for it. But you mustn't destroy the statue. It's for the goddess. She'll turn her back on us if we burn it."

Priam looked long into the old man's eyes. With a word, he could send Antenor to his death. With another word he could light a fire beneath the horse that would be seen as far away as Tenedos. He was angry enough to do both of these things, and perhaps, if he were a younger man, he would have done them. But he was not young; the wrinkled countenance he gazed into was a mirror of his own. He no longer needed to set examples, to prove authority, to show decisiveness. Age had brought him weariness, to be sure, and pains, but it had also brought him a slim measure of wisdom, and, perhaps more important, a large measure of patience. Antenor had been the companion of his youth, and then, when Priam had become king, his first counsellor. Together they had formed the Trojan council, and together they watched it work. When the Greeks came, both had seen their sons go off to fight, and both had watched them die. Priam lifted his head slightly and smelled the salt breezes wafting in from the shore, vacant of enemies for the first time in a decade. And he heard, even at this distance, the sound of birds in the far woods.

The king gazed so long in Antenor's face that the people became restless and shifted nervously. Finally, Priam dropped his hand from the old man's sleeve and looked around at the crowd. He could no longer speak in a voice that would carry through the ranks of those assembled, but in the loudest voice he could muster he said, "Antenor is no traitor."

An expression of relief rose from the crowd. Although they had been shocked by Antenor's revelation, they still felt a great affection for the old man. Many of them had known him as the king's wise counsellor for all their lives.

"But the horse," shouted Laocoön. "Let us burn it, my lord."

Priam looked at Antenor again. "Perhaps it would be better," he said quietly to his old friend.

Deiphobus, who was standing close enough to hear, now spoke to his father, softly and respectfully. "My lord, it *is* our only prize. If we burn it, we have nothing to show for a ten-year struggle. Wouldn't it mean something in years to come that we possessed this statue, built by our enemies, and testifying to the invulnerability of our city? People will come from everywhere to see it, and it will show that in the end we prevailed."

The argument meant very little to Priam, who no longer cared for such symbols of triumph and power, but he understood his son's reasoning. Deiphobus was preparing the world he would live in, reign in too, probably, when Priam was dead, since Hector's son was too young. Should Priam deprive him of this trophy? Was it right for Priam to intrude on a world he would not live in? And yet, he liked the horse no more than Laocoön did. The old king wished Hector were here. Hector would have known what to do.

He looked back to his old friend and saw the silent plea still there in his eyes. He sighed, then said quietly, "All right, Deiphobus, see to it."

With that, he turned his back on the crowd and the horse and mounted his chariot. Deiphobus, meanwhile, entered the center of the circle. The people's attention, which had been centered on the king, now fell on his son.

"Fetch ropes!" Deiphobus shouted. "And someone

bring a ladder so we can remove that spear. *The war is over!* We've won, and we've got a prize, a magnificent prize. Fetch the ropes, and we'll bring it into the city!"

There was a roar of approval, and a stampede of citizens rushed back toward town. Ahead of them in the distance was the solitary chariot of the king, which entered the Scaean Gates without ceremony and disappeared.

But the people's joy could not be diminished. Those who returned to Troy did not just get ropes and a ladder. This was a holiday to end all holidays, and they brought back food and drink by the wagon-load, fruits, meats, bread, cheese, milk, wine: all those commodities that had been hoarded and doled out so sparingly in the previous ten years. And they brought flowers. Some flowers they strewed in the path of the great beast; others they threw on its platform; still others they strung into garlands, and when the ladder was raised to remove the spear, the climber was prevailed upon to place the garlands around the horse's neck.

The dragging of the horse became the labor of the entire city. Everyone wanted a turn at the ropes, and those who did not pull helped to remove the log rollers from behind the platform and run them up to the front again. The great beast moved slowly and fitfully toward the city.

Getting the great wooden figure across the plain and up the small rise to the city gates took the better part of the day, and it was only when they were near the threshold that they realized it was too tall to get through. A stone lintel overtopped the Scaean Gates, and this was several feet lower than the horse's head. After so long and arduous a journey, however, the Trojans were not to be stopped. Over Laocoön's objection, Deiphobus ordered the lintel dismantled. The crowd cheered as the great limestone blocks came crashing to the ground.

Some of the people rolled these away, and the rest took up the ropes again, heaving the beast through the gates. Four times the horse stuck crossing the threshold, and men with stout poles pried away the obstructions. During this time, citizens who were watching the work marveled at the look of the thing, half-in, half-out of the city, its tall head peeking over the great wall.

It was near sunset when they finally got the horse through the gates and into the city, too late to bring it the rest of the way up the broad streets to the temple of Athena, so Deiphobus ordered the work stopped for the night. Then the citizens, pleased with their accomplishment, abandoned themselves to celebration. Wine flowed freely, and the people sang and danced around the horse in the broad square of the marketplace. Their shadows, cast by the torchlight, played on the great wooden flanks, and their music could be heard in the far suburbs of the city. The reveling lasted well into the night, and when the Trojans finally retired to their homes, they went to sleep happy in the knowledge that they were a free people once more.

The gates were locked, of course, and the guard was set as usual, but on this night, the lookouts did not talk of the Greeks. Some talked about their farms, which they could return to now, and others about the trading they would take up again, now that commerce would reopen in the city. They talked about trips they would make, relatives and friends they would visit in distant towns. They talked, they laughed, and they planned for the future. Troy, so long on the brink of death, was alive again.

The darkness and cramped quarters inside the horse did not bother the men nearly as much as the heat. Although Epius had left several air holes in the neck, tail, and legs, he'd purposely put none in the central cavity where he and his companions would be, for fear they might be detected. Thus, the men had air to breathe, through a circuitous inner route from the extremities, but hardly any ventilation for cooling. When the midsummer sun began beating on the horse's back that day, the temperature inside rose murderously high. It was only the certainty of instant death that kept them from abandoning the horse even while it was ringed with Trojans.

They could hear imperfectly the discussions that took place around them during the morning. They heard Cassandra's cry, and they heard Laocoön's shouts. Pyrrhus whispered to Odysseus that if he smelled smoke, he would leap out and die a soldier's death rather than be burnt alive, but Odysseus told him to be quiet. He obeyed, even when the spear point penetrated the horse dangerously near his head. Finally, they heard Deiphobus's voice commanding that the horse be taken into the city. Had not the citizens themselves been cheering the next moment, they might have heard a brief, stifled cry of joy coming from within the wooden beast.

The ten men felt every bump of the jarring ride up the field, and their greatest fear was that the horse would come apart. They feared the unwieldy head, loosened by the vibrations, might come toppling down, or that the great body, slung between the pairs of legs would collapse. They heard the creaking of the timbers, and they prayed to the gods that the pegs and bindings would hold until they reached their destination. When the horse stuck so many times at the Scaean Gates, they thought it was the end. They feared the Trojans would dismantle the horse to take it into the city piecemeal, but then it rolled free.

They felt no more movement once they were inside the gates. Instead, they began to hear the sounds of revelry. They heard the muffled strains of music and singing, and through the great legs of the horse they could feel the vibration of the Trojans' dance as some of the citizens leapt upon the platform. They listened to the celebration for hours, and then the laughing voices outside grew more and more faint. Finally they heard the most welcome sound of all—silence.

The debate on the field, the perilous journey into the city, and the stifling heat inside the wooden chamber had been an ordeal for the Greeks, but their wait in the quiet citadel was worse. The plan was that they would not emerge from the horse for some time after the Trojans went to bed. This delay was to allow ample time both for their comrades out at sea to put ashore, and for the Trojans to fall asleep. Since the occupants of the horse could not see the night sky and thus mark the passage of time accurately, they did not know precisely what hour it was, or how many hours it lacked until dawn. They had to depend on their best estimate from within. Nor did they dare speak during this time, or move in such a way that might be noted from the outside, for the Trojans may well have set guards around the horse, guards who were even now standing beside the tall legs. So the Greeks waited in their dark womb.

The Trojans had set no guard around the horse, however. The sentries on the wall occasionally glanced over their shoulders at the great beast whose head was on their own level, and even they did not note the lone figure far below who approached the horse after everyone else had gone to sleep.

Helen had not joined her fellow citizens in the festivities of the day. She was as pleased as anyone that the war was over, but she feared to go among them lest they be reminded of the reason for the war. Now, however, she was drawn to the horse, which she had seen only from afar.

She looked at the great angular body, so different from the graceful curves of a real horse, and she shuddered a little. It was Greek, she thought. Though constructed on the Trojan plain, and of Trojan timber, the creation was thoroughly Greek. The art she had become used to in Troy, the tapestries, the wall paintings, the statuary, all had a kind of joyous frivolity and lightness, so different from what she grew up with at home. Greek art was serious and solid, solid as these ponderous tower-like legs.

Yet the horse held a morbid attraction. She stepped up on the platform and touched one of the legs. As much as the thing frightened her, she felt a strange kinship with it. Both were now orphans in Troy, both trophies of war. But tomorrow this horse would be enshrined before the Temple to Athena as a lasting symbol of victory. What would become of her, however? Made of flesh instead of wood, she needed to fill ten thousand more days here, get up every morning and live every hour of every one of them until she grew old and died.

It was not that she disliked Troy. The city was still beautiful, and its people a happier, more civilized and gentle breed than her countrymen, but what could life hold for her here now? Could the Trojans ever forgive her for all that had happened? Would wives forgive her their lost husbands, children their lost fathers? Would the royal family continue to welcome her now that Paris and Hector were dead, and Priam old? Her coming here ten years ago had been a desperate assertion of independence and freedom. But now it looked as though she was doomed to spend the rest of her life a prisoner of her past.

She leaned back against the pillar-like leg and stared out into the vacant city streets. She thought of Sparta, the only other home she had ever known. She thought of the palace there, crude by Trojan standards, and the small stand of wooden dwellings that made up the town. She thought of her old servants, many of whom must be dead, and of her favorite horses. She thought of the hills where she used to ride, and she thought of her Spartan husband who never objected to her long, solitary jaunts into the country. Soldiers had reported that Menelaus had not been seriously injured by Pandarus's arrow. She wondered where he was right now. He must be sailing home at this moment, home to Sparta. Thinking of her? She shook her head. If so, it would be with curses. He would be surprised, she thought, if he knew how much she missed Sparta this night.

She smiled. He had been so proud of being king of Sparta, a younger brother who never expected to be a king. She remembered how much he enjoyed showing off Sparta's simple beauties to strangers, and how she would feel an odd affection for him at those times. It wasn't love. No, not love. She might wish sometimes that she could lie to herself, but she couldn't. She didn't love him. Her love, for all it was worth, had been reserved for the crazy Trojan prince, the foolish, selfish, egotistical, charming boy. But she did have tender feelings toward Menelaus. He was, after all, the only person who had ever given her the freedom she wanted.

She lifted her hands and nearly prayed, but she stopped herself. The gods had ceased listening to her prayers long ago, and her pride would not allow her to keep asking in vain. She wanted to pray that she be whisked over the sea to that Spartan ship, and be forgiven by that husband who had let her ride in the hills. Unconsciously she said his name aloud.

In the darkness inside the horse's belly a man's unseeing eyes glared. He had not heard the voice for ten years, and the first sound it uttered was his own name. He stirred, and a hand suddenly clapped over his mouth, the fingers digging painfully into his cheeks. He froze. A moment passed. Then he patted the arm attached to the hand to let Odysseus know that he was calm and would make no noise. Odysseus slowly loosened his grip.

Below them, Helen walked back to the edge of the platform and stepped off. She turned one last time to look at the great wooden figure. It seemed still another cruel joke of the gods that she, who so loved horses, would have this grotesque effigy to gaze upon for the rest of her days as a reminder of her shame.

XI

The Fall

IN THE STILLNESS of the night, the men inside the horse had heard Helen's footfalls on the platform and then the faint sounds of her steps as she walked away. Odysseus pulled Menelaus by the neck toward him so that he could whisper in his ear. "Her coming was a godsend. Now we know there aren't any guards, or they would have spoken to her."

Menelaus nodded.

Odysseus waited a few minutes longer to give Helen time to leave the vicinity. The he tapped Epius's shoulder. The carpenter carefully opened the trap door slightly so that he could look out. Though it lacked two days to full, the moon shone very brightly that night on the flat surface of the platform beneath them. Epius opened the hatch a bit more and could make out the oak tree that was in the center of the marketplace. This meant that the hatch faced away from the wall and thus away from the sentries on the wall. He opened the hatch all the way.

Immediately a rush of cool night air relieved the stuffiness inside the cavity, and the men, their clothing sweat-soaked and sticking to them, felt revived. Those nearest the trap door looked out. Except for Odysseus, none had ever seen the inside of the city before. All they could see now were the dark outlines of buildings, but even these seemed impressive, colored as they were by the stories the men had heard of Troy's splendor. They remained motionless for a moment, then Epius dropped one end of the rope ladder.

Pyrrhus was the first to climb out. He lowered himself quickly to the platform, then ducked behind one of the legs on the opposite side so he could look up at the wall. There were two sentries on the battlements near the Scaean Gates, both leaning over the wall and looking out toward the plain. Pyrrhus ducked back to the other side again and signaled to his companions. One by one they silently climbed down to the platform, Epius last of all.

Odysseus had instructed the men in what they were to do if they got into the city. None of them knew, of course, where their wooden vehicle might end up in Troy, and they had devised plans for negotiating the city streets back to the Scaean Gates if the horse were placed near the temple. But they had known for hours, now, that those plans were unnecessary. The Trojans had left the horse in the best possible location, right near the very gates the Greeks had to secure.

Odysseus took Pyrrhus, Antilochus, and Idomeneus with him and made for the stairway that led up to the wall. Epius was sent across the marketplace to where a small fire was still smoldering from the evening's festivities. He carried with him wood shavings and a long staff topped by a cloth, twined around tinder. He fell to the ground and began blowing into the embers. Meanwhile, Menelaus, Diomedes, Sthenelus, and Machaon ran to the gates. Only Philoctetes hung back beneath the horse, where he had the best view of the sentries on the wall.

During the celebration, the lookouts had had difficulty keeping their minds on their task. Though they never abandoned their posts, citizens brought them food and drink so that they could take part in the merriment. Then, when the rest of the populace had gone to bed, they spent a good part of the night talking to each other about the time of peace that had arrived. Now, however, in the longest hours of the night just before dawn, when even the best conversation flags, they had not exchanged a word in forty minutes. Ten feet from each other, they looked into the gloom, each buried in his own thoughts.

The one to the right, nearest the stairway, was thinking about his wife. She had carried wine up to him during the festivities. It was one of the few nights of the war that he'd seen her, and they had laughed together, even though he was on duty. Now that peace was restored and the watch could be lightened, he looked forward to spending many more nights at home with her.

The sentry on the left was not married. His thoughts were of sailing. He wanted to buy a boat now that the seacoast was clear, and he wondered how much his armor might be worth if he were to offer it in trade. He was just turning to his companion to ask his opinion when a twang from below broke the silence. The arrow severed his vocal chords before he could speak, and the last thought in his mind was the handsome figure he would cut standing in the bow of his own boat, framed by the blue waters of the Aegean.

The other sentry heard the twang, but he was distracted by the sound of his fellow slumping over. He smiled, thinking that the other had finally given way to sleep after too much wine. He approached his companion to wake him with a jest, when the breath was knocked out of him from behind and he was pushed to the floor. He felt the cold stones of the rampart against his cheek, and then something even colder drawn across his throat.

From the platform, Odysseus signaled to Epius, who then held the staff over the reawakened fire. When it caught, he ran to the wall with it, clambered up the stairs, and waved the now flaming torch back and forth over the battlements. At another signal from Odysseus, the four men below slid the great bolt and opened the gate. Then they all stood still and waited.

They heard nothing; and despite the moonlight, they could see nothing, either. Odysseus told Epius to wave the torch again, and he did so, furiously back and forth. Again they waited, but their comrades didn't appear. Odysseus had told Agamemnon that, once he beached his ships, he should take his forces as far inland as he dared without being seen by the lookouts on the wall, and then wait for a signal. Any number of things could account for the delay. Agamemnon, out of caution, might have held the armies further down the field than he had originally planned, and they were now taking longer to cover the ground to the city. Or perhaps the ships had landed late, and the troops were presently assembling on the shore to cross the field in answer to the signal. There was no telling in the dim light how far away they were. But delays were not what the men feared. They feared their comrades were not there at all, that they had not returned. They feared a shipwreck off Tenedos, or a mutiny that forced the captains to return to Greece. In short, they feared they had been abandoned in the enemy's citadel.

Odysseus told Epius to wave the torch yet again, and he did so, but the more he waved it, the more quickly it consumed its fuel, and they had brought only one.

"If the fire goes out," whispered Pyrrhus to Odysseus, "and they haven't seen it, they'll never come."

Odysseus looked around for a moment. Then he said, "The fire won't go out. We'll light a torch they can see right through the gates." He gestured to Epius, and the carpenter knew what the command was.

He descended the steps silently and strode back to the horse with the torch. He hesitated, looking at his creation one last time, the greatest thing he had ever built. He had accepted the fact long ago that he would never be able to see it again once they returned to Greece, but he had consoled himself with the thought that at least it might stand here for others to see in years to come. Perhaps they would even admire it, once the stigma of its use had been forgotten. But that was not to be. It was to be an engine of Troy's destruction to the very end, becoming now a beacon to the invading army. He hurled the flaming brand into the hatch. It lit the inside of the horse a hellish orange.

The men had been needlessly anxious, however, for even as Epius walked back to the gate, he saw what they all saw at that moment—ghostly legions striding toward them, thousands of them, materializing out of the darkness. The only indication that they were men at all was the muffled clinking of their armor as they moved. Epius shot a glance back at the horse with an idea of rescuing it, but the inside had already caught.

Odysseus rushed down the stairs and reached the gate just as Agamemnon entered it. He clasped the chief's hand, and in the moonlight each could perceive the glint of mad ecstasy in the other's eye. For Odysseus, the master trickster, his greatest ruse of all had worked; for Agamemnon, the king of kings, Troy was about to fall to him.

In their original battle plan for this night, Odysseus and Agamemnon had intended to maintain the secrecy of their attack as long as possible, infiltrating the town quietly and killing as many Trojans in their sleep as they could before an alarm was raised, but now that they had found it necessary to set fire to the horse, they could no longer hope for a delayed discovery. So Agamemnon quickly assigned sectors of the city to those of his captains who were near him. The square began to fill with soldiers, and they stumbled over each other in the shadows. As more and more crowded in, movement through the gates slowed, leaving the majority of Greeks still outside the city in one large mass. Agamemnon, not daring to shout orders, tried in lowered tones to get his captains to move the soldiers out of the square and into the streets, but the captains themselves were restricted in movement, and, using lowered voices, could only direct those soldiers nearest to them.

In the midst of this confusion, the fire inside the horse, sucking air through the hatch and the secret holes Epius had bored into it, finally burned up through the interior of the neck. Flames shot from the holes in the eyes, and then quickly enveloped the head. Suddenly the whole square was illuminated, and the faces of the men, surprised by the sudden glare, were lit a ghastly red.

No one could tell precisely where the scream came from. It was a woman's scream, and it emanated from one of the buildings adjoining the square. She had been awakened by the crackling of the fire and the light playing upon the wall. She left her husband's side and went to the window to investigate. Then she saw the most horrifying sight of her life, and in a night which would be filled with shrieks, hers was the first.

Agamemnon was almost relieved at the sound, for it unlocked his voice at long last. He began to shout orders freely, and then his captains did likewise. The soldiers, having direction once more, followed their leaders up the streets of Troy. And the square, which so recently had resembled a pen of cattle milling nervously in the dark, now became a thoroughfare, filling from the Scaean Gates and emptying into the avenues of the city that fanned out from the marketplace like rays of light from the sun. But the strange beacon which was at the focus of these rays was nothing like the heavenly orb, said to be the fiery chariot of Apollo. Its madly dancing flames, now lapping at every part of the wooden body, seemed to rise from Erebus, for they lit up Troy, its beautiful buildings, and broad streets, in the lurid and unnatural glow of the underworld.

Priam had slept fitfully most of the night. For many hours the sound of jubilation in the square kept him awake, and while the rest of the city celebrated, he lay in bed thinking of the sons he'd lost in the war. He thought of Antiphus, who had been killed by Agamemnon. He thought of Mestor. He thought of Echemmon and Chromius, who both fell before Diomedes on the same day. He thought of Troilus, young Troilus, cut off so early in the war. He thought of Hector. He thought of Paris. The king was too old to be hopeful, too old to think of the future. Even with these thoughts in his head, however, his tired eyes did finally close, and during the last watch of the night, he lay quietly and peacefully next to his sleeping wife. Torches were being lit around the palace and servants were already up and preparing for the morning when the cries reached the palace. Priam did not hear them, but others in the household did. When the two guards at the palace gate realized that the alarm was real, one rushed inside to alert the royal family, while the other went for reinforcements. In the interim, a few members of the household took the opportunity to slip from the premises, to seek escape or asylum in another place.

The guard did not wait to knock at the royal chamber, but burst in unceremoniously. "My lord, my lady, get up! Save yourselves! The Greeks are in the city!" Without waiting for a response, he bounded to the next apartment, and the king and queen, now sitting bolt upright in their bed heard the alarm being repeated down the hall. They sat for a moment, not looking at each other, not looking at anything, but wondering if this hobgoblin of the night might disappear if they lay back in their bed once more. But the alarm inside the palace, echoed now by that from the city outside, was not a phantasm.

A frightened servant with a torch entered the chamber and awaited orders. The royal couple looked blankly at him for a moment. Then Priam roared, "My armor!"

The servant stared at the old king, astonished. Hecuba grabbed her husband, who was getting out of bed. "My lord, you can't!"

"My armor!" he shouted at the servant again. "Can't you hear?"

The servant disappeared.

"What can you do?" cried Hecuba, who got up now too. "You're old. You can't do anything."

"I can die," he said, putting on his sandals, "as my sons have. At least I can die."

The servant returned with the ancient armor and weapons, kept bright by continual polishing, but not used now for a quarter-century. The king hurriedly put on the armor, slung the shield over his shoulder, and then rushed into the corridor, his old ash wood spear in his hand.

"My lord, what will happen to your people if you die?" said Hecuba, following him. "What will happen to me?"

Ignoring her, Priam headed down to the courtyard. They could hear already the clash of arms and the sounds of fighting outside, and on their way they passed various panic-stricken members of the royal household who were looking for a place to hide or a way to escape. In the courtyard they found many of the palace women, including Andromache and her child, Astyanax. They had congregated under the sacred laurel tree at the altar to Zeus, hoping the most high god would provide them refuge. Here it was that Hecuba grabbed her husband once more.

"You must stop, my lord! This is madness!"

She clung to his arm, and it was a measure of her strength and his weakness that he could not shake free. Perhaps it was the realization of that feebleness that filled the old man with rage. Instead of trying to pull free, he turned on her angrily and grasped her arms tightly, holding her in front of him. The old queen winced audibly with the pain and her eyes filled with tears. It was the first time he had ever handled her roughly, and the sound of her faint cry shocked him. The anger drained from his face, and he loosened his grip.

"Please, my lord," she sobbed quietly. "Take off your armor. Stay with us here by the laurel tree. They will not hurt you on Zeus's altar. You must not die. Your people need you now more than ever."

Priam hung his head sadly for a moment, then took off his helmet. She helped him remove the rest of the armor, and then piled it neatly under the laurel. He joined the women, and fell to his knees before the altar. He prayed silently to Zeus that the most high god would take care of his wife, his queen, his companion of forty years, if he himself should die.

Few inside the palace knew how well it was protected, or even if it were protected at all. The guard who had gone for reinforcements returned only to find Pyrrhus and the Myrmidons already at the gate. A battle ensued, but the palace guards, greatly outnumbered, could delay the Greeks but little. When the Trojans were all killed or dispersed, the Myrmidons picked up a stout plank, and in four thrusts battered down the gate. Inside, they met the palace's last defense, a hastily-gathered band of Trojans under the leadership of Deiphobus. These fought the Myrmidons at the threshold, and were able to hold them off awhile, since the Greeks could not put into play their numerical advantage. But eventually the Trojans

218

were driven back. Deiphobus himself stumbled as he was retreating, and a Myrmidon soldier, wielding a club, struck his skull, crushing it.

Priam's youngest son, Polites, was among the Trojans at the gate. He had come there with a weapon in his hand, but a boy of thirteen was no match for experienced swordsmen. He stayed in the back, and when this last bastion of the palace collapsed, he ran. Pyrrhus, seeing him flee, pursued him. There was of course nowhere to go. The palace, like the city itself, was a fortress, as good at locking people in as locking them out. But the boy sought the only refuge he knew, the sacred precinct in the courtyard, and it was here that Pyrrhus caught up with him. Achilles' son took only hasty note of the others gathered there in the moonlight, the women and the old man. His attention was on the boy, whose age he did not guess at. He only knew that he had lately been among the palace defenders, but now he was leaning over with both hands on the altar, catching his breath. Pyrrhus drew back his spear. There was an impassioned cry of "*No!*" from the group of women, but the spear was already in the air. It transfixed the boy from back to front, and he fell upon the altar, his blood flowing onto the smooth stone.

Hecuba ran screaming to her son, and the other women gathered around her, but her husband went calmly to the trunk of the laurel tree where the queen had piled his armor. He lifted his ash spear and stepped out to face the Greek.

Pyrrhus, his sword in hand and ready now to leave the courtyard to explore other parts of the palace, was taken aback by the sight of one so ancient brandishing a weapon. "Who are you, old man?" he asked.

The Myrmidons had now gathered in the courtyard

behind their young chief, and one of them told him that it was the king who faced him, Priam of Troy.

Achilles' son looked at the old man. "Come, Priam," he said, "I'll take you prisoner. Put down your spear. You're no match for me." Pyrrhus had, however, thrown his shield in front of him when he first saw the spear, and now Priam recognized it, even in the dim light of the courtyard. It was Hector's shield, the ceremonial shield his son had never worn in battle. Now it was stained with the blood of his people. Priam raised his spear, so heavy in his old arms, and heaved it at the Greek. It fell harmlessly to the ground several feet short of where the young warrior stood.

Pyrrhus now hardened his features and took on the dark look that so many had quaked to behold in his father. He cried out an incoherent sound and lunged at the old king. Hecuba left her bleeding son, and would have run between the two men, but she was held back by the other women. Priam, with neither armor nor shield, stood without defense, and it was only because of a reckless swing on Pyrrhus's part that he was able to dodge the first blow. The awkward movement, however, was a strain on his old limbs, and Priam's legs crumpled beneath him. Pyrrhus then bestrode him. He was enraged first by the king's defiance, and now by his own faulty blow, which all his men had witnessed.

He raised his sword over his head but then stopped for a moment before letting it fall. He looked around the courtyard. The women gazed at him horror-struck, and in their midst, Hecuba, sobbing, pleaded with all the gods of Olympus to grant her husband another hour's life. On the other side, the Myrmidon troops also watched him. The significance of the moment was not lost upon them. After ten years of war, they had finally penetrated the great citadel of Troy, penetrated its very palace, and now had Troy's proud king in their power. In a moment, the last trace of Trojan sovereignty, Trojan integrity, would be gone. And yet, though they had strived so mightily for just this end, some of the soldiers were mortified by the sight before them: a pitiful old man lying prostrate at the feet of their young leader. They watched the sword. It hung motionless in the air for one eternal instant between past and future, life and death, all that had been and all that would be.

Pyrrhus looked at the king once more, and with all his might swung the blade. Priam gazed at his son's fine shield, with its wondrous surrounding wall, its beautiful images of the gods, and its lovely horse at the center. The old man's head, severed from his body, rolled to the side, while his heart pumped the last of his blood onto the grass of the courtyard.

Pyrrhus bent over and was about to lift the head by its white hairs to display it in triumph to his troops, but then hesitated and decided to let it be. He straightened himself, stepped over the body, and rejoined his army. Leaving a few men to guard the women, he led the rest out of the courtyard to search the remainder of the palace.

Greeks ranged through the streets of Troy, and the night was filled with shrieks, some from men dying, others from women raped in their beds while their husbands bled upon the floor. Soldiers entered buildings looking first for resistance, then women, then loot. When everything of value had been removed, they set the buildings afire, and Troy burned.

The sack of a city, then as now, is not the mission of an army; it is the reward. It follows no rules; it is the ultimate prize in the game. Though it was true that captured men were usually killed, captured women usually taken alive as concubines or slaves, and children killed or sold into slavery depending on their ages, this procedure did not develop from some ethical code. It was merely the result of crude logic. Men, if left alive, could live to take revenge, something women and children rarely did. And after a city had been thoroughly unpeopled and looted, it was usually destroyed. Soldiers did not burn a city to prevent it from rising again and threatening their children, but merely for the ecstatic joy humans find in destruction.

It was the Locrians, a contingent from central Greece, who reached the Temple to Athena first. They were led by a man of diminuitive stature named Ajax, who often suffered the jests of his fellow captains for having the same name as the great fighter from Salamis. While the other Ajax lived, the Locrian chief had been called "Little Ajax" to distinguish him, and this appellation so irked him that he was secretly happy when his namesake killed himself.

Ajax had asked Odysseus for directions to the temple. The Palladium was now gone, but he hoped the building might still contain some treasures, though his men were somewhat timid about ransacking such a sacred place. Greeks and Trojans worshipped the same gods, and feared retribution if they angered the powerful war goddess. But the Locrians also feared their chief's temper, and so they followed, torches in hand, as he led them into the great structure.

Even amid the noise of this terrible night, the crackling fires and the dreadful cries, the temple seemed to offer a haven, a place apart. The horrible sounds were muffled inside, and they seemed to die among the massive columns. Of course, the Locrians were disappointed by the barrenness they found within. There was neither statuary nor ornamentation of any kind, just a large central cavity, surrounded by pillars. The Trojans had purposely kept the area clear so that they could use it for dancing and processions in honor of the goddess. Ajax was particularly disgusted, but lest he leave a stone unturned, he had his men walk through the temple to search for anything of value that might lay hidden in the shadows. The soldiers searched, and, way at the back, they found the only treasure the temple had to offer.

Cassandra was crouching down, shivering, holding onto one of the great pillars, and she screamed when they laid their hands on her. So dire was the scream that the soldiers released their grip, but the cry brought their chief, and he marveled at the find. His status was not high among the Greeks, and his rewards at the divisions of spoil had never been equal to those of Diomedes, or of Odysseus, or of his namesake. Never had he been given a beautiful girl such as this.

"Bring her out onto the floor," he ordered them.

They laid hold of her again, and again she screamed: "Don't! Please don't!"

Again the men hesitated, and one of them spoke timorously to their chief. "My lord, she might be a priestess or a votary of the goddess."

"A priestess? So what!" roared Ajax.

"It would be sacrilege," the soldier whispered.

Sneering at his men's timidity, Ajax pushed them aside and grabbed one of the girl's arms himself. He jerked it away from the pillar, and she cried again: "Don't, please! The lady will punish you!"

"Punish me?" he said as he tried to pry her other hand away. "Why punish me? I'm not going to hurt you. What do you think I am?"

"A toad," she cried, "an ugly toad, and the lady will punish you."

One of the soldiers snickered. Ajax heard it and looked around at them, enraged. The men avoided his eyes. Then he frowned at the girl, drew back his hand, and gave her a blow to the face that sent her sprawling. Blood bubbled from her lips onto her chin, and a tooth spilled out onto the polished floor of the temple. Ajax dragged her away from the columns and tore open her garments. She screamed once more.

"Be quiet!" he yelled, and when she continued shrieking, he hit her in the face again, and the blow made a hideous cracking sound. She began to gag on the blood in her mouth, and coughed uncontrollably. Ajax, undeterred, pushed her legs apart, and when she felt his rough hand on her most tender, most private part, she screamed again, an astonished, hopeless scream that sent shudders through the men watching. Despite the throbbing pain in her jaw, she tried to sit up to push him away, but he hit her a third time, knocking her down, and before she could rise again, she felt his whole weight come down on top of her. She felt his face and his breath hotly near her own, and she tried to scream, but he put his hand over her mouth. Then she felt another pain, worse than that in her jaw. She looked widly at the soldiers standing around them, as if entreating one of them to save her, but they did not help. Some looked at her sadly in silence. Others, fearful of sacrilege, turned away uneasily, not daring to watch.

Agamemnon did not take an active part in the sack. In a sense, his reward had already come. A share of the women and the loot would be set aside for him in any case, when the best prizes were distributed at the end. So once his officers and men had been dispersed to the various sectors of town, and the destruction had begun, he was content to walk the streets alone. He had never seen the inside of this city, which he had sought for so many years. The streets were wide, as he had heard, and the buildings, illuminated now by a hundred fires, were stately.

He made his way up the main thoroughfare that led to the palace, and along the way he met Odysseus and a small band of Ithacans. Under his orders, Odysseus had gone to Antenor's house to make certain the old man was not harmed. Since Zeus had ordained that Antenor would be the means by which they gained the city, the chief felt the old man should be spared in duty to the god. Agamemnon had, in fact, told Odysseus to protect the whole family, but the Ithacan reported that one son, his last, Laocoön, had resisted even their protection, and had to be killed. Antenor and his wife, however, were safe.

Agamemnon and Odysseus then continued toward the palace, and they reached the vicinity of the temple just as Ajax was leaving it with his men and with Cassandra. She was being supported by two of the soldiers as they descended the steps.

"It looks like Little Ajax has found a prize already," said Odysseus.

"Who is she?" asked the chief.

The Ithacan squinted his eyes. In the firelight he could see the dress of a princess, and the long, disheveled hair. "I think it's Cassandra, Priam's daughter."

"The mad one?"

"I think so. She must have gone to the temple for sanctuary."

Agamemnon looked at the girl, so helpless in the hands of the soldiers, her garments torn and bloodstained. He approached the Locrian, and when Ajax saw him coming toward him, he stopped where he was on the steps and eyed the chief suspiciously.

"Do you know who she is?" Agamemnon shouted to him.

Ajax looked puzzled. "No. A priestess or something. I don't know."

"And you took her from the temple by force?"

"Why not? I found her. She's mine."

Agamemnon narrowed his eyes at the little man. "You're a fool, Ajax. Let her go. And if you know what's good for you, you'll get back in that temple and pray the goddess doesn't take revenge on you and your men—for what you did to her."

Ajax was about to resist, but he heard his soldiers murmuring. He knew they agreed with Agamemnon, and he could not make them stand against the chief. He motioned disgustedly to his two men to release her, and when they did, she crumpled to the steps. Then Ajax turned to his superior once more. "Take her. She's yours. But I'll be damned if I'll pray to Athena for her." With that he left, and his relieved men followed him.

When they were gone, Agamemnon approached her. Her face was purple and swollen with bruises, and her chin caked with blood. He knelt down on the steps in front of her, but she did not appear to see him. Though her eyes were wide open, they seemed blank. The chief looked deeply into her face, and without turning away said quietly to Odysseus, "Guard her. See that no more harm comes to her."

It was in the eastern suburbs of the city, near the Dardanian Gates, that the Trojans had the most warning. Aeneas lived in this district, as did most of his fighting forces. Like many other Trojans, he had drunk his fill of wine the night before, to celebrate but also to forget the long years of war and the loss of so much and so many. If the wine banished such thoughts from his waking brain, however, it had little effect on his dreams, for he dreamt of Hector this night.

He would never have counted his cousin Hector as a close friend. The tension between the two branches of the family, the faint reverberations of a feud long past, had always stood between them. While Hector lived, the two treated each other with correctness and respect, but never with warmth. Aeneas was sorry when Hector died, of course, but he did not mourn as one would for a friend.

In this dream, however, Hector was looking at him cordially, as he never had in life. Aeneas had just walked into a room in the palace where the prince was giving orders to some of his lieutenants. Hector might have been irked by the interruption and merely given Aeneas a cool glance, but instead he smiled pleasantly, almost shyly, at his cousin. Aeneas was surprised at such a show of friendliness, and stood there for what seemed like a long time enjoying the warmth of his smile. But then he noticed Hector's clothing. It was torn and covered with blood and dust. It looked just as it had the last time Aeneas had seen Hector, as his cousin was being dragged behind Achilles' chariot. He wondered why Hector had not changed his garments, and he was about to ask him how he had escaped Achilles, when Hector raised his hand to his cousin. He motioned for Aeneas to leave the room, yet it was such a mild gesture and accompanied by such a friendly smile that Aeneas could take no offence.

He was just turning to leave the room when he heard his name called. It was being called loudly, from outside the room, outside the palace, indeed, outside the whole universe of his dream.

"My lord, Aeneas, wake up! There are cries in the street!"

It was his wife, Creusa. Even in his bewildered state, still partly in his dream, still affected by the wine, he could hear the cries. He stumbled out of bed and to the window, but he could see nothing. Then he made for the ladder and mounted to the roof of the house. Several of his neighbors were also on their roofs, all looking toward the threatening red glow in the distance.

"The city's on fire!" he heard one of his neighbors say.

Someone had been careless the night before, Aeneas thought. Someone who had drunk too much had left his fire blazing, and now the city was in flames. They had defeated one foe only to succumb now to another. Aeneas was about to climb down to join in whatever rescue operations there would be when he heard a cry: "The Greeks! The Greeks are in the city!" He ran back to the edge of the roof to look down, and there he saw citizens fleeing from the heart of the city toward the Dardanian Gates. "The Greeks!" he heard again.

He bolted down to his rooms and strapped on his armor, barely aware of his wife's questions. In the street he met many of his men who had also been awakened by the alarms. Since their district lay the furthest from the Scaean Gates, he had time to organize them into a small resistance. They hastened in the direction from which the crowd ran, and they encountered the enemy several streets away. It was Diomedes' army that they met.

Diomedes was surprised to find a mass of armed troops in his way, but he was not displeased. He did not much like the idea of slitting men's throats in their sleep, and he had purposely volunteered to take his contingent into the farthest reaches of the city to search for any real fighting forces. Agamemnon agreed with the plan, and sent his own herald, Talthybius, with Diomedes to guide him. Talthybius was the only Greek besides Odysseus who had been in Troy before and who knew his way around. Now that they had found an actual army to fight, Diomedes ordered an attack, and the battle was joined, the first of the whole war to take place at night.

Both the darkness and the narrowness of the fighting space, which prevented outflanking maneuvers, helped the Trojans, but these benefits were balanced by their much smaller numbers and their poor fighting condition. Most of them had been sleeping off the effects of too much wine and too much food a mere twenty minutes before. The best they could hope for was to delay the Greek forces a little while and then succumb to a soldier's death, content at least that they did not die in their beds. For a while, as he swung his sword in the confused darkness, Aeneas was content with such a conclusion. He would have lived an honorable life, died an honorable death, a defender of Troy to the last.

What made him change his mind and decide to escape was not fear. Like most warriors, he had made his peace with death long ago, and no longer trembled at it. Perhaps it was the opportunity he had to save his men and his family—his wife, his son, his father. He had the power to keep them from death or slavery, and he loved them enough to do it. Or perhaps it was the last ember of that smoldering resentment his family felt for their kinfolk in the palace. He had, after all, given ten years of his life so that his cousins could remain princes and he their subject. Perhaps ten years was enough, and eternity too much. Perhaps the idea even crossed his mind that with the other line extinguished, he would take their place as the rightful king of the Trojans, should any Trojans survive. Perhaps most important of all, though, was the glimpse Aeneas had of futility, the futility of the war fought and lost, and now the futility of his own death. Though he was no philosopher, Aeneas was intelligent enough to see that the city was doomed, and nothing he could do would change that.

He called some of his lieutenants around him and told them they were going to retreat. At an appointed signal, the Trojan line would fall back, and all would fly in different directions, trusting to the darkness and their superior knowledge of the city streets to make good their escape. They were to gather their families and whatever goods they could take quickly and make for the Dardanian Gates. The lieutenants spread the word, and when Aeneas was confident that all knew the plan, he gave the signal.

Diomedes was near the front when the Trojan line

suddenly evaporated. So quickly did they disappear into the darkness that he suspected a trap, and held his men where they were for several moments before pursuing. When he finally did pursue, he saw that the massed force they had been fighting was completely dispersed. Yet he did not dare allow his own army to disperse in pursuit while in so heavily armed a sector of the city. Instead, he kept his men together and, following Talthybius's directions, proceeded slowly through the streets. The slowness of his progress allowed Aeneas's plan to succeed.

Word of the escape spread quickly, and when Aeneas reached his own house, Creusa was already waiting at the door with their son and all that the servants could gather from within. Only old Anchises was missing.

"Where's my father?" shouted Aeneas.

"He's inside," said Creusa. "I can't get him to leave."

"Take the boy," said Aeneas. "Take the servants and everything. When you get out of the gates, go up into the hills. My men will be there. I'll find you." He embraced his wife once, briefly, and then lost her in the darkness. He entered the house.

The old man was seated by the window, from which he could see the glare of the fires as they approached this easternmost part of the city. When he heard Aeneas enter, he did not turn to look at him, but acknowledged his presence only by beginning to speak. "Damn Priam," he said. "It was the horse, wasn't it?"

"I don't know."

"Zeus the Cloud Squatter! It must have been the horse. Damned fool, Priam. Always a damned fool. And now the city's on fire. My city as much as his."

"Father, you've got to leave."

"You go. I don't care to." He said it offhandedly, as if he were refusing a joint of mutton instead of his life. "Well, he'll die for it, damned fool; that's for sure. Him and all his sons. They'll die for it, and so will we."

"Father, we don't have to. The Greeks haven't reached here yet. The Dardanian Gates are still open."

"You go. I'm too old. I'll just slow you down."

"Slow me down? I've seen you walk to those gates a thousand times. What's the matter?"

The old man hesitated, then said quietly, "I fell down. Probably broke my damn leg. I can't go."

"I'll carry you."

"You can't carry me. Just leave me."

Aeneas ignored the command. He went to his father and bent over in front of him. Anchises hesitated momentarily, then cursed under his breath and put his arms reluctantly around his son's neck. Aeneas hoisted him up.

"You should have been king, you know," Anchises said. "You would have been a good one. So would I," he added. "Zeus the Cloud Squatter, I would."

Diomedes wanted to cut off the Trojans' last avenue of retreat. At a good run, his army could easily reach the Dardanian Gates before many of the citizens, but his progress was bogged down by the maze of streets in this sector of the city. Though Talthybius knew the Trojan market area well, and the broad thoroughfare that led to the palace and the temple, his knowledge of the old Dardanian suburbs was scanty. He knew where the gates were only in a general way, and negotiating the narrow alleys and lanes to get there, especially in the dark, was extremely difficult. Rather than taking the whole army on a circuitous route, Diomedes called a halt and sent the herald ahead to find the shortest way.

Talthybius did not like the idea of venturing out into the hostile streets alone, but there was no point in disputing the idea with Diomedes. He left the army and directed his steps to the only place in this sector that he knew how to get to with any certainty, Aeneas's house,

231

where he had stayed on a previous visit to Troy. He was fairly sure that it was close to the Dardanian Gates, and he might find his way from there. The herald stuck close to the buildings, lest he be seen and recognized as a Greek, but he need not have worried. When he finally did encounter Trojans a few streets away, they took no notice of the solitary figure. They were too intent on their flight, as the noise and the flames got closer to this last remaining section of the city.

When Talthybius reached Aeneas's house, there was no reason to go any further. The shortest path to the gates was clearly indicated by the crowds of fleeing citizens clogging the streets. Some were in horse-drawn wagons, which they had filled with their possessions. Others rode horses, upon which they'd slung merely food and blankets. But most were on foot, content to escape with their lives. Many carried children, or pulled them at their side, and the children, who could comprehend only the terror, cried and shrieked. Animals, too, were racing for the gates, cows, goats, sheep, horses, as if the very livestock were afraid of the Greeks.

Content that he'd accomplished his mission, the herald was about to turn and retrace his steps to Diomedes when he saw the strange figure emerge from the doorway. Too tall to negotiate the portal at its full height, it had to duck to come out onto the street, and once out it heaved its upper part a bit higher as if to right itself. The herald recognized the monster to be a man carrying another on his back, and even in the dim light and the confusion he recognized the bearer to be Aeneas. The herald ducked into the shadow so that his erstwhile host would not see him, but Aeneas, encumbered as he was, did not even turn to look around. Once he had shifted the weight to a more manageable position, he joined the frenzied multitude and headed up the street toward the gates.

Talthybius stood in the darkness and watched Aeneas go, watched till the unwieldly figure was swallowed up by the crowd and borne out of sight, and even then the herald did not move. He stayed and watched the strange procession of humanity until it thinned to a mere trickle, and the sound of their clamor faded into the distance. It was only when the streets both in front of him and behind were finally deserted that he quit his vantage point and made his way back to the waiting Greek army.

XII

The Fire

By morning, the whole city was in flames. So rapid was the progress of the fire that the loot and captives had to be herded out of Troy so they would not be consumed. A hasty village of tents was constructed on the plain before the city to house the Greeks during the division of spoils, and all morning long a steady stream of men and material flowed from the Scaean Gates down to the shore. The cries of the previous night were replaced by the shouts of soldiers and the clatter of wagons as the city's wealth was removed from Troy.

Agamemnon stood inside the gates, in the great open square of the marketplace, protected from the fire by its very openness, but ringed now by buildings in flames or in smoldering ruins. He could hear the creaking sound as structures leaned over, their supports burned out from under them. He could hear the occasional crash as a building collapsed, sending up a cloud of dust and smoke. He stood near the oak tree that had grown in the center of the square and had offered shade to citizen and foreign merchant alike. Now it was only a black skeleton, but shade was not needed today. The smoke and ash in the air obscured the sun, which would otherwise have shone brightly on this summer morning. The smoke burned in Agamemnon's lungs, but he felt a compulsion to stand here, *inside* the city gates, near the wall that had thwarted him so long. He stood and watched as the city burned and crumbled before his eyes.

Near him on the ground lay the charred remains of the wooden horse. Only the rollers survived, their tops scorched, but the logs otherwise intact. The trick had worked. It had been an absurd idea, and he hadn't liked it, but it had worked, and now Troy was his. Yet he wished he had been able to conquer the city some other way. He knew now why he had objected to the ruse, though he hadn't been aware of his reasons at the time. The more lunatic the scheme, the more certain it would be remembered if it succeeded. The story of Odysseus's trick would someday overshadow the story of his own victory. The fate of Troy would be forever linked not with his own name as the conqueror, but with the means by which he conquered. The gods had not lied to him. He did indeed take the city, but the undying fame he had hoped for would reside instead in the monstrous horse.

He stared at the embers and thought of home. All had not been well in Greece when he left ten years ago. Mycenae had once dominated the other Greek states, dominated in fact all the eastern Aegean, but things had been changing. There was strife and feuding and discontent throughout the Greek peninsula, and it was mirrored in his own land, even in his own family. When he was chosen to lead this grand expedition, he convinced himself that victory abroad would end the troubles at home. Now victory was attained, but he wondered if a few shiploads of loot and captive women would really change anything. He had learned over the last ten years what little control he or anyone else actually had over events. If he had such limited power as supreme head of a vast army, could he hope to have more when he went back to being a peacetime leader of a single province? He shook his head and had a momentary vision of his own civilization crumbling into ruin, just as the city around him was collapsing at his feet.

From behind him, a voice suddenly demanded, "Where is she?"

The chief turned around. It was Menelaus. Were Agamemnon less distracted by his own thoughts, he might have been shocked by the look on his brother's face. It was a look of terror. To be sure it was hidden behind a mask of anger and indignation, but the fear beneath the mask was palpable.

"She's in my tent," said the chief.

Menelaus opened his mouth as if he would speak again, but then abruptly turned on his heel and left. Without emotion, Agamemnon watched him as he headed in the direction of the tents. Then the chief turned back to the pile of smoldering timbers before him, and in the rising smoke he saw the image of his daughter, Iphigenia. He saw her as he had seen her so many times, her head thrown back and singing at the top of her lungs in the woods around Mycenae. Of all the thousands who had died for the attainment of this prize, this city, she had been the first. Agamemnon tried to recall what her voice sounded like, but he could not. Her image dissolved, in any case, and he watched as the thin wisps of smoke rose to join the unnatural dark cloud overhead.

Helen had been surprised by the youth of the warrior who had found her. He was Achilles' son, she gathered, a boy not even twenty, yet he ordered around men who were more than twice his age. Pyrrhus had found her in her apartment during his search of the palace the previous night. She had made no attempt to hide or escape. Nor had she sought refuge at the altar as the other palace women had. She seemed content to perish in her room if no one found her. Many in the army, no doubt, would have been happy had she done so, or if the chief had

236

summarily dispatched her. Many of the captive women, too, probably wished her dead, but the chief was happy to leave her fate up to her husband.

Pyrrhus had treated her courteously. He told her to find a veil among her things, and once she had it on, he conducted her out of the palace and out of the city. She remained under guard on the plain until the tents were pitched, and then she was escorted to Agamemnon's own. Pyrrhus, however, was the only Greek captain she had seen. Even the chief had not visited her.

She knew the interview that was coming. She had imagined it many times over in the last ten years. She had imagined what her husband would say to her, and how she would respond. She imagined a hundred things she wanted to say to him but would not say. How could she tell him that she had never hated him, never wanted to cause him pain? How could she explain that her own shortcomings had made her leave him, and not any failings on his part? She couldn't say these things, because they would sound like excuses and lies, self-serving lies, and maybe that's what they were. She no longer knew.

But it wasn't just excuses she wanted to tell him. Oddly enough, she wanted to tell him about Troy, the lovely city she had lived in for ten years, the city the Greeks had just destroyed. Oh, the ten years of war had taken their toll on the city and its citizens, to be sure, but still, it was Troy, and she wanted to describe it to him. She wanted to tell him about the people, what a happy people they were, and the pride they had in their city—its wide streets, its gardens, its handsome buildings. She wanted to tell him about the things she had seen, the music and poetry she'd heard, the beautiful hymns to the gods and wonderful stories of the ancient heroes. Who would she ever tell these things to if not to him? But she could never tell him. Perhaps she would not even live long enough to tell him.

He could, in a rage, kill her. He could easily justify it both as revenge for what she'd done to him and as a small atonement for all the men who had died contesting over her. Or he might spare her life for what might be a worse fate, to bring her home and make her a menial and concubine in her own house, serving him both in bed and in the kitchen, lower than the servants who had once served her, lower than her daughter, who could now order her about. Who would blame him for degrading her this way?

Perhaps she deserved either fate, perhaps neither. She didn't ponder such things anymore. She had reached the age where the unresolvable ambiguities of life supplant the simple glories of right and wrong. There was really only life, and there was death.

The tent was furnished sparingly enough, but there was a chair for her to sit in, and she sat facing away from the entrance. She heard the flap of the cloth as her husband entered, but she did not move.

Menelaus stood for a long moment watching her from behind, as if trying to recognize her first from that perspective. He noted her hair, which was the same color it had been, but it was shorter now, and did not shine as it had. He looked at her shoulders, and he remembered them. They were bare except for the two ends of her bodice, held up by brooches. He had always admired her shoulders for not sloping like so many women's, and he used to enjoy stroking them when it was his right.

"Stand up," he ordered.

She obeyed, and turned to face him.

It was this moment that he had been dreading, more, perhaps, even than she. They looked into each other's eyes, but only briefly. Helen, to avoid any appearance of defiance, lowered hers immediately, but Menelaus continued to stare at her face. She was older. Her beauty had been so legendary that he had half-expected her never to age at all, but she had aged. She could no longer be taken for a girl, as she might have been when he saw her last. She was a woman now, well into her thirties. He noted her dress, which, of course, he had never seen before. It was dyed a deep blue, a color the city was known for. In the days before the war, Trojan blue cloth was prized throughout the Aegean. He could make out her thin figure under the dress. It had not changed. He remembered the first time they had ever been like this, alone in a room facing each other. He pushed the thought from his mind.

He said slowly, "I'm going to have to kill you."

Helen did not respond, either in word or gesture.

"You can't be allowed to survive this," he continued. "You understand that."

She nodded quickly, resignedly, and did not raise her eyes.

"Too many have died," he went on. "Everyone will expect it." He paused, then asked, "Do you have anything to say to me?"

Without raising her head, she said, "I only wish I'd died ten years ago, my lord."

Her voice was as he remembered it. Hearing her say his name the night before had put him in mind of it, but now to hear her speak a complete sentence brought back the full memory. She had a distinctive voice, lower and deeper than was common in women. It had always been a source of pleasure to him, but he put this thought out of his mind too.

"Yes," he said quietly, "it would have been better if you had died then."

They stood together in silence. Menelaus wanted to say more, ask her more questions, hear more from her, but he knew there was no reason. There could be no extenuation for what she'd done, and to prolong the interview further merely showed his own weakness. She deserved to die, and he must be the one to kill her. He reached for his dagger.

Though Helen remained silent with her eyes cast down, her senses were alive to every sound and motion. As she heard him draw his weapon, her mind raced.

"Would you rather sit down?" he asked.

She closed her eyes and shook her head.

"Very well," he said. He paused, then stepped up to within striking distance of her. He paused again.

Beauty, she kept thinking, beauty had to be the answer. The gods had given it to her, and the gifts of the gods cannot be scorned. Paris had always said that. Others saw beauty as a blessing; she had seen it as a curse, but it was the same gift, wasn't it? Never in her life had she used her beauty for her own advantage—never—because to do so would be to admit that it was a blessing as well as a curse. But now her life was about to end.

Menelaus raised the dagger.

Blessing? Curse? What's the difference, she thought. It was both. It had to be, because nothing is ever just one thing or another.

She looked up at him, and as she did so, she lifted her hands to the top of her bodice and undid the two brooches which held it up. The garment fell to her waist.

Her breasts were small. They had always been small. In her early adolescence, she had hoped they would never grow at all, and she almost got her wish. Later, when she learned that most men preferred large breasts, she wondered that Menelaus and then Paris could find hers so very beautiful, small as they were. She wondered no longer.

Menelaus stared at her. A look of bewilderment came over his face, and he lowered the knife.

She breathed deeply. There is, after all, only life, and there is death.

The boy was happy to reenter the city. Too young to comprehend what had befallen it, he enjoyed seeing the dancing fires, which still raged everywhere except in the open marketplace. He rather liked the jolly, balding man who accompanied him, too. The man asked him if he could climb the steps to the wall by himself, and the boy said he could, even though the height of each step was nearly up to his waist. When he tried to pull himself up the first one unsuccessfully, the jolly man laughed, then heaved him up onto his shoulders.

"I'll carry you, like a horse," he said, and the boy laughed to see the grown man snort and whinny as if he were a beast.

When they reached the top, Odysseus sat Astyanax on the wall so that both of them could look out. The division of the treasure and captives had taken up most of the day, but now it was done, and the Greeks loading the ships with their booty cast long shadows in the late afternoon sun. The man and the boy watched them move about on the shore.

Odysseus was pleased with the outcome of the disposition, especially of the palace women, who were the most important prizes and might have caused the most rivalry. The other captains were surprised that Agamemnon chose for himself the mad girl Cassandra, whom Little Ajax had raped in the temple, but Odysseus wasn't. He had seen the way the chief looked at her on the steps the previous night. The other captains were equally surprised that Odysseus chose Hecuba instead of a younger woman. The old queen's incessant moans and curses alarmed all those around her, and the soldiers had begun referring to her as "the Stygian bitch" after one of the furies of the underworld. But Odysseus didn't care about her complaints; her scolding put him in mind of his old nurse. She'd stop moaning eventually, in any case, and then she'd be more useful and do more work around his palace in Ithaca than a girl would. Besides, there was his wife, Penelope, to consider. Let the others choose young concubines if they wanted. There was nothing Odysseus valued more than peace at home.

He wasn't at all surprised that Menelaus decided to take Helen back and let her resume her former life as queen. The chief's brother was a fool anyway, and he'd gotten what he deserved. Odysseus would never have let her survive the war if she were his wife, but then Odysseus would never have gone to such lengths to retrieve her in the first place. Well, good riddance to both of them, in any case, Odysseus thought. It wasn't his concern any longer.

Pyrrhus asked for Hector's widow, Andromache, as his prize, even though she was several years older than he. The chief agreed. On Odysseus's advice, however, the disposition of Hector's son, Astyanax, was withheld from Pyrrhus, and mother and child were separated, despite the passionate entreaties of Andromache. The closest the Greeks came to trouble was when Pyrrhus asked to sacrifice one of Priam's daughters on Achilles' tomb. Even after a night of slaughter, this seemed especially brutal to the other captains. To Odysseus it seemed merely pointless. But Pyrrhus's status and the respect the others still had for his father induced Agamemnon to agree to it, so a young woman named Polyxena was chosen, and Pyrrhus dragged her up the coast to the burial mound and wielded the knife himself.

Diomedes alone among the great captains declined to take one of the palace women. He seemed unusually moody since the sack, and so the others did not question him about it. He accepted only treasure enough to reward his men, and then seemed anxious to go home.

When the disposition was over, old Antenor and his wife, Theano, were set free. During the sack, Odysseus had kept them under close guard to protect them from the Greek soldiers, and during the disposition he kept them no less closely guarded to protect them from the Trojan captives, who suspected them of treachery and might have tried to kill them. Antenor, for his part, gladly would have accepted such a sentence, realizing that it was through his agency that the city was lost. Odysseus told him not to blame himself for what had happened. It was the will of the gods, after all, and Antenor had merely done what he thought was right. But Antenor would take no consolation. Agamemnon offered the old couple passage anywhere the Greeks were sailing on their homeward jouney. They chose Cyrene, and Odysseus offered to land them there himself on his way back to Ithaca, but they would under no circumstances sail with him. So it was decided they would travel with Menelaus instead, which suited Odysseus just fine anyway. He had no use for grudges.

So now the job was done, all but one last duty. Agamemnon could go home to rule again in Mycenae, Menelaus in Sparta. Old Nestor could live out the rest of his days in retirement in Pylos while his stout sons went about his business. Diomedes could return to Tiryns, Philoctetes to Thessaly. Pyrrhus could go to Achilles' kingdom of Phthia and wield the scepter his father never got to hold, and even Little Ajax could return to Locris, the only place where he could play king. Odysseus would take longer to get home, of course, than the others, since his rocky island lay far on the other side of the Greek mainland, but he was a good sailor, and he would enjoy the journey. Besides, he would be bringing home more than enough wealth to justify his absence.

Odysseus smiled and looked at the boy, whose small legs dangled over the side of the wall. "What do you see out there?"

"Horses," said Astyanax, and he pointed to where a brace of snowy white mounts was being led from the plain to the shore.

"Ah," said Odysseus nodding, "you're a horseman like your father. Do you remember your father?"

Not taking his eyes from the plain, the boy patted the top of his head with his hand and pronounced the word, "Helmet."

Odysseus laughed. "Yes. I've seen the helmet. I even owned his shield for a while. Did you ever see his shield?"

The boy shook his head vigorously.

"Oh, it was a fine shield, a very fine shield, until Pyrrhus got it all battered up. Now it looks like the bottom of an old pot, the kind you cook vegetables in." He laughed again, and the boy laughed too.

"Your father was going to be king, you know."

"King!" the boy repeated.

"Yes, and you too. You would have been king, and worn a crown, like your grandfather."

The boy looked at him quizzically.

"But you couldn't be king of Troy anymore," said Odysseus. "We'd have to call this 'Pyropolis.' " He put together the two Greek words meaning "fire" and "city." "Yes, you'd be king of Pyropolis!"

The boy realized that the jolly man was making a joke again. Astyanax laughed at the sound of the funny word the man had made up.

"Yes," said Odysseus. "Pyropolis. But Pyropolis doesn't need a king." Still smiling, the Ithacan stepped behind Astyanax, slipped his hands under the boy's arms, and lifted him high into the air over his head.

244

"Come on," he said, "take a better look at those horses."

Astyanax giggled, partly because of the tickling sensation under his arms, and partly because the jolly man was whisking him around like his father used to when the two would play together. Odysseus laughed again and then held Astyanax over the edge of the wall, the boy squirming with delight.

"No," said Odysseus, "Troy doesn't need a king anymore."

Miles away on the slopes of Mt. Ida a small group of people looked for shelter in the wooded hills on this, their first night away from Troy. Many had found friends and relatives among their fellow survivors, for almost all of them were of the Dardanian tribe and had lived near each other in the eastern sector of Troy. They settled down on the hillside and took an inventory of the stores they had rescued from the city. One among them, however, a close relative of the royal family and now their leader, looked for his wife.

The servants told Aeneas that Creusa had become separated from them in the rush for the gates, and though they had his son, his wife had never rejoined them. He searched all day among the various groups of survivors inquiring about her. By sunset he had seen each individual who escaped, but none had seen her leave the city. He gave up his search and returned to his father.

The old man had had his leg set by a physician, and now he sat by himself on a slope overlooking the still-burning city. Aeneas came and sat by his side, and both watched the fire in silence.

After a long time, the old man said simply, "I'm sorry."

Aeneas nodded. "Maybe she's better off dead. God knows what'll happen to us."

His father was quiet for a few moments more, then said, "We could go to Chrysa. They were an ally. They might let us settle."

Aeneas folded his arms over his knees and rested his chin on his arms.

"Or if you don't want to settle on the coast," continued Anchises, "we could go further south. We could go to Pergamum. They've always been friendly to us."

Without looking at him, Aeneas said, "For someone who was ready to die yesterday, you're awfully anxious to live now."

"Yesterday I thought I had a son who could take care of himself without me."

Aeneas did not respond, and the two fell silent again as they watched the city burn far below them on the plain.

Troy burned all night. It was burning the next morning when a ragged group of refugees made their way slowly down the far side of Mt. Ida and away from Ilion. Parts of the city were still smoldering two days later when the Greeks weighed anchor, the holds of their vessels filled to bursting. And when the last ship departed and sailed westward, a profound silence descended on the plain.

There was movement, however. From the woods east of Troy, a solitary horse picked its way toward the citadel. It was probably one of the terrified animals that had fled through the Dardanian Gates on the night the Greeks entered the city. Now, obeying some mysterious internal command, it left the sheltering forest to return to its home. Perhaps it expected to find its stall again, where hay and oats and water were abundant. Perhaps it even looked forward to the familiar sound of its owner's voice and the prickling strokes of the brush on its back. When the beast reached the Scaean Gates, however, it stopped.

Living cities, like living people, are each different,

each unique, but ruined cities all look alike. The walls of the star-shaped fortress still stood; no weeds had yet taken root beneath them, but within, everything that had been Troy was gone. The broad streets, the handsome buildings, the gardens, the trees, the statues, the paintings, all was now a charred, black nightmare of twisted debris and rubble.

The horse nodded its head vigorously and snorted to clear its nostrils of the acrid smoke that still hung in the air. Then, after one more brief glance at the desolate landscape inside the city, it turned away and began a leisurely walk back in the direction from which it had come.

Troy received no other visitors after that. Wisps of smoke rose from scattered quarters for another week until a soaking rain cooled the timbers down and put out the fire for good. Then the gods, having mercy on the city at last, covered it, ever so slowly, in a shroud of earth.